The Albert Gate Mystery

Being Further Adventures of Reginald Brett, Barrister Detective

By Louis Tracy

Originally published in 1904

The Albert Gate Mystery
Being Further Adventures of Reginald Brett, Barrister Detective

© 2010 Resurrected Press
www.ResurrectedPress.com

Published by Intrepid Ink, LLC

Intrepid Ink, LLC provides full publishing services to authors of fiction and non-fiction books, eBooks and websites. From editing to formatting, to publishing, to marketing, Intrepid Ink gets your creative works into the hands of the people who want to read them.
Find out more at www.IntrepidInk.com.

ISBN 13: 978-1-935774-33-4

Printed in the United States of America

FOREWORD

The Albert Gate Mystery features Reginald Brett in a case with international implications. Reginald Brett, Barrister Detective has featured in another Resurrected Press book, *The Stowmarket Mystery*, as has the Scotland Yard detective Winter who again plays second fiddle to the brilliant lawyer.

In this case, a fortune in diamonds belonging to the Turkish Sultan has been stolen from a house near the Albert Gate in London. The Foreign Office official coordinating security has gone missing. If the diamonds are not recovered it would have severe political repercussions, not only in London, but also in Turkey where it might result in the overthrow of the Ottoman government.

At the time of this story, 1904, the Ottoman Empire of the Turks had long been considered the "sick man of Europe." In the previous century it had lost much of it territory including Egypt, the Balkans, and Greece. The government of the Sultan was more known for its corruption and intrigue than for good governance. Much of the remaining empire held the seeds of revolt, which were to flare up so dramatically during the First World War.

A group, mostly drawn from younger officers in the military, known as "young turks" sought to overthrow the Sultan and replace him with a secular government along modern lines. This would finally occur after the First World War, when the caliphate was replaced with a republic led by Mustafa Kemal Ataturk.

That Tracy should anticipate these events by almost twenty years is an example of life imitating art. The period leading up to the First World War was full of intrigues by the major powers of Europe as they jockeyed

for power and position. Given the precarious position of
the Sultan, it is not farfetched to imagine a conspiracy to
embarrass him to bring about his removal.

The novel, itself, is full of action, disguises and
misdirection as the plot plays out across Europe. We at
Resurrected Press hope that you enjoy *The Albert Gate
Mystery*.

About the Author

Louis Tracy (1863-1928) was a British journalist and
author. He wrote numerous books both under his own
name and using the pseudonyms Gordon Holmes and
Robert Fraser. He shared these pseudonyms and
collaborated with P.M. Shiel on a number of works.
Among his books are *The Wings of Morning* (1903), *The
Stowmarket Mystery* (1904), and *Number Seventeen*
(1916).

Greg Fowlkes
Editor-In-Chief
Resurrected Press
www.ResurrectedPress.com

TABLE OF CONTENTS

1
A Mysterious Crime

Reginald Brett, barrister-at-law and amateur detective, had seldom been more at peace with the world and his own conscience than when he entered the dining-room of his cosy flat this bright October morning.

Since the famous affair of Lady Delia Lyle's disappearance and death, he had not been busy, and the joy of healthy idleness is only known to the hard worker. Again, while dressing, he had received a letter inviting him to a quiet shoot at a delightful place in the country.

All these things blended with happy inconsequence to render Brett contented in mind and affable in manner.

"It's a fine morning, Smith," he said cheerily, as he settled himself at the table where his "man" was already pouring out the coffee.

"Bee-utiful, sir," said Smith.

"Smith!"

"Yessir."

"Not even the best English autumn weather can stand being called 'bee-utiful.' Don't do it. You will open the flood-gates of Heaven."

Smith laughed decorously. He had not the slightest idea what his master meant, but if it pleased Mr. Brett to be jocose, it was the duty of a servant who knew his place to be responsive.

The barrister fully understood Smith's delicate appreciation—and its limits. He instantly noticed that the morning paper, instead of reposing next to his folded napkin, was placed out of reach on a sideboard, and that the eggs and bacon made their appearance half a minute too soon.

As an expert swordsman delights to execute a pass *en tierce* with an umbrella, so did the cleverest analytical detective of the age resolve to amaze his servitor.

"Smith," he said suddenly, composing his features to their most severe cross-examination aspect, "I think the arrangement is an excellent one."

"What arrangement, sir."

"That Mrs. Smith and yourself should have a few days' holiday, while Mrs. Smith's brother takes your place during my forthcoming visit to Lord Northallerton's—why, man, what is the matter? Is it too hot?"—for the cover Smith had lifted off the bacon and eggs clattered violently on the table.

"'Ot, sir. 'Ot isn't the word. You're a fair licker, that's what you are."

Smith invariably dropped his h's when he became excited.

"Smith, I insist that you shall not call me names. Pass the paper."

"But, sir—"

"Pass the paper. Utter another word and I refuse to accept Mrs. Smith's brother as your *locum tenens*."

Smith was silenced by the last terrible epithet. Yet he was so manifestly nervous that Brett resolved o enlighten him before plunging into the day's news.

"For the last time, Smith," he said, "I will explain to you why it is hopeless for you to think of concealing tradesmen's commissions from me."

The shot went home, but the enemy was acquainted with this method of attack, and did not wince.

"You knew that Lord Northallerton had recently invited me to his October pheasant-shooting. During the last few days a youth, who grotesquely reproduces Mrs. Smith's most prominent features, has mysteriously tenanted the kitchen, ill-cleaned my boots, and bungled over the studs in my shirts. This morning a letter came with the crest and the Northallerton postmark. Really, Smith, considering that you have now breathed the same air as myself for eight long years, I did not expect to be called on for an explanation. Besides, you have destroyed a masterpiece."

"Sir—" began Smith.

"Oh, I understand; there is nothing broken but your reputation. Don't you see that the mere placing of the newspaper at a distance, so that you might have a chance to speak before I opened it, was a subtle stroke, worthy of Lecocq. Yet you demand feeble words. What a pity! Know, Smith, that true genius is dumb. Speech may be silvern, but silence is surely golden."

The barrister solemnly unfolded the paper, and Smith faded from the room. On a page usually devoted to important announcements, the following paragraphs stood forth in the boldness of leaded type:–

"MYSTERIOUS OCCURRENCE IN THE WEST END.

"An affair of some magnitude–perhaps a remarkable crime–has taken place in an Albert Gate mansion.

"Owing to the reticence of the authorities, it is at present impossible to arrive at a definite conclusion as to the nature or extent of the incident, but it is quite certain that public interest will be much excited when details are forthcoming. All sorts of rumours attain credence in the locality, the murder of several prominent persons being not the least persistent of these. Without, however, giving currency to idle speculation, several authentic statements may be grouped into a connected form.

"Four weeks ago a party of Turkish gentlemen of high rank in Constantinople, arrived in London and took up their abode in the house in question, after some structural alterations, pointing at great security within and without, had been planned and executed.

"Attending these Turkish gentlemen, or officials, was a numerous suite of Moslem guards and servants, whilst, immediately following their arrival, came from

Amsterdam some dozen noted experts in the diamond-cutting industry. These were lodged in a neighbouring private hotel, where they were extremely uncommunicative as to their business in London. They were employed during the day at the Albert Gate house. The presence in the mansion, both day and night, of a strong force of Metropolitan police, tended to excite local curiosity to an intense degree, but no clear conception of the business of the occupants was allowed to reach the public.

"Whatever it was that took place, the full particulars were not only well known to the authorities—the presence of the police hints even at Governmental sanction—but matters proceeded on normal lines until yesterday morning.

"Then it became clear that a remarkable development must have occurred during the preceding night, as the whole of the Dutch workmen and the Turkish attendants were taken off in cabs by the police, not to Morton Street Police Station, but to Scotland Yard; this in itself being a most unusual course to adopt. They are unquestionably detained in custody, but they have not yet been charged before a magistrate.

"The police, later in the day, carried off some of these men's personal belongings, from both hotel and mansion.

"A sinister aspect was given to the foregoing mysterious proceedings by the presence at Albert Gate, early in the day, of two police surgeons, who were followed, about twelve o'clock, by Dr. Tennyson Coke, the greatest living authority on toxicology.

"Dr. Coke and the other medical gentlemen subsequently refused to impart the slightest information as to the reasons that led the police to seek their services, and the Scotland Yard authorities are adamant in the matter.

"The representative of a news agency was threatened with arrest for trespass when he endeavoured to gain admission to the Albert Gate house, and it is quite *evident that the police are determined to prevent the facts from leaking out at present–if they can by any means accomplish their wishes."*

Brett read this interesting statement twice slowly. It fascinated him. Its very vagueness, its admissions of inability to tell what had really happened, its adroit use of such phrases as "Turkish gentlemen of high rank," "Noted experts in the diamond-cutting industry," "The greatest living authority on toxicology," betrayed the hand of the disappointed journalistic artist.

"Excellent!" he murmured aloud. "It is the breath of battle to my nostrils. I ought to tip Smith for my breakfast. Had I read this earlier, I would not have eaten a morsel."

He carefully examined the page at the back. It contained matter of no consequence–a London County Council debate–so he took a pair of scissors from his pocket and cut out the complete item, placing the slip as a votive offering in front of a finely-executed bust of Edgar Allen Poe, that stood on a bookcase behind him.

Within three minutes the scissors were again employed. The new cutting ran–

"There is trouble at Yildiz Kiosk. A Reuter's telegram from Constantinople states that a near relative of the Sultan has fled to France. The Porte have asked the French Government to apprehend him, but the French Ambassador has informed Riaz Pasha that this course is impracticable in the absence of any criminal charge."

"These two are one," said the barrister, as he turned towards Poe's bust and laid the slip by the side of its predecessor. This time he had mutilated a critique of an Ibsensite drama.

The rest of the newspaper's contents had no special interest for him, and he soon threw aside the journal in order to rise, light a cigarette, and muster sufficient energy to write a telegram accepting Lord Northallerton's invitation for the following day.

He was on the point of reaching for a telegraph form when Smith entered with a card. It bore the name and address—

"The Earl of Fairholme, Stanhope Gate."

"Curious," thought Brett. "Where is his lordship?" he said aloud—"at the door, or in the street?"

(His flat was on the second floor.)

"In a keb, sir."

"Bring his lordship up."

A rapid glance at "Debrett" revealed that the Earl of Fairholme was thirty, unmarried, the fourteenth of his line, and the possessor of country seats at Fairholme, Warwickshire, and Glen Spey, Inverness.

The earl entered, an athletic, well-groomed man, one whose lines were usually cast in pleasant places, but who was now in an unwonted state of flurry and annoyance.

Each man was favourably impressed by the other. His lordship produced an introductory card, and Brett was astonished to find that it bore the name of the Under-Secretary of State for Foreign Affairs.

"I have come—" commenced his lordship hesitatingly.

But the barrister broke in. "You have had a bad night, Lord Fairholme. You wish for a long and comfortable chat. Now, won't you start with a whiskey and soda, light a cigar, and draw an easy chair near the fire?"

"'Pon my honour, Mr. Brett, you begin well. You give me confidence. Those are the first cheerful words I have heard during twenty-four hours."

The earl was easily manoeuvred into a strong light. Then he made a fresh start.

"You have doubtless heard of this Albert Gate affair, Mr. Brett?"

"You mean this?" said the other, rising and handing to his visitor the longer paragraph of the two he had selected from the newspaper.

"That is very curious," said the earl, momentarily startled. But he was too preoccupied by his thoughts to pay much heed to the incident. He merely glanced at the cutting and went on:

"Yes, that is it. Well, Edith–Miss Talbot, I mean–vows that she won't marry me until this beastly business is cleared up. Of course, we all know that Jack didn't slope with the diamonds. He's tied up or dead, for sure. But–no matter what may have become of him–why the dickens that should stop Edith from marrying me is more than I can fathom. Just look at some of the women in Society. They don't leave it to their relatives to be mixed up in a scandal, I can tell you. Still, there you are. Edith is jolly clever and awfully determined, so you've got to find him, Mr. Brett. Dead or alive, he must be found, and cleared."

"He shall," said Brett, gazing into the fire.

The quiet, self-reliant voice steadied the young peer. He checked an imminent flow of words, picked up the newspaper slip again, and this time read it.

Then he blushed.

"You must think me very stupid, Mr. Brett, to burst out in such a manner when you probably have never heard of the people I am talking about."

"You will tell me, Lord Fairholme, if you get quietly to work and try to speak, so far as you find it possible, in chronological sequence."

His lordship knitted his brows and smoked in silence. At last he found utterance.

"That's a good idea of yours. It makes things easier. Well, first of all, Edith and I became engaged. Edith is the daughter of the late Admiral Talbot. She and Jack, her brother, live with their uncle, General Sir Hubert Fitzjames, at 118, Ulster Gardens. Jack is in the Foreign Office; he is just like Edith, awfully clever and that sort of thing, an assistant secretary I think they call him. Now we're getting on, aren't we?"

"Splendidly."

"That's all right. About a month ago a chap turns up from Constantinople, a kind of special Envoy from the

Sultan, and he explains to the Foreign Office that he has
in his possession a lot of uncut diamonds of terrific value,
including one as big as a duck's egg, to which no figures
would give a price. Do you follow me?"

"Each word."

"Good. Well–I can't tell you why, because I don't
know, and I could not understand it if I did–there was
some political importance attached to these gems, and the
Sultan roped our Foreign Office into it. So the Foreign
Office placed Jack in charge of the business. He fixed up
the Envoy in the house at Albert Gate, got a lot of
diamond cutters and machinery for him, gave him into
the charge of all the smart policemen in London; and
what do you think is the upshot?"

"What?"

"The Envoy, his two secretaries, and a confidential
servant were murdered the night before last, the
diamonds were stolen, and Jack has vanished–absolutely
gone clean into space, not a sign of him to be found
anywhere. Yesterday Edith sends for me, cries for half an
hour, tells me I'm the best fellow that ever lived, and then
I'm jiggered if she didn't wind up by saying that she
couldn't marry me."

The Earl of Fairholme was now worked up to fever
heat. He would not calm down for an appreciable period,
so Brett resolved to try the effect of curiosity.

He wrote a telegram to Lord Northallerton:–

*"Very sorry, but I cannot leave town at present.
Please ask me later. Will explain reason for postponement
when we meet."*

He had touched the dominant note in mankind.

"Surely!" cried the earl, "you have not already decided
upon a course of action?"

"Not exactly. I am wiring to postpone a shooting
fixture."

"What a beastly shame!" exclaimed the other, in
whom the sporting instinct was at once aroused. "I'm

awfully sorry my affairs should interfere with your arrangements in this way."

"Not a bit," cried Brett. "I make it a sacred rule of life to put pleasure before business. I mean," he explained, as a look of bewilderment crossed his hearer's face, "that this quest of ours promises to be the most remarkable affair I have ever been engaged in. That pleases me. Pheasant-shooting is a serious business, governed by the calendar and arranged by the head-keeper."

An electric bell summoned Smith. The barrister handed him the telegram and a sovereign.

"Read that message," he said. "Ponder over it. Send it, and give the change of the sovereign to Mrs. Smith's brother, with my compliments and regrets."

2
MEHEMET ALI'S NOTE

Then he turned to Lord Fairholme.

"Just one question," he said, "before I send you off to bed. No, you must not protest. I want you to meet me here this evening at seven, with your brain clear and your nerves restored by a good, sound sleep. We will dine, here or elsewhere, and act subsequently. But at this moment I want to know the name of the person most readily accessible who can tell me all about Mr. Talbot's connection with the Sultan's agent."

"His sister, undoubtedly."

"Where can I find her?"

"At Ulster Gardens. I will drive you there."

The barrister smiled. "You are going to bed, I tell you. Give me a few lines of introduction to Miss Talbot."

The earl's face had brightened at the prospect of meeting his *fiancee* under the favourable conditions of Brett's presence. But he yielded with good grace, and promptly sat down to write a brief note explanatory of the barrister's identity and position in the inquiry.

The two parted at the door, and a hansom rapidly brought Brett to the residence of Sir Hubert Fitzjames.

A stately footman took Reggie's card and its accompanying letter, placed them on a salver with a graceful turn of his wrist, which oddly suggested a similar turn in his nose, and said:

"Miss Talbot is not at home, sir."

"Yes, she is," answered Brett, paying the driver of the hansom.

The footman deigned to exhibit astonishment. Here was a gentleman—one obviously accustomed to the manners of Society—who declined to accept the courteous disclaimer of an unexpected visit.

"Miss Talbot is not receiving visitors," he explained.

"Exactly. Take that card and the letter to Miss Talbot and bring me the answer."

Jeames was no match for his antagonist. He silently showed the way into a reception room and disappeared. A minute later he announced, with much deference, that Miss Talbot would see Mr. Brett in the library, and he conducted this mysterious visitor upstairs.

On rejoining Buttons in the hall he solemnly observed:

"That's a swell cop who is with the missus—shining topper, button-hole, buckskin gloves, patent leathers, all complete. Footmen ain't in it with the force, nowadays."

Jeames expanded his magnificent waistcoat with a heavy sigh over this philosophical dictum, the poignancy of which was enhanced by his knowledge that the upper housemaid had taken to conversing with a mounted policeman in the Park during her afternoons off.

The apartment in which Brett found himself gave ready indications of the character of its tenants. Tod's "Rajasthan" jostled a volume of the Badminton Library on the bookshelves, a copy of the Allahabad *Pioneer* lay beside the *Field* and the *Times* on the table, and many varieties of horns made trophies with quaint weapons on the walls.

A complete edition of Ruskin, and some exquisite prints of Rossetti's best known works, supplied a different set of emblems, whilst the room generally showed signs of daily occupation.

"Anglo-Indian uncle, artistic niece," was the barrister's rapid comment, but further analysis was prevented by the entrance of Miss Edith Talbot.

The surprise of the pair was mutual.

Brett expected to see a young, pretty and clever girl, vain enough to believe she had brains, and sufficiently well endowed with that rare commodity to be able to twist the good-natured Earl of Fairholme round her little finger.

Young, not more than twenty—unquestionably beautiful, with the graceful contour and delicately-balanced features of a portrait by Romney—Edith Talbot bore few of the marks that pass current as the outward and visible signs of a modern woman of Society. That she should be self-possessed and dressed in perfect taste were as obvious adjuncts of her character as that each phase of her clear thought should reflect itself in a singularly mobile face.

To such a woman pretence was impossible, the polite fictions of fashionable life impossible. Brett readily understood why the Earl of Fairholme had fallen in love with this fair creature. He had simply bent in worship before a goddess of his own creed.

To the girl, Brett was equally a revelation.

Fairholme's introductory note described the barrister as "the smartest criminal lawyer in London—one whose aid would be invaluable." She expected to meet a sharp-featured, wizened, elderly man, with gold-rimmed eye-glasses, a queer voice and a nasty habit of asking unexpected questions.

In place of this commonplace personality, she encountered a handsome, well-groomed gentleman—one who won confidence by his intellectual face, and retained it by invisibly establishing a social equality. Fortunately, there is yet in Britain an aristocracy wherein good birth is synonymous with good breeding—a freemasonry whose passwords cannot be simulated, nor its membership bought.

Brett read the wonder in the girl's eyes, and hastened to explain.

"The Earl of Fairholme," said Brett, "thought I might be of some service in the matter of your brother's strange disappearance, Miss Talbot. I am not a professional detective, but my friends are good enough to believe that

I am very successful in unravelling mysteries that are beyond the ken of Scotland Yard. I have heard something of the facts in this present affair. Will you trust me so far as to tell me all that is known to you personally?"

"My uncle, General Fitzjames, has just gone to Scotland Yard," she began, timidly.

"Quite so. Perhaps you prefer to await his return?"

"Oh, no, I do not mean that. But it is so hard to know how best to act. Uncle expects the police to accomplish impossibilities. He says that they should long since have found out what has become of Jack. Perhaps they may resent my interference."

"My interference, to be exact," said Reggie, with the pleasant smile that had fascinated so many women. Even Edith Talbot was not wholly proof against its magic.

"I, personally, have little faith in them," she confessed.

"I have none."

"Well, I will do as you advise."

"Then I recommend you to take me into your confidence. I know Scotland Yard and its methods. We do not follow the same path."

"I believe in you and trust you," said the girl.

So ingenuous was the look from the large, deep eyes which accompanied this declaration of confidence, that many men would have pronounced Miss Talbot to be an experienced flirt. Brett knew better. He simply bowed his acknowledgements.

"What is it that you want to know?" she continued. "We ourselves are no better informed than the newspapers as to what has actually happened, save that four men have been killed as the result of a carefully-planned robbery. As for my brother—"

She paused and strove hard to force back her tears.

"Your brother has simply vanished, Miss Talbot. If the criminals did not scruple to leave four dead men behind, they would not draw the line at a fifth. The clear inference is that your brother is alive, but under restraint."

"I can see that it is possible he was alive until some time after the tragedy at Albert Gate. But–but–what connection can Jack have with the theft of diamonds worth millions? These people used him as their tool in some manner. Why should they spare him when success had crowned their efforts?"

"We are conversing in riddles. Will you explain?"

"You know that my brother is an assistant Under-Secretary in the Foreign Office?"

"Yes."

"Well, early in September, his chief placed him in charge of a special undertaking. The Sultan had decided to have a large number of rough diamonds cut and polished by the best European experts. They were all magnificent gems, exceedingly valuable it seems, being rare both in size and purity; but one of them was larger than any known diamond. Jack told me it was quite as big as a good-sized hen's egg. Both it and the others, he said, had the appearance of lumps of alum; but the experts said that the smaller stones were worth more than a million sterling, whilst the price of the large one could not be fixed. No one but an Emperor or Sultan would buy it. His Excellency Mehemet Ali Pasha was the especial envoy charged with this mission, and he brought credentials to the Foreign Office asking for facilities to be given for its execution. He and the two secretaries who accompanied him have been killed."

"Yes?" said Brett, whose eyes were fixed intently on the hearthrug.

"Jack was given the special duty of looking after Mehemet Ali and his companions during their residence in London. It was his business to afford them every assistance in his power, to procure them police protection, obtain for them the best advice attainable in the diamond trade, and generally place at their disposal all the resources which the British Government itself could command if it undertook such a curious task. He had been with them about a month–not hourly engaged, you understand, as once the preliminary arrangements were made, he had little further trouble–but he used to call there every morning and afternoon to see if he could render any assistance. Matters had progressed so favourably until the day before yesterday, that in another month he hoped to see the last of them. He was always saying that he would be glad when the business was ended, as he did not like to be officially connected with the fate of a few little bits of stone that happened to be so immensely valuable."

"Did your brother call there as usual on Monday afternoon?" said Brett.

"Yes; he came straight here from Albert Gate, and had tea with uncle and myself. He sat in the very chair and in the very position you now occupy. I can remember him saying: 'By jove! the hen's egg'–that is what he used to call the big diamond–'is turning out in fine style.' He even discussed the possibility of bringing us to see the collection when it was finished and before it left this country."

"Did your brother say why the diamonds were brought to this country in the first instance?"

"Yes; the Sultan and his advisers seemed to think the work of cutting them could be performed more safely and expeditiously here than anywhere else. Even the Turk has a high regard for the manner in which law and order are maintained in Britain. Yet the sequel has shown that the diamonds and their guardians were perhaps in greater danger here than they would have been in Constantinople."

"Was that the only reason?" said Brett, who had apparently made up his mind with reference to the pattern of the carpet, and was now gazing into the bright fire which danced merrily in the grate, for the day though fine was chilly.

The girl wrinkled her brows in thought before she answered: "I think I do remember Jack saying that he believed there was some State business mixed up in the affair, but I am quite sure he did not know the exact facts himself."

"Can you recollect any of the special precautions taken to protect the gems? Your brother may have mentioned some details in conversation, you know."

"Oh, I think I know all about them. In the first instance, the house at Albert Gate had previously been tenanted by a rich banker, and it was well defended by all ordinary means against the attacks of ordinary burglars. But, in addition to this, before the diamonds left the safe at the Bank of England, the building was practically torn to pieces inside by workmen acting under the direction of the Commissioner of Police. It was absolutely impossible for anyone to enter except through the front door, unless they flew out of the second storey window. Servants and workmen, like everybody else, had to use this door alone, as the windows and doors in the basement had all been bricked up. Inside the entrance-hall there were always twelve policemen, and an inspector in charge.

"Every one who left the house was searched by the inspector on duty, and Jack used to say that he was very glad he invariably insisted upon this examination, although the police were at first disinclined to meet his wishes in the matter, he being, so to speak, their direct superior for the time. Beneath the entrance-hall were rooms occupied by several Turkish and other servants. Mehemet Ali himself, in the presence of his secretaries, used to open the door leading to the suite of apartments in which the diamond cutters worked, and two of the Turkish gentlemen would remain there all day until the men left in the evening. The Envoy and both secretaries used to meet Jack when he visited the place, and for the last three weeks he had nothing to do but see the diamonds, count them, drink an excellent cup of coffee, and smoke a wonderful cigarette, made of some special Turkish tobacco, cultivated and prepared only for the Imperial household."

"Ah!" sighed Brett, with a note of almost unconscious envy in his voice. He knew exactly what that coffee and those cigarettes would be like. "I beg your pardon," he went on, perceiving that Miss Talbot did not understand his exclamation. "Will you tell me as nearly as you can the occurrences of Monday evening?"

"They were simple enough," said the girl. "My brother dined at home. We had one or two guests, and were all in the drawing room about 10 15, when a note came for him from Mehemet Ali. I know exactly what was in it. I looked over his shoulder whilst he read it. The words were: 'I wish to see you to-night on important business. Come, if possible, at once.' I have to tell you that it was in French, but this is an exact translation."

"Your brother was quite sure that it was from Mehemet Ali himself?" said Brett.

"Quite sure," was the reply. "He knew his handwriting well, having had several communications from him during the progress of the business."

"Did your brother leave the house immediately?" asked Brett.

"That instant. He went downstairs, put on his overcoat and hat, and got into a cab with the messenger who brought the note."

"Do you know who this messenger was?"

"One of the policemen on duty in the house itself."

A slight pause ensued, and Brett was about to take his departure, having no further questions to ask at the moment, when some one was heard hastily ascending the stairs, talking to a companion as he advanced.

"This is my uncle," exclaimed Miss Talbot, rising to go to the door. Before she could reach it an elderly gentleman entered, bearing upon him all those distinguishing tokens that stamp a man as a retired major-general.

He exclaimed impetuously—

"I have brought a gentleman from Scotland Yard, my dear." Then he caught sight of Brett. "Who is this?"

Edith was about to explain, when another man entered—a strongly-built, bullet-headed man, with keen eyes and firm mouth, and a curious suggestion in his appearance of having combined pugilism with process-serving as a professional means of existence. His face extended into a smile when his eyes fell upon the barrister.

"Ah, Mr. Brett," he cried. "Now we have something to do that is up to your mark. You are on the spot first, as usual, but this time I can honestly say that I am glad to see you."

Sir Hubert Fitzjames glanced in astonishment from his niece to the barrister. He could find nothing better to say than—

"This, my dear, is Mr. Winter, of Scotland Yard."

3
WHAT THE POLICE SAW

Brett promptly cleared the situation by explaining to Sir Hubert, in a few words, the reason for his unexpected presence, and when the Major-General learnt the name of the distinguished personage who had sent Lord Fairholme to the barrister he expressed a ready acquiescence in the desire to utilise his services. Nor was the effect of such a notable introduction lost on Mr. Winter, whose earlier knowledge of the barrister's remarkable achievements in unravelling the tangled skein of criminal investigation was now supplemented by a certain amount of awe for a man who commanded the confidence of His Majesty's Government.

"Well," said Sir Hubert Fitzjames, with the brisk animation of one accustomed to utter commands that must be instantly obeyed, "we will now proceed to business."

For the moment no one spoke. The Scotland Yard detective evidently wished his distinguished colleague to take the lead. No sooner did Brett perceive this than he rose, bowed politely to Miss Talbot and her uncle, and said—

"The first thing to do is to trace the whereabouts of Mr. Talbot, and this should be a comparatively easy task. The other features of this strange occurrence impress me as highly complex, but it is far too early a stage in the investigation to permit any definite opinion being expressed at this moment."

Every one seemed to be surprised by Brett's attitude.

"Where are you going to, sir?" asked Mr. Winter.

"That depends largely upon you," was the smiling reply. "If you come with me we will go direct to Albert

Gate, but if you decide to prosecute further inquiries here, I will await your arrival at my flat."

"That is as much as saying that there are no facts worth inquiring into to be learnt here?"

"Exactly so. Miss Talbot has told me all that is material to our purpose. Her brother was unexpectedly sent for after dinner on Monday night, and left the house hurriedly, without affording any clue to his subsequent proceedings beyond that contained in a brief note sent to him by Mehemet Ali Pasha. Indeed, it was impossible for him to afford any explanation, as he himself was quite unprepared for the summons. Meanwhile, every moment lost in the endeavour to follow up his movements is precious time wasted."

The barrister's manner, no less than his words, impressed Mr. Winter so greatly that he too rose from the seat which he had occupied, with the intention of conducting a long and careful examination of each member of the household.

"Then I will come with you at once," he said.

"Oh," cried the Major-General, "I understood you to say as we came here that there were many questions which required immediate inquiry in this house, on the principle that the movements of the missing man should be minutely traced from the very commencement."

Mr. Winter looked somewhat confused, but Edith Talbot broke in–

"I think, uncle dear, it would be well to defer to Mr. Brett's judgment."

"Do you really believe," she said, turning to the barrister, "that you will soon be able to find my brother?"

"I am quite sure of it," he replied, and the conviction in his tone astonished the professional detective, whilst it carried a message of hope to the others. Even Sir Hubert, for some reason which he could not explain, suddenly experienced a strong sense of confidence in this reserved, distinguished-looking man. He stepped forward eagerly and held out his hand, saying–

"Then we will not detain you, Mr. Brett. Act as you think fit in all things, but do let us have all possible information at the earliest moment. The suspense and uncertainty of the present position of affairs are terribly trying to my niece and myself." The old soldier spoke with dignity and composure, but his lips quivered, and the anguish in his eyes was pitiful.

Brett and Mr. Winter quitted the house; they hailed a hansom, and drove rapidly towards Albert Gate.

"Do you know," said the man from Scotland Yard, breaking in on his companion's reverie, "you surprised me by what you said just now, Mr. Brett?"

"I thought you were too old a hand to be surprised at anything," was the reply.

"Oh, come now, you know well enough what I mean. You said you thought it would be a comparatively simple matter to find Mr. Talbot, whilst the other features of the crime are very complex. Now the affair, thus far, impresses me as being the exact opposite to that statement. The crime is simple enough. A clever gang of thieves get into the place by working some particularly cool and daring confidence game. They don't hesitate at murder to cover up their tracks, and they make away with the plunder under the very noses of the police. All this may be smart and up-to-date in its methods, but it is not unusual. The difficult question to my mind is, what have they done with Mr. Talbot, and how did they succeed in fooling him so completely as to make him what one might almost call a party to the transaction?"

The barrister pulled out a cigar-case.

"Try one of these, Winter," he said. "You will find them soothing."

"I never smoke whilst on business," was the testy reply.

"I invariably do." He proceeded to light a cigar, which he smoked with zest.

"I do not know how it is," went on Mr. Winter, "but whenever I happen to meet you, Mr. Brett, in the course of an inquiry, I always start by being very angry with you."

"Why?" There was an amused twinkle in Brett's eyes, which might have warned the other of a possible pitfall.

"Because you treat me as if I were a precocious youth. You listen to my theories with a sort of pitying indulgence, yet I have the reputation of being one of the best men in Scotland Yard, or I should not have been put on this job. And I am older than you, too."

"I may surely pity you," said Brett, "even if I don't indulge you too much."

"There you go again," snapped the detective. "Now, what is there silly about my theory of the crime, I should like to know."

"You shall know, and before you are much older. Bear with me for a little while, I beg of you. You may be right, and I may be quite wrong, but I think there is much beneath the surface in the investigations we are now pursuing. My advice to you is to drop all preconceived theories, to note every circumstance, however remote it may appear in its bearing upon events, and in any case not to act precipitately. Whatever you do, don't arrest anybody."

"But," said the other, somewhat mollified by Brett's earnestness, "half a dozen people may be arrested at any moment."

"Pray tell me how?"

"Descriptions of the stolen diamonds and of the suspected persons are in every police office in Great Britain and in most Continental centres by this time. Passengers by all steamers are most carefully scrutinised. Every pawnbroker and diamond merchant in the country is on the look-out, and, generally speaking, it will be odd if somebody does not drop into the net before many hours have passed."

"It will, indeed," murmured Brett; "and no doubt the somebody in question will experience a certain amount of inconvenience before he proves to you that he had nothing whatever to do with the matter. Now, don't answer me, Winter, but ponder seriously over this question: Do you really think that the intelligence which planned and successfully carried through an operation of such magnitude will be trapped by plain-clothes constables watching the gangways of steamships, or by any pawnbroker who has ever lent half the value of a pledge?"

Almost impatiently the barrister waved the subject out of the hansom, and the detective had sense enough to leave him alone during the few remaining minutes before the vehicle pulled up near the Albert Gate mansion.

Brett stopped the driver some little distance short of the house itself, as he did not wish to attract the attention of a knot of curious sightseers in the street. He asked Winter to precede him and make known the fact that he was coming, so that there would be no delay at the door. This the detective readily agreed to, and Brett rapidly took in the main external features of the house which had become the scene of such a remarkable tragedy.

It was a palatial structure, built on the sombre lines of the Early Victorian period. Miss Talbot's brief description of the measures taken to protect its occupants from interference was fully borne out by its aspect. There was no access to the basement; the main entrance was situated at the side; all the ground-floor and first-storey windows facing into the street were fitted with immovable wooden venetians. Presumably those on the Park side were similarly secured, whilst the back wall abutted on to that of another mansion, equally large and strongly built, tenanted by a well-known peer.

Truly, it required a genius almost unrivalled in the annals of crime to murder four people and steal diamonds worth millions in such a place whilst guarded by twelve London policemen and under the special protection of the Home Office.

The appearance of Winter at the door caused the gaping idlers in the street to endeavour to draw nearer to the mysterious portals. Thereupon three policemen on duty outside hustled the mob back, and Brett took advantage of the confusion thus created to slip to the doorway almost unperceived. One of the police constables turned round to make a grab at him, but a signal from a *confrere* inside prevented this, and Brett quickly found himself within a spacious entrance hall with the door closed and bolted behind him.

Winter was talking to two uniformed inspectors, to whom he had explained the barrister's mission and credentials.

"We have here, Mr. Brett," he said, "Inspector Walters, who was on duty until ten o'clock on Monday night, and Inspector Sharpe, who relieved him. They will both tell you exactly what took place."

"Thank you," said the barrister, "but it will expedite matters if you gentlemen will first accompany me over the scene of the crime. I will then be able to understand more accurately what happened. Suppose we start here. I presume that this is where the police guard was stationed?"

Inspector Walters assumed the *role* of guide.

"I was in charge of the first guard established a month ago," he said, "and the arrangements I then made have been adhered to without deviation night and day ever since."

From the outer door a short passage of a few feet led up half a dozen steps into a large reception room, the entrance to which was closed by a light double door, half glass. On both sides of the first short passage were two small apartments, such as are often used in London mansions for the purposes of cloak-rooms. The doors from these rooms opened into the inner hall. A large dining-room was situated on the left or Park side, and on the right was a breakfast or morning-room. At the back of the reception hall a handsome staircase led from left to right to the upper floors, whilst a doorway beneath the staircase gave access to the kitchens and basement offices.

"Here," said the inspector, pointing to the foot of the staircase, "two police-constables were constantly stationed. Another stood there," indicating the passage to the kitchen, "and a fourth at the glass door. As the outer basement entrance was not only securely fastened by bolts and bars, but actually bricked up inside, it was absolutely impossible for any person to enter or leave the house save by the front door, nor could any one go from the kitchen to the upper part of the house without passing under the observation of all four constables. I arranged my guards in military fashion, having three men for each post, with one hour on duty and two hours off, but the same men were never on guard together at definite hours, as they were relieved at varying times. You will understand that I considered it a very responsible task to safeguard these premises, and thought it best to render it impossible for any section of the force under my command to take part in a conspiracy, although such a thing was in itself most improbable."

They then ascended the staircase and found themselves on the first floor.

There were six spacious apartments on this storey, and all of them had originally opened on to the landing. The special precautions taken to guard the diamonds of the Turkish mission had altered all that. Five doorways had been bricked up, the result being that admission to the whole set of rooms could only be obtained through the first door that faced the top of the staircase.

This apartment was luxuriously furnished, and Inspector Walters explained that the Turkish Envoy and his suite passed the working hours of each day there after they had personally thrown open the other apartments to the diamond polishers and unlocked the safes in which the gems were stored, when work ceased on the previous day.

"His Excellency," said the inspector, "kept the keys of this room and the others, together with those of the safes, in his own possession night and day. He slept upstairs, and so did the other two gentlemen. No one was allowed to come to this floor except the confidential servant, named Hussein, who used to bring coffee, cigars, and newspapers or other things the gentlemen might require, together with their lunch in the middle of the day. The workmen brought their lunch with them, so that they came in and out once a day only."

"Where did this confidential servant sleep?" said Brett.

"I believe he used to lie curled up on the rug outside his Excellency's door."

"And the other servants?"

"They all slept in the basement."

"What were they, Turks or Christians?"

"Well, sir," said the inspector with a smile, "two of them were Turks in costume, whilst three were Christians in appearance. That is the best I can say for the Christians, as they were Frenchmen, though certainly the cook was a first-rate *chef*. Of course, we all got our meals here whilst on duty."

"Did his Excellency and the other members of the mission eat food prepared in the ordinary way?"

"Oh, yes; they appreciated French dishes as keenly as anybody might do."

"It was in this room, then," continued Brett, "that the murders took place?"

"Yes; I suppose that must be so," said the inspector. "But my friend here," pointing to Inspector Sharpe, "can tell that part of the story better than I can."

They passed into the inner rooms, which were quite silent and deserted, and presented a strange appearance considering the character of the house and its locality. Although the ceilings were decorated with beautiful paintings and fringed with superbly emblazoned mouldings, although the walls were papered with material that cost as much per yard as good silk, each apartment was occupied with workmen's benches, and curious devices for cutting and polishing diamonds.

In the first room were two small safes, one of which was intended to receive the gems under treatment at the close of each day's work; the other held certain valuable materials required in the diamond cutter's operations. Three of the rooms were on the Park side, and it was here that the small colony of skilled artisans had been installed.

The other two rooms were not tenanted, nor had any communicating doors been broken through the walls in order to gain access to them.

The windows of the three apartments occupied by the workmen were not only guarded by strong iron bars, but possessed the additional security of external wire blinds of exceedingly small mesh. Each window admitted plenty of light, and could be raised to allow a free circulation of air, but it was seemingly quite impossible for any active communication to take place with the outside. The three rooms looked out over a small enclosed lawn, which was separated from the park by a brick wall surmounted by iron railings. All the fireplaces had been closed with bricks and mortar.

"You will see, sir," said the inspector, when he had called Brett's attention to these details, "that mysterious though the murders were, they were as nothing compared with the disappearance of the diamonds. Every person who came downstairs was most carefully and methodically searched each time he passed the constable on duty at the bottom. It may be admitted that a few small stones could be so secreted as to escape observation, but some of these stones were so large that such a notion

is not to be thought of, whilst the size of the great
diamond which Mr. Talbot christened the 'Hen's Egg'
rendered its transference past the searchers beneath
absolutely impossible. There was no humbug about the
search, you will understand, Mr. Brett. People had to
take their boots off, open their mouths, and hand over
their hats, coats, sticks, or umbrellas for inspection.
Every part of their clothing was scrutinised, and the
contents of their pockets, money, watches, keys, and the
rest, thoroughly examined. These were our orders, and
they were strictly obeyed, Mr. Talbot himself being the
first to insist that the regulation should be carried out
rigidly, so far as he was concerned. Why, one day a
Cabinet Minister came here to see the diamonds. He was
elderly and stout, and did not at all like having to take off
his boots, I can assure you, as he nearly got apoplexy
whilst lacing them up again."

During the inspector's running comments Brett had
carefully scrutinised each of the windows. He at once
came to the conclusion, by a simple analysis of the
possibilities, that by no other means than through the
barrier of iron wire had the diamonds passed out of the
house; but the most thorough examination failed to reveal
any loophole by which this achievement had been
accomplished. He opened each of the windows, tested
every iron bar, and saw that the fastenings of the
external blind were undisturbed, whilst the fine wire
mesh showed no irregularities in its hexagonal pattern
wherein any defect would at once be visible.

"We have done all that long since, sir," said the second
police officer, smiling at the obviousness of an amateur's
method of inspection, for it happened that he had never
met the barrister before, though he had often heard of
him.

"You have?" said Brett, with the slightest tinge of
sarcasm in his voice. "Did you do this?" and he
commenced to thump with a clenched fist upon every
portion of the external screen that he could reach.

"No, we did not," said the policeman, "and I don't see that it is going to accomplish anything except hurt your hand."

"That may be so," murmured Brett; "but the diamonds went this way and none other."

He tested every portion of one window screen in this manner without effect. Then he approached the second window, and, beginning at the left-hand top corner, did the same thing. Suddenly an exclamation came from the three interested watchers. In the centre of the lower part of the screen Brett's hand made a visible impression upon the iron wire. Using no more force than had been applied to other portions, the blow served to tear a section of the blind about eight inches across. Instantly the barrister ceased operations, and, producing a pocket-microscope, minutely examined the rent.

"I expected as much," he said, taking hold of the torn part of the screen and giving it a vigorous pull, with the result that a small piece, measuring about eight inches by six, came bodily out. "This has been cut away, as you will see, by some instrument which did not even bend the wire. It was subsequently replaced, whilst the fractured parts were sufficiently cemented by some composition to retain this section in its place, and practically defy observation. There was nothing for it but force to reveal it thus early. No doubt in time the composition would have dried, or been washed away, and then this bit of the screen would have fallen out by the action of wind and weather. Here, at any rate, is a hole in your defensive armour." He held out the *piece de conviction* to the discomfited Sharpe, who surveyed it in silence.

It was no part of Brett's business in life, however, to snatch plaudits from astounded policemen.

"This is a mere nothing," he continued. "Of course, there must have been some such means of getting the diamonds off the premises. Let us return to the ante-room

and there you can tell me the exact history of events on
Monday evening."

4
THE MURDERS

In less confident tones Inspector Walters resumed his narrative—

"On Monday evening, sir," he said, "about eight o'clock, his Excellency and the two secretaries were dining downstairs, and matters had, thus far, gone on with the same routine as was observed every preceding day. The workmen quitted work at six o'clock. The three gentlemen went out for a drive as soon as everything was locked up, and came in again at a quarter to eight. They did not change their clothes for dinner, so there was no occasion to search them, as no one had gone upstairs since they had descended soon after six. They had barely started dinner when some one called at the front door, and I was sent for. The door bell, I may explain, was always answered by one of the house servants, and he, if necessary, admitted any person who came, closing the door; but the visitor had to be examined by the policeman stationed in the passage before he was permitted to come any further. On this occasion I went out and found three gentlemen standing there. They were Turks, as could be easily seen by their attire, and appeared to be persons of some consequence."

"What do you mean by the words 'their attire'?" interrupted Brett. "Were they dressed in European clothes or in regular Turkish garments?"

"Oh," said the inspector, "I only meant that they wore fezzes; otherwise they were quite accurately dressed in frock coats and the rest, but they were unmistakably Turks by their appearance. Two of them could speak no English, and the third, who acted as the leader of the party, first of all addressed me in French. Finding I did not understand him, he used very broken, but fairly intelligible, English. What he wanted was to be taken at once to his Excellency, Mehemet Ali Pasha. I said that his Excellency was dining and that perhaps he had better call in the morning, but he replied that his business was very urgent, and he could not wait. He made me understand that if I sent in the cards of himself and his companions they would certainly be admitted at once. I did not see any harm in this, so I took the three cards and gave them to Hussein, who was crossing the hall at the moment."

"As the cards were printed in Turkish characters you could not, of course, tell what the names were," said Brett.

A look of blank astonishment crossed the inspector's face as he replied: "That is a good guess, but it is so. The hieroglyphics on the piece of pasteboard were worse than Greek. However, Hussein glanced at them. He appeared to be surprised; he went into the dining-room, returning with the message that the gentlemen were to be admitted. Of course I had nothing else to do but to let them in, which I did, accompanying them myself to the door of the dining-room, and making sure, before the door was closed, that their presence was expected."

"How did you do that?" said Brett.

"Well, although they spoke in what I suppose was Turkish, it is not very difficult to distinguish by a man's tones whether his reception of unexpected visitors is cordial or not, and there could be no doubt that the visiting cards had conveyed such names to his Excellency as warranted the introduction of the party into the house. The six gentlemen remained in the dining-room until 9.17 (I have the time noted here in my pocket-book). They then came out and went upstairs in a body to the ante-room, where they all sat down, as I could tell by the movement of chairs overhead, and in a few minutes Hussein was rung for to bring cigarettes and coffee. This was at 9.21. Hussein was searched as he came downstairs after receiving the order, and again at 9.30 when he returned after executing it. I was relieved at ten o'clock, and beyond describing the three gentlemen, I know nothing more about the business."

"They were well dressed?" inquired Brett; "they impressed you as Turkish gentlemen by their features, and they wore fezzes?"

"Yes," said the policeman, with a smile; "but there was a little more than that."

"It is of no importance," said Brett.

"But really it must be," urged the inspector. "One of them, the man who spoke to me, had a bad sword-cut across his right cheek, whilst another squinted horribly; besides, they were all elderly men."

"Pardon me, inspector," said Brett, "but you admit, no doubt, that this is a very remarkable crime I am investigating."

"I should just think it is, sir," was the answer.

"Well, now, does it not strike you that the perpetrators thereof, who were not afraid to be scrutinized by yourself and by several other policemen, and to be searched and further scrutinized by a different set of officers when they came out again, would be very unlikely persons to bear about them such distinguishing characteristics as would lead to their arrest by the first youthful police-constable who encountered them? I do not want to be rude, or to indicate any lack of discretion on your part, but, from my point of view, I would vastly prefer not to be furnished with any description of these three persons, nor would I care to have seen them as they entered or left the house."

"Well, that is very curious," said Inspector Walters, dropping his hands on his knees in sheer amazement at such an extraordinary statement from a man whose clearness and accuracy of perception had been so fully justified by the incident of the window-blind.

"And now, Mr. Sharpe," said Brett, turning to the other officer, "what did you observe?"

"I came on duty at ten o'clock, sir; posted my guards, and received from Inspector Walters an exact account of what had taken place before my arrival. Inspector Walters had hardly quitted the house, when one of the junior members of the mission came downstairs with a note which he asked me to send at once by a constable to Mr. Talbot."

"You are quite sure he was one of the members of the mission?" said Brett.

"Perfectly certain. I have seen him every previous night for nearly a month, as the gentleman often went out late to the Turkish Embassy, and elsewhere. I sent the note, as requested, and Mr. Talbot came back with the constable in about twenty minutes. Mr. Talbot went upstairs accompanied by Hussein; Hussein came down, was searched, went down to the kitchen, brought up more coffee, and never appeared again. The next time I saw him was about noon yesterday, when we broke open the door, and found his dead body. At 11.25, Mr. Talbot, accompanied by the one whom Inspector Walters has described as the spokesman of the strangers, came down the stairs. Mr. Talbot looked somewhat puzzled, but not specially worried, and submitted himself to the searching operation as usual. The other man seemed to be surprised by this proceeding, but offered no objection when his turn came, and said something laughingly in French to Mr. Talbot, when he had to take his boots off. The two gentlemen went outside and called a cab. Mr. Talbot got in, and the constable at the door heard the foreigner tell the driver to go to the Carlton Hotel. He repeated the address twice, so as to make sure the man would make no mistake.

"Then they drove off, and there was no further incident to report until five minutes past twelve, when the other two foreigners came downstairs. Then we had a bit of a job. They knew no English, and one of our men, .

who could speak French, found that they did not
understand that language. However, at last in dumb
show we got them to perceive that everybody who came
downstairs had to be searched. They submitted at once,
and I took special care that the investigation was
complete. There was nothing upon them to arouse the
slightest suspicion, no weapons of any sort beyond a
small pocket-knife carried by one man, and not much in
the way of either papers or money. Before going out one of
them produced a small card on which was written,
'Carlton Hotel.'

"I took it that this was their residence, so I instructed
a constable to see them into a cab and tell the driver
where to take them. I also showed them how much money
to give the cabman. None of the gentlemen upstairs put
in an appearance, nor did I hear them retire to rest. To
make quite sure that all was right, I and a sergeant who
looked in a little later, went upstairs and tried the door of
the ante-room. This was locked and everything was quiet
within, so we returned to the hall, and the night was
passed in the usual manner. Hussein always made his
appearance about eight o'clock in the morning, when he
came down to procure coffee for his Excellency and the
others. As he did not show up I wondered what had
become of him. When nine o'clock came, I determined to
investigate matters. By that time the diamond cutters
had put in an appearance, and were gathered in the hall,
undergoing a slight search preparatory to their day's
work."

"How many of these men were there?" broke in Brett.

"Fourteen exactly. They were mostly Dutchmen, with,
I think three Belgians. Taking a constable with me, I
went upstairs, and ascended to the second storey, where I
knew his Excellency's suite was situated, and where I
expected to find Hussein asleep on a mat in front of the
bedroom door. The mat was there, but no Hussein. Then I
went higher up to the rooms occupied by the two

assistants. I knocked, but received no answer. One door was locked; the other was open, so I went in, but the room was empty, and the bed had not been slept upon. This seemed so strange that I knocked loudly at the other door, with no result. I returned to his Excellency's floor and hammered at the door, which was locked, sufficiently to wake the soundest sleeper that ever lived. This again was useless, so I returned downstairs and sent off two messengers post haste—one to Mr. Talbot, and the other to the Commissioner of Police at Scotland Yard. The man who went to Mr. Talbot's house returned first, bringing the startling information that Mr. Talbot had not been home all night, and that his uncle and sister were anxious to know where he was, as they had received no message from him since he quitted the house the previous night at 10.15. The Commissioner of Police came himself a little later. By that time Inspector Walters had reached here for his turn of day duty, and after a hasty consultation we decided to break in all the doors that were locked, commencing with that of the second assistant. His room was empty, and so was his Excellency's, neither apartment having been occupied during the night. We then returned to the first floor and forced the door of the ante-room, which, we discovered, was only secured by a spring latch, the lower lock not having been used. As soon as we entered the room, we found the four dead men. Hussein, the servant, was nearest the door and was lying in a crumpled-up position. He had been stabbed twice through the back and once through the spinal column at the base of the neck. His Excellency and the two assistants were seated in chairs, but had been stabbed through the heart. The instrument used must have been a long thin dagger or stiletto. There was no sign of it anywhere in the room, and most certainly none of the men who came out the previous night had such a weapon concealed upon him.

"Doctors were at once sent for, and the first medical gentlemen to arrive said that each of the four had been dead for many hours, but they also imagined that the coffee, the remains of which we found in some cups on the table, had been drugged. So, before disturbing the room and its contents in any way, the Commissioner sent for Dr. Tennyson Coke. After careful investigation Dr. Coke came to the same conclusion as the other gentlemen. He believes that his Excellency and his two assistants were first stupefied by the drug and then murdered as they sat in their chairs, whilst the appearance of Hussein and the nature of his wounds seemed to indicate that he had been unexpectedly attacked and killed before he could struggle effectually or even call for assistance.

"Of course, the diamonds had vanished, whilst in the safes or on the tables we found the keys which had evidently been taken from his Excellency's pockets. We were all puzzled to account for the disappearance of the diamonds and the dagger, but you have clearly shown the means whereby they were conveyed off the premises. Dr. Coke took away the coffee for analysis. The four bodies were carried to the mortuary in Chapel Place, and the fourteen workmen were conveyed to Scotland Yard, not because we have any charge against them, but the Commissioner thought it best to keep them under surveillance until the Turkish Embassy had settled what was to be done with them, in the matter of paying such wages as were due and sending them back to Amsterdam. The men themselves, I may add, were quite satisfied with our action in the matter. That is really all I have to tell you."

"It is quite clear, then," said Brett, "that two men succeeded in murdering four and in getting away with their plunder and arms without creating the slightest noise or exciting any suspicion in your mind."

"That is so," admitted Inspector Sharpe ruefully.

"Then," said Brett, "there is nothing else to be done here. Will you come with me, Mr. Winter?"

"Where to, sir?" inquired the detective.

"To find Mr. Talbot, of course."

"Easier said than done," remarked Inspector Walters, as the door closed behind the visitors.

Inspector Sharpe was less sceptical.

"He's a very smart chap is Brett," he said. "Neither you nor I thought of punching that wire screen, did we?"

5
A STARTLING CLUE

Once clear of the Albert Gate mansion, the barrister was bound to confess to a sense of indefiniteness, a feeling of uncertainty which seldom characterised either his thoughts or his actions. He admitted as much to his companion, for Brett was a man who would not consent to pose under any circumstances.

"It is quite true," he explained, "that our first duty must be to find Mr. Talbot, and it is still more certain that we will be able to accomplish that part of our task; but there are elements in this inquiry which baffle me at present."

"And what are they, sir?" said the detective.

"I fail to see why Mr. Talbot was dragged into the matter at all. On the straightforward assumption that Turks were engaged in the pleasant occupation of taking other Turks' lives—an assumption to which, by the way, I attach no great amount of credence—why did they not allow Mr. Talbot to go quietly to his own home? It was not that they feared more speedy discovery of their crime. The hour was then late; it was tolerably certain that he would make no move which might prove injurious to them until next morning, and then the whole affair was bound to be discovered by the police in the ordinary course of events."

"I don't quite follow you, sir," said Winter, with a puzzled tone in his voice. They had, for the sake of quietude, turned into the Park, and were now walking towards Hyde Park Corner. "What do you mean by saying that Mr. Talbot would make no move in the matter until next morning?"

"Oh, I forgot," said Brett. "Of course, you don't know why the diamonds were stolen?"

"For the same reason that all other diamonds are stolen, I suppose."

"Oh, dear no," laughed the barrister. "This is a political crime."

"Political!" said the amazed policeman.

"Well, we won't quarrel about words, and as there are perhaps no politics in Turkey, we will call it dynastic or any other loud-voiced adjective which serves to take it out of the category of simple felony. Why? I cannot at this moment tell you, but you may be perfectly certain that the disappearance of those diamonds from the custody of Mehemet Ali Pasha will not cause the Sultan to sleep any more soundly."

"What beats me, Mr. Brett," said the detective, viciously prodding the gravel path with his stick, "is how you ferret out these queer facts–fancies some people would call them, as I used to do until I knew you better."

"In this case it is simple enough. By mere chance I happened to read this morning that there had been some little domestic squabble in royal circles at Constantinople. I don't know whether you are acquainted with Turkish history, Mr. Winter, but it is a well-recognised principle that any Sultan is liable to die of diseases which are weird and painfully sudden; for instance, the last one is popularly supposed to have plunged a long sharp scissors into his jugular vein; others drank coffee that disagreed with them, or smoked cigarettes too highly perfumed. In any case, the invariable result of these eccentricities has been that a fresh Sultan occupied the throne. Now, don't forget that I am simply theorising, for I know no more of this business than you do at this moment, but I still think that you will find some connection between my theory and that which has actually occurred. At any rate, I have said sufficient to prove to you the importance of not being too ready to make arrests."

"I quite see that," was the thoughtful rejoinder. "But you must not forget, sir, that we in Scotland Yard are bound by rules of procedure. Perhaps you will not mind my suggesting that a word from you to the Foreign Office might induce the authorities to communicate officially with the Home Department, and then instructions could be issued to the police which would leave the matter a little more open than we are able to regard it under the existing conditions."

"I will see to that," said the barrister. "When does the inquest take place?"

"This evening at six."

"It will be adjourned, of course?"

"Oh, yes; no evidence will be given beyond that necessary for purposes of identification, and this can be supplied by the police themselves and an official from the Turkish Embassy."

"Very well. You will mention to no one the theory I have just explained to you?"

"Not if you wish it, sir."

"I do wish it at present. Which way are you going?"

"Straight to the Yard."

"In that case I will accompany you a portion of the distance."

They had now reached Hyde Park Corner, and, hailing a hansom, Brett told the driver to stop outside the Carlton Hotel. The man whipped up his horse and drove in the direction of Constitution Hill, evidently intending to avoid the congested traffic of Piccadilly and take the longer, but more pleasant, route through the Green Park and the Mall.

"By the way," said Brett, "did the driver of the hansom which conveyed Mr. Talbot and his companion from Albert Gate on Monday night tell you which road he followed?"

"Yes," said the detective, "he went this way."

Brett rubbed his hands, with a queer expression of thoughtful pleasure on his keen face.

"Ah," he said, "I like that. It is well to be on the scent."

He did not explain to his professional *confrere* that it was a positive stimulant to his abounding energy and highly-strung nerves to find that he was actually following the path taken by the criminal whom he was pursuing. The mere fact lent reality to the chase. For a mile, at any rate, there could be no mistake, though he might expect a check at the Carlton. Arrived there, Brett alighted.

"Are you going to make any inquiries in the hotel, sir?" said Mr. Winter.

"Why should I?" said Brett. "You have already ascertained from the management that no person even remotely resembling any of the parties concerned is staying at the hotel."

"Yes, confound it, I know I did," cried the other, "but I never told you so."

"That is all right," laughed Brett. "Come and see me at my chambers this evening when the inquest is finished. Perhaps by that time we may be able to determine our plan of action."

Once left to himself, Brett did not enter the hotel. Indeed, he hardly glanced at that palatial structure, having evidently dismissed it from his mind as being in no way connected with the tragedy he was investigating. He made it an invariable rule in conducting inquiries of this nature to adopt the French method of "reconstituting" the incidents of a crime, so far as such a course was possible in the absence of the persons concerned. He reasoned that a very plausible explanation of the unexpected appearance of the three strangers in the Albert Gate mansion on Monday night had been given to Jack Talbot. This young gentleman, it might be taken for granted, had not been selected by the Foreign Office to carry to a successful issue such an important and delicate matter as that entrusted to him, without some good grounds for the faith in his qualities exhibited by his superiors. Brett thought he could understand the brother's character and attributes from his favourable analysis of the sister, and it was quite reasonable, therefore, to believe that Talbot was a man not likely to be easily duped. The principals in this crime were evidently well aware of the trust reposed in the Assistant Under-Secretary, and they, again, would not underrate his intelligence. Hence there was a good cause for Talbot to accept the explanations, whatever they were, given him during the conclave in the dining-room; the effect of which, in Inspector Sharpe's words, had been to "puzzle" the young Englishman. Further, there must have been a very potent inducement held out before Talbot would consent to drive off with a stranger at such a late hour, and when the cab was dismissed at the Carlton, the excuse given would certainly be quite feasible.

"It must surely be this," communed Brett. "The man explained that he was a stranger in London, that he lived quite close to the Carlton Hotel, and that he found it convenient not only for the purpose of giving directions that would be understood, but also for paying fares, to direct the drivers of hired vehicles to go there and not to his own exact address, which he had found by experience many of them did not recognize, whilst his knowledge of the language was not ample enough to enable him to describe the locality more precisely. It follows, then, in unerring sequence that Talbot was conveyed to some place within a very short distance of the spot where I now stand."

He looked along Pall Mall, up the Haymarket, and through Cockspur Street, and he noted with some degree of curiosity that there were very few residential buildings in the neighbourhood. Clubs, theatres, big commercial establishments and insurance offices occupied the bulk of the available space. It was a part of his theory that none of the other great hotels in this district could harbour the criminals, otherwise there would have been no excuse to stop the hansom outside the Carlton.

Brett did not take long to make up his mind once he had decided upon a definite course. He stood at the corner barely three minutes, and then walked off through Pall Mall and down the steps near the Duke of York's Column into the Horse Guards' Parade, intending to walk quietly to his Victoria Street flat. A call at the Foreign Office procured him an official authorization from the Under-Secretary to inquire into the circumstances of Talbot's disappearance and a promise that the Home Office should be communicated with.

He desired to review the whole of the circumstances attending this strange mystery of modern life, and the result of his reflections quickly became apparent when he reached his residence, for in the first instance he despatched a telegram, and then made several notes in his private diary.

The telegram, in due course, produced an elderly pensioned police inspector, a quiet reserved man, whom the barrister had often employed. He explained briefly the circumstances attending Mr. Talbot's disappearance, and added—

"I want you to find out the names, and if possible the business—together with any other information you may happen to come across—of every person who lives within a distance, roughly speaking, of two hundred yards from the Carlton Hotel. The Post Office Directory and your own observation will narrow down the inquiry considerably. It is the unrecorded balance of inhabitants with whom I am particularly anxious to become more definitely acquainted." The man saluted and withdrew.

Brett imagined that he would now be left in undisputed enjoyment of a few hours' rest before the Earl of Fairholme kept the appointment fixed for seven o'clock. But in this he was mistaken.

Smith brought in some tea, which was refreshing after his walk, for the engrossing nature of the morning's occupation caused him to forget his lunch. A cigar and evening paper next claimed his attention, but he had barely settled down to the perusal of a garbled account of events at Albert Gate when his man again entered, announcing in mysterious tones the presence of Mr. Winter. Smith's attitude towards the myrmidons of Scotland Yard who occasionally visited the barrister on business, was peculiar. He regarded them with suspicion, tempered by wholesome awe, and he now made known the arrival of the detective in such a manner as caused his master to laugh at him.

"Show him in, Smith," he said cheerily; "he has not come to arrest me this time."

Winter entered, and a glance at his face brought Brett quickly to his feet.

"What is the matter?" he cried when the door had closed behind the servant. "You have received important news?"

"I should think I have," replied the detective, dropping into a seat. "I was just writing a report in the Yard when I was sent for by the Chief, and you could have knocked me down with a feather when I heard the reason. I suppose I am acting rightly in coming at once to tell you, although in my flurry at the time I quite forgot to ask the Chief's permission, but as you are mixed up in the case at the request of the Foreign Office, I thought you ought to learn what had happened."

"Well, what is it?" cried Brett, impatient of the other's careful provisos.

"Simply this," said the detective. "Mr. Jack Talbot bolted from London on Tuesday in company with a lady. They crossed over from Dover to Calais by the midday boat, and went direct to Paris. Mr. Talbot calmly booked rooms for himself and the girl in the Grand Hotel, had the nerve to write 'Mr. and Mrs. Talbot, 118, Ulster Gardens, London, W.,' in the register, and both of them disappeared forthwith. But we will soon lay hands on the gentleman, no fear. I have somehow suspected, Mr. Brett, that your notion of a political crime was all poppy-cock. It is a good big brazen-faced steal."

"Is it?" said Brett, his face glistening with excitement at the intelligence so suddenly conveyed to him. "Would you mind explaining to me how this precious information reached you?"

"There is no use, sir, in fighting against facts," said the detective, with dogged insistence. "This time you are dead wrong. Mr. Talbot was recognized at Calais by a Foreign Office messenger returning from France. Seeing him with a lady, and knowing that he was not married, the messenger—Captain Gaultier by name—did not speak to him, especially as Mr. Talbot seemed rather to avoid recognition. Captain Gaultier thought nothing of the matter until this morning, when he visited the Foreign Office on duty and heard something of the affair. He then saw the Under-Secretary, the same gentleman who sent the Earl of Fairholme to you, and told him what had happened. The Under-Secretary could hardly refuse to believe such a credible witness, so telegrams were despatched to the Embassy in Paris and the police at Dover. From Dover came the information that exactly such a couple as described by Captain Gaultier had crossed to France on Tuesday morning; and a few hours later a wire from Paris announced the discovery of the registered names at the Grand Hotel. The Paris telegram went on to say that the gentleman had told the manager his luggage was following from the Gare du Nord, and that his wife and himself were going out for half an hour, but would return in time to dress for dinner. When his traps arrived they were to be taken to his room. No luggage ever came, nor was either of the pair seen again; but we will lay hands on them, never fear."

Brett took a hasty stride or two up and down the room.

"So you think," he burst forth at last, "that Mr. Talbot has not only taken part in some vulgar intrigue with a woman, but that he has also bolted with the Sultan's diamonds, sacrificing his whole career to a momentary impulse and imperilling his neck for the sake of a few gems, which he cannot even convert into money?"

"Why not? It is not the first time in the history of the world that a man has made a fool of himself over a woman, or even committed a murder in order to steal diamonds."

"My dear Winter, do be reasonable. Where is the market for diamonds such as these are supposed to be? You know, even better than I do, that the slightest attempt to dispose of them at any figure remotely approaching their value will lead to the immediate detection and arrest of the person rash enough to make the experiment. Don't you see, man, that the Foreign Office and its messenger, its Under-Secretary, your Commissioner, and the Embassy officials in Paris have been completely and abjectly fooled–fooled, too, in a particularly silly fashion by the needless registration of names at the hotel?"

"No, I do not see it. One cannot go against facts, but this time the evidence looks so strong that I shall be mightily mistaken if Mr. Talbot does not swing for his share in the matter. Anyhow, I have done my duty in letting you know what has happened, so I must be off."

"To arrest somebody, of course?" cried Brett, with an irritating laugh; but Mr. Winter was already hurrying down the stairs.

The momentary feeling of annoyance soon passed, to be succeeded by profound pity for the household at 118, Ulster Gardens. He well knew that once the police became convinced that a particular individual was responsible for the commission of a crime it required the eloquence of several counsel and the combined intelligence of a judge and jury at the Old Bailey to force them to change their opinion. Brett had never, to his knowledge, seen Talbot, yet he felt that this bright, alert and trustworthy young official was innocent of the slightest voluntary complicity in a crime which must shock London when its extent became known.

The testimony of the Foreign Office messenger was, of course, staggering at first sight, especially when backed up by the hurried investigations made at Dover and Paris. But there must be an explanation of Talbot's supposed journey, and, even assuming the most unfavourable view of his actions, why on earth should he so ostentatiously parade himself and his companion at the bureau of the Grand Hotel? There could be but one answer to this question. He acted in this manner in order to make certain that his presence in Paris should be known to the police at the first instant they endeavoured to trace him. Then, who could the woman be? The last thing that a clever criminal flying from outraged law would dream of doing would be to encumber himself with a young and probably good-looking companion of the opposite sex.

The more Brett thought out the complexities of the affair, the more excited he became, and the longer and more rapid were his strides up and down the length of his spacious sitting-room. This was his only outward sign of agitation. When thinking deeply on any all-absorbing topic, he could not remain still. He felt obliged to cast away physical as well as mental restriction on the play of his imagination, and he would at times pace back and forth during unrecorded hours in the solitude of his apartments, finally awakening to a sense of his surroundings by reason of sheer exhaustion.

He was not destined to reach this ultimate stage on the present occasion. With a preliminary cough–for the discreet Smith was well versed in his master's peculiarities–his servant announced the appearance of the Earl of Fairholme.

Brett looked at his watch, and was caught in the act by his visitor. "Yes, I know we fixed on seven o'clock," cried the impetuous young peer, "but I was simply dying to hear the result of your inquiries thus far, and I ventured to call an hour earlier."

The barrister explained that he sought to learn the time as a matter of mere curiosity. "Indeed," he added, "your appearance at this juncture is particularly welcome. I want to ask you many things concerning Mr. Talbot."

"Fire away," said Fairholme. "I'm no good at spinning a yarn, but I can answer questions like a prize boy in a Sunday-school."

"Well, in the first instance, have you known him many years?"

"We were at school together at Harrow. Then I entered the Army whilst he had a University career. My trustees made me give up the Service when I succeeded to the estates, and about the same time Jack entered the Foreign Office. That is three years ago. We have seen each other constantly since, and, of course, when I became engaged to his sister our friendship became, if anything, stronger."

"Nothing could be more admirably expressed. Do you know anything about his private affairs?"

"Financially, do you mean?"

"Well, yes, to begin with."

"He got a salary, I suppose, from Government, but he has a private income of some thousands a year."

"Then he is not likely to be embarrassed for money?"

"Most unlikely. He is a particularly steady chap—full of eagerness to follow a diplomatic career and that sort of thing. Why, he would sooner read a blue-book than the *Pink 'Un*!"

"If you were told that he had bolted with a nondescript young woman, what would you say?"

"Say!" vociferated Fairholme, springing up from the seat into which he had subsided, "I would tell the man who said so that he was a d—d liar!"

"Exactly. Of course you would! Yet here are all kinds of people–Foreign Office officials, policemen, and hangers-on of the British Embassy in Paris–ready to swear, perhaps to prove, if necessary, that Talbot and some smartly-dressed female went to Paris quite openly by the day service yesterday, and even took care to announce ostentatiously their arrival in the French capital."

For a moment the two men faced each other silently, the one amused by the news he was imparting, the other staggered by its seeming absurdity. Then Fairholme flung himself back into his chair.

"Look here, Mr. Brett," he went on, "if Jack himself stood there and told me that what you have said is true I would hardly believe it." A note of agony came into his voice, as he added: "Do you know what this means to his sister? My God, man, it will kill her!"

"It will do nothing of the sort," cried Brett. "Surely you understand Miss Talbot better. She will be the first to proclaim to the world what you and I believe, namely, that her brother is innocent, no matter how black appearances may be. I have no knowledge of him save what I have learned within the last few hours, yet I stake my reputation on the certainty that he is in no way connected with this terrible occurrence save by compulsion."

"It gives one renewed courage to hear you speak so confidently," said the earl, his face lighting with enthusiasm as he looked eagerly at the other, whose earnestness had, for an instant, lifted the veil from features usually calm and impassive, betraying the strength of character and masterful purpose that lay beneath the outward mask.

"Is there anything else I can tell you?" asked Fairholme.

"You are quite sure that his was a nature that could not stoop to a vulgar intrigue?" said Brett. "Remember that in this relation the finest natures are prone to err.

From long experience, I have learnt to place such slips in quite another category than mere lapses of criminality."

"Of course any man who knows the world must appreciate your reasons fully, but from what I know of Jack I am persuaded the thing is quite impossible. Even if it were otherwise, he would never be so mad as to go off when he knew that something very unusual and important was about to occur with reference to a special mission for the successful conclusion of which he had been specially selected by the Foreign Office."

"Ah, there you touch on the strange happenings of coincidence. Circumstantial evidence convicts many offenders, but it has hanged many an innocent man before to-day. I could tell you a very remarkable case in point. Once—"

But Smith appeared to announce dinner, and Brett not only insisted that his new acquaintance should dine heartily, but also contrived to divert him from present anxieties by drawing upon the rich storehouse of his varied experiences.

The meal, therefore, passed pleasantly enough. Both men arranged to visit Sir Hubert Fitzjames during the evening and decide on a definite course of action which would receive the approval of the authorities. Armed with a mandate from the Foreign Office, Brett could enter upon his task without fear of interference from officialdom. Nothing further could be done that night, as the private inquiry agent could not possibly complete any portion of his house-to-house scrutiny in the vicinity of the Carlton until the following morning at the earliest.

They smoked and chatted quietly until 7.30 p.m., when Inspector Winter again put in an appearance, to announce that the coroner's jury had brought in a verdict of "Wilful murder by some two or more persons unknown."

The detective was somewhat quieter in manner now that the sensational turn of events in Paris had assimilated with the other remarkable features of the crime. Moreover, the presence of a peer of the realm had a subduing influence upon him, and he had the good taste not to insist too strenuously that Lord Fairholme's prospective brother-in-law was not only an accessory to a foul murder, but also a fugitive thief.

One new fact was established by the post-mortem examination of the victims. Considerable violence had been used to overcome the struggles of the servant, Hussein. His neck was almost dislocated, and there was a large bruise on his back which might have been caused by the knee of an assailant endeavouring to garrotte him.

They were discussing this discovery and its possible significance when Smith entered, bearing a lady's visiting-card, which he silently handed to his master.

Brett read the name inscribed thereon. He merely said, "Show the lady in." Then he turned to the Earl of Fairholme, electrifying the latter by the words: "Miss Edith Talbot is here."

An instant later Miss Talbot came into the room. The three men knew that she brought momentous, perchance direful, intelligence. She was deathly pale. Her eyes were unnaturally brilliant, her mouth set in tense resolution.

"Mr. Brett," she said, after a single glance at her lover, "we have received a letter from my brother."

"A letter from Jack!" cried Fairholme.

"Well, I never did!" ejaculated Mr. Winter.

But Brett only said—

"Have you brought it with you, Miss Talbot?"

"Yes; it is here. My uncle, who was too ill to accompany me, thought you ought to see it at once," and she handed a torn envelope to him.

He glanced at the postmark.

"It was posted in Paris last evening," he said, his cool utterance sending a thrill through the listeners. "Is the address written by him?" he added.

"Oh, yes. It is undoubtedly from Jack."

Here was a woman moulded on the same inscrutable
lines as the man whom she faced. Seldom, indeed, would
either of these betray the feelings which agitated them.
Then he took out the folded letter. It contained but three
lines, and was undated.

"My dear Uncle and Sister," it ran. "I am in a position
of some difficulty, but am quite safe personally.–Ever
yours,   JACK."

Mr. Winter was the first to recover his equanimity. He
could not control the note of triumph in his voice.

"What do you think of it now, Mr. Brett?"

The barrister ignored him, save for a glance which
seemed to express philosophical doubt as to whether Mr.
Winter's head contained brains or sawdust.

"You are quite positive that both letter and envelope
are in your brother's handwriting?" he said.

"Absolutely positive."

"There can be no doubt about it," chimed in
Fairholme, to whom, in response to a gesture, Brett had
passed the damning document.

"Then this letter simplifies matters considerably,"
said Brett.

Miss Talbot looked at him unflinchingly as she
uttered the next question:

"Do you mean that it serves to clear my brother from
any suspicion?"

"Most certainly."

"I thank you for your words from the bottom of my
heart. Somehow, I knew you would say that. Will you
please come and help to explain matters to my uncle?
Harry, you will come too, will you not?"

The sweet gentle voice, with its sad mingling of hope
and despair, sounded so pathetic that the impetuous peer
had some difficulty in restraining a wild impulse to clasp
her to his heart then and there.

Even Mr. Winter was moved not to proclaim his
disbelief.

"I will see you in the morning, sir," he muttered.

Brett nodded, and the detective went out, saying to himself as he reached the street–

"Nerve! Of course he has nerve. It's in the family. Just look at that girl! Still, it did require some grit to sign his name in the hotel register and then calmly sit down to write a letter telling his people not to worry about him. I've known a few rum cases in my time, but this one—"

The remainder of Mr. Winter's soliloquy was lost in the spasmodic excitement of boarding a passing omnibus, for this latest item of news must be conveyed to the Yard with all speed.

6
A JOURNEY TO PARIS

The sight of Talbot's letter seemed to fire Brett's imagination. He radiated electric energy. Both Lord Fairholme and Miss Talbot felt that in his presence all doubts vanished. They realized, without knowing why, that this man of power, this human dynamo, would quickly dispel the clouds which now rendered the outlook so forbidding. For the moment, heedless of their presence, he began to pace the room in the strenuous concentration of his thoughts. Once he halted in front of the small bust of Edgar Allan Poe, whose pedestal still imprisoned the two cuttings of a newspaper which formed the barrister's first links with the tragedy. His ideas suddenly reverted to the paragraph describing the efforts of the Porte to obtain from the French Government the extradition of a fugitive relative of the Sultan. At that instant, too, a tiny clock on the mantelpiece chimed forth the hour of eight.

"That settles it," said Brett aloud. "Smith," he vociferated.

And Smith appeared.

"Pack up sufficient belongings for a short trip to the Continent. Don't forget a rug and a greatcoat. Have the portmanteau on a cab at the door within three minutes."

"I am sorry, Miss Talbot," he continued, with his charming smile and a manner as free from perplexity as if he was announcing a formal visit to his grandmother. "I have just decided to go to Paris at once. The train leaves Victoria at 8.15. Lord Fairholme will take you home, and you will both, I am sure, be able to convince Sir Hubert that to yield too greatly to anxiety just now is to suffer needless pain."

"You are going to Paris, Mr. Brett!" cried Edith.
"Why?"

"In obedience to an impulse. I always yield to
impulses. They impress me as constituting Nature's
telegraphs. I have a favourite theory that we all contain a
neatly devised adaptation of Marconi's wireless system,
and the time may come when the secret will be
scientifically laid bare. Then, don't you see, it will be
possible for a man in London to ring up a sympathetic
soul in San Francisco. At present the code is not
understood. It is not even properly named, so people are
apt to distrust impulses."

He rattled on so pleasantly that Edith, absorbed by
the agony of her brother's disappearance and possible
disgrace, could not conceal an expression of blank
amazement at his levity.

Brett instantly became apologetic.

"Pray forgive my apparent flippancy, Miss Talbot," he
said. "I am really in earnest. I believe that a flying visit to
Paris just now must unquestionably advance us an
important stage in this inquiry. Let me explain exactly
what I mean. Here is a letter from your brother, in
handwriting which you and others best qualified to judge
declare to be undeniably his. It also bears postmarks
which would demonstrate to a court of law that it was
posted in Paris last night and received here to-day. But it
does not follow that it was written in Paris; it might have
been written anywhere. Now, according to the police,
there is an entry in the visitors' book at the Grand Hotel
which appears to prove that your brother wrote his name
therein on Tuesday night. If the handwriting in the
Grand Hotel register corresponds beyond all doubt with
that in this letter and envelope, then your brother must
be in Paris. If it does not, he is not there. I am convinced
that the latter hypothesis is correct, but to make doubly
sure I will go and see with my own eyes. There now–I
owed you an explanation, and I have barely time to catch
my train. Good-bye. I will wire you in the morning."

He placed the mysterious letter in his note-book, gave them a parting smile, and was gone.

He managed to catch the 8.15, which started punctually, the sole remnant of railway virtue possessed by the Chatham and South Eastern line. A restful porter, quickened into active life by a half-crown tip, found him a vacant seat in a first-class smoking carriage, and Brett's hasty glance round the compartment revealed that his travelling companions, as far as Dover, at any rate, were severely respectable Britons bound for the Riviera.

The harbour station at Dover wore its usual aspect of dejected misery. The hurrying passengers pushed and jostled each other in their frenzied efforts to board the steamer, for the average British tourist has a rooted belief that such pushing and jostling and banging of apoplectic portmanteaus against the legs of others are absolutely necessary if he would not be left behind.

With an experience born of many voyages, Brett quickly noted the direction of the wind and the vessel's bearings. A stiff breeze had brought up a moderate sea, and the barrister dumped down his bag and flung himself into a chair on what a novice would regard as the weather side of the charthouse. He bore the discomfort for a few minutes, and was rewarded for his foresight by possessing the most sequestered nook on deck when the vessel turned her head seawards and began one of the shortest, but perhaps the most disagreeable, voyages in the world.

Having retained his seat long enough to establish a proprietary right therein, Brett rose and made a short tour of the ship. To distinguish any one on deck was almost out of the question. The passengers were huddled up in indefinable shapes, and there was hardly light sufficient to effect a stumbling progress over the multitude of hand-baggage. So the barrister dived down the companion-way and cannoned against a burly individual who had propped himself against a bulkhead on the main deck saloon.

Something hard in the man's pockets gave Brett a sharp rap, and when they separated with mutual apologies, he laughed silently.

"Handcuffs!" he murmured. "Scotland Yard is always prepared for emergencies. I will wager a considerable sum that as soon as Winter reached headquarters his story about the letter caused a telegram to be despatched to Dover. Here's a detective bound for Paris and prepared to manacle Talbot the moment he sees him. What a fearful and wonderful thing is the English police system. A crime, obviously clever in its conception and treatment, can be handled by a sharp policeman wearing regulation boots and armed with handcuffs. Really, I must have a drink."

Clinging to the hand-rails and executing some crude but effective balancing feats, he reached the dining saloon, which was woefully denuded of occupants, for the English Channel that night had sternly set its face against the indiscriminate use of cold ham and pickles.

Near the bar, however, solemnly digesting a liqueur, stood a man to whom the choppy sea evidently gave no concern. He had the square shoulders, neat-fitting clothes and closely clipped appearance at the back of the neck which mark the British officer; but he also stood square on his feet and swayed with unconscious ease whether the vessel pitched or rolled or executed the combined movement.

"Now, I wonder," said Brett, "if that is Captain Gaultier. He must be. Gaultier, from his name, should be a Jersey man, hence his facility in foreign languages and his employment as a Foreign Office messenger. It's worth trying. I will make the experiment."

He reached the bar and ordered a whisky and soda. Turning affably to the stranger, he remarked–

"Nasty night, isn't it? I hope we shan't be much behind time."

The stranger glanced at him with sharp and inquisitive eyes, but the glance evidently reassured him, for he replied quite pleasantly–

"Oh, no. A matter of a few minutes, perhaps. They usually manage to make up any delay after we leave Calais."

"That's good," said Brett, "because I want to be in Paris at the earliest possible moment."

The other man smiled.

"We are due there at 5.38," he said. "Rather an early hour for business, isn't it?"

"Well, yes," assented the barrister, "under ordinary circumstances, but as my only business in Paris is to examine an hotel register and then get something to eat before I return, I do not wish to waste time unnecessarily on the road."

The other man nodded affably, but gave no sign of further interest.

"So," communed Brett, "if it be Gaultier, he has not heard the latest developments. I must try a frontal attack."

"Does your name happen to be Gaultier?" he went on.

The stranger arrested his liqueur glass in the final tilt.

"It does," he said; "but I do not think I have the pleasure of knowing you."

"No," said Brett, "you haven't."

"Well?" said the other man.

"The fact is," said Brett, "I heard you had been in London. I guessed from your appearance that you might be a King's messenger, and it was just possible that the Captain Gaultier in whom I was interested might start back to the Continent to-night, so I put two and two together, don't you see, with the result that they made four, a thing which doesn't always happen in deduction if in mathematics."

Now, Foreign Office messengers are not chosen for their simplicity or general want of intelligence. Captain Gaultier eyed his questioner with some degree of stern suspicion as he said from behind his cigar–

"May I ask who you are?"

"Certainly," replied Brett, producing his card.

After a quick glance at the pasteboard, Gaultier continued–

"I suppose, Mr. Brett, you have some motive in addressing me? What is it?"

"I am interested in the fate of a man named Talbot," was the straightforward reply, "and as you told the Under-Secretary that you had seen Talbot crossing to Paris in company with a lady last Tuesday, I hoped that perhaps you would not mind discussing the matter with me."

Captain Gaultier was evidently puzzled. Private conversations with Under-Secretaries of State are not, as a rule, public property, and his momentary intention to decline further conversation with this good-looking and fascinating stranger was checked by remembrance of the fact.

"Really, Mr. Brett," he said, "although I do not question the accuracy of your statement, you will readily understand that I can hardly discuss the matter with you under the circumstances."

"Naturally. You would not be holding a responsible position in His Majesty's service if you were at all likely to do any such thing. But I propose, in the first instance, to reassure you as to my bona fides, and I may point out, in the second place, that as I have met you by a fortunate chance, you can hardly deem it a breach of confidence to discuss with me the mere accidental appearance on a cross-Channel steamer of a man known not only to both of us, but to society at large."

Gaultier clearly hesitated, but did not refuse to accept the Under-Secretary's letter, which Brett handed to him, with the words–

"You know the handwriting, no doubt?"

"That speaks for itself." The King's messenger smiled when he returned the note. "It is an odd coincidence," he added, "and still more curious that you should spot me so readily. However, Mr. Brett, we have now cleared the air. What can I do for you?"

"Simply this," said the barrister; "do you mind telling me how you came to recognize Mr. Talbot?"

"Well, for one thing," was the thoughtful reply, "I knew his overcoat. I often met Talbot in the Foreign Office, and one day he drove me to his club wearing a very handsome coat lined with astrachan. It struck me as a peculiarly comfortable and well-fitting one, and although there are plenty of men about town who may possess astrachan coats, it is a reasonable assumption that this was the identical garment when it happened to be worn by the man himself."

"Then you are quite certain it was Talbot?" went on the barrister.

"Quite certain."

"Would you swear it was he, though his life depended on your accuracy?"

"Well, no, perhaps not that; but I would certainly swear that I believed it was Mr. Talbot."

"Ah, that is a material difference. The only way in which you could be positively certain was to enter into conversation with him, was it not?"

"Yes, that is so."

"I do not want you to think, Captain Gaultier, that I am cross-examining you. Let me tell you at once that I believe you saw someone masquerading in Talbot's clothes, and made up to represent him. Was there anything about his appearance that might lend credence to such a view?"

The other reflected a little while before answering.

"There was only one thing," he said—"he did not seem to notice me. Now, he is a sharp sort of chap, and as it was broad daylight and a fine day, he must have seen me, for he knows me well. Again, from all that I have heard of him, I do not think that he would either pass an acquaintance without speaking to him, nor take flying trips to the Continent with ladies of the music-hall persuasion."

"You have supplied two very powerful reasons why the individual you saw should not be Jack Talbot. Yet, as you say, it was broad daylight, and you had a good look at him."

"No, no," interrupted the other. "I had a good look at his coat–and the lady. Whoever the man was, he appeared to be wrapped up in both of them, and he certainly did not court observation. I naturally thought that the feminine attachment accounted for this, and for the same reason, I did not even seek to scrutinize him too closely. To put the thing in a nutshell, I saw a man whom I believed to be Jack Talbot–and who certainly resembled him in face and figure–attired in Talbot's clothes, and wearing a coat which I had noted so particularly as to be able to describe it to my tailor when ordering a similar one. Add to that the appearance of an attractive lady, young and unknown, and you have my soul laid bare to you in the matter."

"Thank you," said Brett. "I am much obliged."

He would have quitted the saloon, but Captain Gaultier laughed–

"Hold on a bit: it is my turn now. Suppose I try to pump you."

A giant wave took hold of the vessel and shook her violently, and Brett, though an average amateur sailor, felt that the saloon was no place for him.

"Between you and the ship, Captain Gaultier," he said, "the success of the operation would be certain. I have secured a quiet corner of the deck. If you wish for further talk we must adjourn there."

The transit was effected without incident, much to Brett's relief. After a minute or two he felt that a cigar was possible. He turned to his companion with a quiet observation—

"The vessel has failed. You can start now."

"Well," said Gaultier, "tell me what is the mystery attaching to Talbot's movements. I only heard the vaguest of rumours in the Department, but something very terrible appears to have happened, and, indeed, I heartily wished I had kept my mouth shut concerning my supposed meeting with him last Tuesday, as the affair was no business of mine. Moreover, you have now somewhat shaken my belief in his identity, although I can hardly tell you why that should be so."

Brett paused to make sure that no one would overhear him, but the fierce wind whistling round the chart house and bridge, the seas that smote the ship's quarter with a thunderous noise, the all-pervading sense of riotous fury in the elements, rendered the precaution almost unnecessary. In any case, there was no one near enough to act the part of eavesdropper, and Brett, exercising the rapid decision which frequently impressed others as a gift of divination, determined that to let such a man as the King's messenger into the secret could not possibly be harmful to the interests of his client, whilst his help might be beneficial.

In the fewest possible words, therefore, he poured the tale into the other's wondering ear. When he had finished, Gaultier remained silent a few minutes.

Already the clear radiance of the magnificent light at Calais was sending intermittent flashes of brightness over the deck, and the long shoulder of Cape Grisnez was thrusting the force of the gale back into mid-Channel.

"I think," said Gaultier, speaking slowly and thoughtfully, "that your view is the right one, Mr. Brett. There is much more in this business than meets the eye, and any man who believes that Jack Talbot would mix himself up in it must be a most determined ass. Of course, such people do exist, but they shouldn't be in the police force. You are going on to Paris, you said?"

"Yes."

"Then we can travel together. All that you have said is quite new to me. Curiously enough, I have just returned from Constantinople, and I may be able to assist you."

Brett silently thanked his stars for the gratuitous circumstance which threw him into the company of Captain Gaultier. He recognized that the King's messenger, with the precaution that might be expected from one whose daily life demanded extreme prudence, desired to mentally review the strange facts made known to him before he committed himself further. With ready tact the barrister changed the conversation to matters of the moment until they reached the pier at Calais, when both men, not encumbered with much luggage, were among the first flight of passengers to reach the station buffet.

On their way they captured a railway official and told him to reserve a *coupe lit* compartment. In the midst of their hasty meal the Frenchman arrived, voluble, apologetic. The train was crowded. Never had there been such a rush to the South. By the exercise of most profound care he had secured them two seats in a compartment, but the third had already taken itself. He was sorry for it; he had done his best.

When they entered their carriage the third occupant was in possession. He was French, aggressively so. Phil May might have used him for a model. The poor man had been wretchedly ill from the moment he left Dover until the vessel was tied to her berth in the harbour at Calais. He paid not the least attention to the newcomers, being apparently absorbed in contemplation of his own misery. The two Englishmen, though experienced travellers, were sufficiently insular to resent the presence of the stranger, whom Brett resolved to put to the language test forthwith.

"It is very cold in here," he said. "Shall I turn on the hot air?"

The Frenchman seemed to understand that he was addressed. He looked up with a shivering smile and explained that he had only booked one seat. The remainder of the compartment was at their disposal. He was evidently guiltless of acquaintance with the English tongue, but Brett did not like his appearance.

Though well-dressed and well-spoken he was a nondescript individual, and the flash of his dark eyes was not reassuring. Yet the man was so ill that Brett forthwith dismissed him from his thoughts, though he took care to occupy the centre seat himself, thus placing Captain Gaultier on the other side of the carriage. After a visit from the ticket examiner, the Frenchman disposed himself for a nap and the train started.

Captain Gaultier by this time had made up his mind as to the information he felt he could give his new acquaintance.

"It is very odd," he said, "that those diamonds should disappear just at the moment when there is every sign of unrest in Turkey. You know, of course, the manner of the last Sultan's death?"

Brett nodded.

"And you have heard, no doubt, something of the precautions taken by the present Sultan to safeguard his life against the attacks of possible assassins?"

"Yes," said Brett.

"Well, these have been redoubled of late, and the man never goes out that he is not in the most abject state of fear. He is a pitiful sight, I assure you. I saw him less than a fortnight ago, driving to the Mosque on Friday, and his coachman evidently had orders to go at a gallop through the streets, whilst not only was the entire road protected by soldiers, but every house was examined previously by police agents. There is something in the wind of more than usual importance in the neighbourhood of Yildiz Kiosk just now, I am certain. I suppose you did not chance to see any mention of the fact that Hussein-ul-Mulk, the Sultan's nephew, has recently fled from Turkey, and is now under the protection of the French Government?"

"Yes, I noticed that."

"You don't seem to miss much," was Gaultier's sharp remark, pausing in his narrative to light a cigar.

"One of my few virtues is that I read the newspapers."

The train was slowing down as it neared the town station in Calais, and Gaultier's voice could be momentarily heard above the diminishing rattle.

"Well," he said, "I happen to know Hussein-ul-Mulk, and if we find out where he lives in Paris I will introduce you to him."

Brett looked at the slumbering Frenchman out of the corner of his eye. The man appeared to be dozing peacefully enough, but the alert barrister had an impression that his limbs were not sufficiently relaxed under the influence of slumber. Indeed, he felt sure that the Frenchman was wide awake and endeavouring to catch the drift of their conversation.

"I will be most pleased to meet your friend, Captain Gaultier," he said, "and lest it should slip your memory I will give you a reminder."

He opened his card-case and wrote on the back of a card: "Grand Hotel. Breakfast 11.30. No more at present."

The quick-witted King's messenger read and understood.

"It seems to me," he went on, "that he is the very man for your purpose. Though he is not in favour at Court just now he has plenty of friends in the various departments, and he could give you letters which would be certain to secure you some excellent orders. I suppose you are going to the East as the result of the rumoured intention of the Turkish Government to reconstitute the navy."

Brett made a haphazard guess at Gaultier's meaning.

"Yes," he said, "we ought to place a good many thousand tons with them."

Gaultier leant forward to strike a match and glanced at their companion. For some indescribable reason he shared Brett's views concerning this gentleman, and immediately started a conversation of general significance. They soon discovered that they had several mutual acquaintances, and in this way they passed the dreary journey to Paris pleasantly enough.

At the Gare du Nord, their knowledge of French methods enabled them to get quickly clear of the *octroi*, as neither of them had any baggage which rendered their presence necessary at the Custom-house. The Frenchman, who seemed to be thoroughly revived by the air of his beloved Paris, hurried out simultaneously with themselves. He had no difficulty in hearing Brett's directions to a cabman. Gaultier entered another vehicle.

Brett was the first away from the station. He fancied he saw his French travelling companion hastily whisper something to a lounger near the exit, so he suddenly pulled up his *voiture*, gave the driver a two-franc piece and told him to go to the Grand Hotel and there await his arrival. The cab had halted for the moment in the Rue Lafayette, at the corner of the Place Valenciennes, and the cabman, recognizing that his fare was an Englishman and consequently mad, drove off immediately in obedience to orders.

Though nearly six o'clock in the morning, it was quite dark, but as Brett walked rapidly back towards the station he had no difficulty in picking out Gaultier, who occupied an open vehicle. Some little distance behind came another, and herein the barrister thought he recognized the man to whom the Frenchman in the train had spoken. By this time many other cabs were dashing out of the station-yard, so Brett took the chance that he might be hopelessly wrong.

He hailed a third vehicle and told the driver to follow the other two, which were now some distance down the Rue Lafayette. Not until the three cabs had crossed the Place de l'Opera and passed the Madeleine could Brett be certain that the occupant of the second was following his friend Gaultier. Then he chuckled to himself, for this was surely a rare stroke of luck.

Quickly reviewing the possibilities of the affair, he came to the conclusion that the travelling Frenchman really understood little, if any, English, but that he had caught the name of the fugitive from the Sultan's wrath and had forthwith betrayed an interest in their conversation which was, to say the least, remarkable. At the exit from the Gare du Nord the stranger had readily enough ascertained Brett's destination, but he clearly regarded it as important that Gaultier—the man who claimed Hussein-ul-Mulk as a friend—should be tracked, and had given the necessary instructions to the confederate who awaited his arrival.

Although Gaultier had not said as much, Brett guessed that his destination was the British Embassy in the Rue du Faubourg St. Honore. The route followed by the cabman led straight to that well-known locality. The Frenchman in the second cab evidently thought likewise, for, at the corner of the Rue Boissy he pulled up, and Brett was just in time to give his driver instructions to go ahead and thus avoid attracting undue notice to himself.

Gaultier turned into the Embassy, and Brett himself halted a little further on. Dismissing his *cocher* with a liberal fare, he walked rapidly back, and saw the spy enter into conversation with the night porter on duty. The latter personage, however, was clearly a trustworthy official, for he loudly told the other to be off and attend to his own affairs.

Then followed a most exciting and perplexing chase through many streets, and it was only by the exercise of the utmost discretion that Brett finally located his man at a definite number in the Rue Barbette, a tiny thoroughfare in the Temple district.

By this time dawn was advancing over Paris, and the streets were beginning to fill with early workers. He inquired from a passer-by the most likely locality in which he could find a cab, and the man civilly conducted him to the Rue de Rivoli. Thence he was not long in reaching the Grand Hotel, where he found the astonished *cocher* of his first vehicle still safeguarding his bag and arguing fiercely with a porter that he had unquestionably obeyed the Englishman's instructions.

Tired though he was, Brett did not fail to scrutinize the list of arrivals at the hotel on the preceding Tuesday. He instantly found the entry he sought. The arrival of "Mr. and Mrs. John Talbot, London," was chronicled in the register with uncompromising boldness. Hastily comparing the writing in Talbot's letter with that of the visitors' book, Brett was at first staggered by their similarity, but he quickly recognized the well-known signs which indicate that a man who himself writes a bold and confident hand has been copying the signature of another with the object of reproducing it freely and with reasonable accuracy. There are always perceptible differences in the varying pressure of the pen and the distribution of the ink.

Allowance had evidently not been made for the fact that Englishmen almost invariably write their names very badly in Continental hotel registers, owing to their inability to use foreign pens. The man who not only forged Mr. Talbot's name, but also supplied him with a wife, laboured under no such disadvantage. Indeed, Talbot himself would probably not have written his own name so legibly.

"That is all right," said Brett wearily, traversing a corridor to gain his room. "Now, I wonder if there is any connexion between Hussein-ul-Mulk and the Rue Barbette."

7
The House In The Rue Barbette

Brett was called at ten o'clock. After reinvigorating himself with a bath and a hearty breakfast, he was ready to meet Captain Gaultier, who arrived promptly at 11.30.

In the spacious foyer of the Grand Hotel it was impossible to say who might be looking at them.

"Come to my room," said Brett. "There we will be able to talk without interruption."

Once comfortably seated, Brett resumed the conversation where he had broken it off in the train overnight.

"You say you know Hussein-ul-Mulk," he commenced.

"Yes," replied the King's messenger, "and what is more, I have discovered his residence since we parted. It seems that one of the attaches at the Embassy met him recently and thought it advisable to keep in touch with the Young Turkish party, of which Hussein-ul-Mulk is a shining light. So he asked him where he lived, and as the result I have jotted down the address in my note-book."

Gaultier searched through his memoranda, and speedily found what he wanted.

"Wait a minute," interrupted Brett. "Does it happen to be No. 11, Rue Barbette?"

The barrister had more than once surprised his companion during the previous night, but this time Gaultier seemed to be more annoyed than startled.

"If you know all these things," he said stiffly, "I don't see why you should bother me to get you the information. I certainly gathered from your remarks that the only acquaintance you had with Hussein-ul-Mulk was obtained from the newspapers, and that individual himself has the best of reasons for not publishing his address broadcast."

Brett smiled.

"You mean," he said, "that Hussein-ul-Mulk does live at No. 11, Rue Barbette."

"Why, of course he does," was the irritable answer.

"That is very odd," said the barrister. "It was a mere guess on my part, I assure you."

His assurance evidently did not weigh much with Captain Gaultier, who replaced the note-book in his pocket, and obviously cast about in his mind for a convenient excuse to take his departure.

Brett knew exactly what was troubling him.

"I am quite in earnest," he said, "in telling you that I simply hazarded a guess at the address. To prove that this is so, I must place you in possession of certain incidents which took place after we parted at the Gare du Nord."

Rapidly but succinctly he told the amazed King's messenger of the chase in the cab across Paris, and how he (Brett) had followed the Frenchman who was tracking Gaultier's movements so closely.

"You will understand," he concluded, "that, in view of my preconceived theory, it was not a very far-fetched assumption to connect Hussein-ul-Mulk with the house in the Rue Barbette into which your spy vanished."

"Well," gasped his astonished hearer, "I must say, Mr. Brett, that I owe you an apology. I really thought at first you were fooling me, whereas now I learn that you simply kept your eyes open much wider than other people, perhaps. Nevertheless, you have given me a genuine explanation of circumstances that were otherwise puzzling. For, do you know, I heard about that chap calling at the Embassy last night. The incident was unusual, to say the least, but I paid little attention to it, and certainly failed altogether to connect it with your visit to Paris. Even yet I do not see what reason anyone can have for shadowing my movements."

"I regard it as mere chance. I imagine that our fellow-passenger in the train caught the name of Hussein-ul-Mulk in our conversation, and this decided him to shadow your movements, by means of the confederate who awaited his arrival at the station. As it happened, they simply hit upon the wrong person. It might have paid them much better to follow me. The outcome of the blunder is that I am in a fair way towards ascertaining all I want to know about them, whereas, up to the present, they do not even suspect my existence as an active agent in the affair."

"Well, now, in what way can I help you regarding Hussein-ul-Mulk?"

"Can you introduce me to him?"

"In what capacity?"

Brett reflected for a moment before replying.

"It would best suit my purpose if I met him as a political sympathiser."

Gaultier evidently did not like the idea. Foreign Office messengers do not care to be associated with politics in any shape or form.

"Is there no other way?" he asked dubiously.

"Plenty," said Brett. "I might pose as a friend of yours interested in Turkish carpets, or coffee, or cigarettes, but for the purpose of my inquiry it would be well to jump preliminaries at once and make this chance acquaintance under the guise of a wire-puller."

"All right," said Gaultier. "I don't see that it matters much to me, and the letter you have in your possession from the Under-Secretary is sufficient warrant for me to give you any assistance that lies in my power."

He glanced at his watch. "It is just about time for *dejeuner*," he continued. "What do you say if we drive to the Rue Barbette at once?"

The barrister assented, and they were soon crossing Paris with the superb disregard for other people's feelings that characterises the local cab-driver.

"By the way," inquired Gaultier, "have you learned anything else since your arrival?"

"Only this–it was not our friend Talbot who came here on Tuesday with a lady."

"You are sure?"

"Positive. I have compared the handwriting in the hotel register with a letter undoubtedly written by Mr. Talbot, and the two do not agree. The entry 'Mr. and Mrs. Talbot, London,' in the visitors' book of the Grand Hotel, was a mere trick intended to amuse the police for a few hours until the conspirators had perfected their scheme for final and complete disappearance."

"It was a bold move."

"Very. Quite in keeping with the rest of the details of an uncommon crime."

At last the *fiacre* stopped in front of the house in the Rue Barbette which Brett had already scrutinized during the early hours of the morning.

"Here we are," said Gaultier with a laugh. "If we find Hussein-ul-Mulk at home I don't know what the deuce we are going to say to him. Remember that I depend on you to carry out a difficult situation, because my Turkish friend will become suspicious the minute he finds me dabbling in intrigue. He knows full well that such matters are quite outside of my usual business."

"I think I will be able to interest him," said Brett calmly; and without further preliminary Gaultier ascertained from the *concierge* that the Turkish gentleman was within.

The two men ascended to the second storey.

Gaultier rapped loudly on the first door he encountered, and the summons appeared to scatter some of the inhabitants, judging by the rapid opening and closing of doors that preceded the appearance of an elderly and solemn-looking Turk, who cautiously demanded their business.

Gaultier sent in his card, and the servitor locked the door in the faces of the two men while he went to ascertain his master's orders.

"They evidently do not mean to take many risks," said the King's messenger in a low voice.

"You are right," replied Brett, "though they appear to take the greatest one of all without giving it a thought."

"And what is that?"

"This exhibition of nervousness and precaution before visitors are admitted. The best way to excite suspicion is to behave exactly as they are doing."

But now the door was reopened, and the elderly Turk ushered them into a spacious room on the right of the entrance hall, where they were received by a young man— a tall, dignified Mohammedan, who rose hastily from a chair, having apparently abandoned the perusal of a newspaper.

"Ah! mon brave Gaultier," he cried, "I am so pleased to see you. I did not know you were in Paris. I have been spending an idle moment over smoke and scandal." He spoke excellent French, and appeared to be quite at his ease, but Brett noticed that Hussein-ul-Mulk held the discarded newspaper upside down. He was smoking a cigarette, lighted the instant before their appearance, and notwithstanding his Oriental phlegm he seemed to be labouring under intense excitement.

Nevertheless, Hussein-ul-Mulk could control his nerves.

"Have you had *dejeuner*, or have you time to join me in a cigarette?" he went on.

"We will be delighted," said Gaultier, taking the proffered case. "The fact is, I only heard of your presence in Paris by accident, and I mentioned the fact to my friend here, who has interested himself in the Armenian cause in London. He at once expressed a keen desire to make your acquaintance, so I ventured to bring him here and introduce him to you. This is Mr. Reginald Brett, an

English barrister, and one who keenly sympathizes with the reform movement in Turkey."

"I am delighted to know you, Mr. Brett," said the suave Oriental. "It is naturally a great pleasure to me to make the acquaintance of any influential Englishman who has given sufficient thought to Eastern affairs to understand the way in which my country suffers under a barbarous and unenlightened rule."

He spoke with the glibness of a born agitator, yet all the while he was inwardly wondering what could be the true motive of the visit paid him by this distinguished-looking stranger, and Brett was silently resolving to startle Hussein-ul-Mulk out of his complacency at the earliest possible moment.

"It is an even greater pleasure to me," he said, "to find myself talking to a reformer so distinguished as you. Your name is well known in England. Indeed, in some quarters, it has come to be feared, which in this world is one of the signs of success."

Hussein-ul-Mulk was puzzled, but he remained outwardly unperturbed.

"I was not aware," he purred, "that my poor services to my country were so appreciated by my English friends."

"Ah," said Brett, with a smile that conveyed much, "a man like you cannot long remain hidden. I have good reason to know that at the present moment your achievements are earnestly attracting the attention of the Foreign Office."

Hussein-ul-Mulk became even more puzzled. Indeed, he exhibited some slight tokens of alarm lest Brett's vehement admiration should reach the ears of others in the adjoining room.

"Really," he said, "you flatter me. Will you not try these cigarettes? They are the best; they are made from tobacco grown especially for the Sultan's household, and it is death to export them. I understand that the cigarette habit has grown very much of recent years in England?"

"Yes," said Brett, "it certainly has developed with amazing rapidity. In trade, as in politics, this is an astounding age."

Gaultier knew that there was more behind the apparent exchange of compliments than appeared on the surface. Having fulfilled his pledge to Brett, he said hurriedly, "Both of you gentlemen will understand that I cannot very well take part in a political discussion. With your permission, Hussein, I will now leave my friend with you for a half-hour's chat, as I have an appointment at the Cafe Riche."

Although Hussein was profoundly disconcerted by Brett's manner no less than his utterances, he could not well refuse to accord him a further audience, so Gaultier quitted the apartment and the Englishman and the Mussulman were left face to face.

Brett felt that the situation demanded a bold game. Under some circumstances he knew that to throw away the scabbard and dash with naked sword into the fray was the right policy.

"I came to see you, Hussein-ul-Mulk," he said, speaking deliberately, "not only because I have an interest in the progressive policy voiced by the young Turkish party, but on account of matters of personal interest to you, and to friends of mine in England."

The Turk bowed silent recognition of the barrister's motives.

"You are aware," said Brett, "that a large number of valuable diamonds were stolen from the special Envoy of his Majesty the Sultan, in London, last Tuesday night, and that the theft was accompanied by the murder of four of the Sultan's subjects and the abduction of a prominent official in the British Foreign Office?"

It is difficult for an olive-skinned man to turn pale, but Hussein-ul-Mulk did the next most effective thing for one of his race. His face assumed a dirty green shade, and his full red lips whitened.

For some few seconds he strove hard to regain his composure and frame a reply, but Brett, nonchalantly puffing a cloud of smoke into the intervening space, and thus helping his hearer to control his emotions, went on—

"Pray do not trouble to deny your knowledge of the fact. It is far better for men of the world like you and me to discard subterfuge when engaged in grave and difficult negotiations. I do not purpose wasting time by describing to you the details of a crime with which you are thoroughly acquainted. Let me say, in a sentence, that my chief, perhaps my only, motive in coming here to-day is to secure the release of my friend Mr. Talbot from the place where he is at present confined, and at the same time to obtain from you a statement which will satisfactorily clear Mr. Talbot in the eyes of his superiors of all personal complicity in the Albert Gate incident."

Again there was a breathless silence.

Hussein-ul-Mulk had regained his nerve. He was now considering how best he could dispose of this Englishman who knew so much. To purchase his silence was too hopeless. He must die as speedily and unostentatiously as possible. So he answered not, but thought hard as to ways and means.

Brett, in imminent danger of his life, disregarded all semblance of danger. He leaned back in his chair, closed his eyes in complete enjoyment of Hussein's cigarettes, which were really excellent, and said, in the even, matter-of-fact tones of one who discusses an abstract problem—

"Of course, my dear friend, you are thinking that the best answer you can give me is to strangle me or to shoot me, or adopt some other drastic remedy which finds favour in Constantinople. But let me point out to you that this will be a serious error of judgment. I have not come here without safeguarding my movements. You are aware that Captain Gaultier, a trusted Foreign Office messenger, brought me here in person. Some members of the British Government, and several important officials of Scotland Yard know that I am in your house and discussing this matter with you. If any accident interferes with my future movements, you will simply precipitate a crisis quite lamentable in its results to yourself, to your association, and to your cause. You will see, therefore, Hussein, that to kill me cannot really be thought of. A man of your penetration and undoubted sagacity must surely admit this at once, and we can then proceed to discuss matters in a friendly and pleasant manner."

At last Hussein found his tongue. "I have never met you before, Mr. Brett," he said, "but you interest me."

Brett smiled and bowed in acknowledgment of the compliment.

"Of course, I admit nothing," went on the Mohammedan.

"Of course."

"Least of all do I admit that I contemplated any breach of hospitality towards yourself."

Brett waved his hand in deprecation of such a pernicious thought.

"But you will understand," went on Hussein-ul-Mulk, "that it is quite impossible for me to even attempt to discuss the very interesting facts you have brought to my notice without some inquiry on my part, and on yours some proof that the events concerning which you have informed me have really happened. You see, one cannot trust newspapers. They get such garbled accounts of occurrences, particularly of State affairs; they are misleading—"

"Excuse me, I am sure you will admit that although I dispensed with details in my brief statement, the facts were undeniable. I can tell you exactly how and why Mehemet Ali and his two secretaries, together with Hussein, his confidential servant, were murdered. But the circumstances were revolting, and need not be unduly discussed between gentlemen. I can tell you how the diamonds were obtained from the Albert Gate mansion, and how they were conveyed to Paris. But as they are probably in your possession, and the main object of your enterprise has thus been accomplished, it seems to me that all these otherwise dramatic effects are needless. I have told you exactly the object of my visit, and I still await an answer."

Hussein-ul-Mulk laughed a trifle uneasily.

"On my part, monsieur, I might attempt to question the extent of your knowledge, but as you are mistaken in one part of your summing-up of evidence, you may be wrong in others."

"To what do you allude?"

The Mohammedan reflected for a moment, and then answered–

"I can see no harm in telling you that I am not aware of any diamonds in which I am personally interested having arrived in Paris."

"Indeed!" said Brett, leaning forward in his chair, and instantly dropping the listless air which had hitherto characterized his utterances. "That is a very curious thing, because the diamonds have been in Paris at least two days, and if they are withheld from the possession of those who employed certain agents to secure them, there must be a powerful reason to account for the delay. Speaking quite disinterestedly, monsieur, I would advise you to inquire into the matter at once."

His words evidently perturbed the Turk.

"Will you object," he said, "if I leave you alone a few minutes? I wish to consult with a friend of mine who happens to be staying here."

"Assuredly," said Brett; "but let me beg you to leave your cigarettes behind. They are exquisite."

Hussein-ul-Mulk had never before encountered such a personality as Reginald Brett. His eyebrows became perfectly oval with surprise and admiration for the man who could thus juggle with a dangerous situation.

"Here is my case," he said, "and when we have concluded this most interesting conversation I hope you will leave me your address, so that I may have the extreme pleasure of sending you a few hundreds."

Then he quitted the room. He was absent fully five minutes.

On his return he said—

"In the opinion of my friend, Mr. Brett, it is impossible for us to do anything at the present moment. We must inquire; we must verify; we must consult others. You will see that the negotiations you have undertaken require on our part some display of the extreme delicacy and tact in which you have given us so admirable a lesson. Suppose, now, we agree to meet here again to-morrow at the same hour. Am I to understand that what has transpired this morning remains, we will not say a secret, but a myth, a mere idle phantasy as between you and me?"

"That is precisely my idea," said Brett. "One hates to mention such a brutal word as 'police' in an affair demanding finesse. Personally I hate the blunderers. They rob life of its charm. They have absolutely no conception of art. Romance with them can end only in penal servitude or on the gallows. Believe me, Hussein, I am very discreet." In another minute he was standing in the street, and inhaling generous draughts of the keen air of Paris.

"I wonder how much my life was worth during the first five minutes?" said he to himself; and then he made his way to a telegraph office, whence he despatched the following message—

"TO THE EARL OF FAIRHOLME,
"STANHOPE GATE, LONDON.

"Have received definite intelligence which confirms my views. Expect our friend will be discovered within forty-eight hours. If possible, join me at Grand Hotel, Paris, to-night, eleven o'clock.

"BRETT."

8
WHAT HAPPENED IN THE RUE BARBETTE

Pending Fairholme's arrival, Brett was not idle. He visited a prominent jeweller in the Rue de la Paix, and, after making some trivial purchases, led the conversation to the question of diamonds. By skilful inquiry he ascertained a good deal about precious stones, both in their crude and their finished states. The accommodating Frenchman showed him a good many samples of South African, Brazilian, and Indian stones, and explained to him the various tests which were used to determine their value.

Brett had no special object in seeking this information. When engaged in elucidating any mystery he made it an invariable rule to post himself as accurately as possible concerning all minor details which might, by any straining of circumstances, become useful.

He returned to his hotel and jotted down some notes of this conversation. Whilst engaged in the task a telegram arrived from the Earl of Fairholme announcing that nobleman's departure from London by the afternoon train service via Boulogne.

Punctually at the time appointed the earl reached the hotel. He was all eagerness to learn what had happened since they parted in London, and why Brett had so suddenly summoned him to Paris.

"I really have not much definite information," said the barrister. "Thus far I am building chiefly on surmise, but I have undoubtedly come into contact with the persons who organized and planned, if they did not actually carry out, the raid on the Albert Gate mansion."

"Then you have news of Jack?" broke in Fairholme excitedly.

"Not exactly. All I can do at present is to assure you that the scent is hot, and we may run our quarry to earth some few minutes after eleven o'clock to-morrow morning."

"I am jolly glad that there is a chance of my being useful in this matter," said the earl gleefully. "If only I am a little bit instrumental in recovering her brother, Edith hasn't got a leg to stand on in the matter of getting married. That's awkwardly put, isn't it? What I mean is that when Talbot is restored to his family and everything is satisfactorily cleared up, Edith and I can get spliced immediately, can't we?"

"I regard it as the most assured fact we have yet encountered," said Brett, pleasantly.

"But you haven't told me yet the exact manner in which I can be useful."

"No," said the barrister. "I have been revolving in my mind the possibilities of to-morrow morning, and you must play an important part in what, by chance, may turn out to be a melodrama. Now, listen to me carefully. In the neighbourhood of the Porte St. Martin there is a street known as the Rue Barbette. At eleven o'clock to-morrow I go to the house No. 11 in that street, and you will accompany me as far as the door. It will be your duty to stand outside and take note of all persons who enter or leave the house once I have disappeared from view in the interior. You must exercise your powers of observation most minutely, paying heed to the height, build, complexion, and clothing of any individual, male or female, who enters or leaves No. 11, Rue Barbette, after you have taken your stand in the street. It is more than probable that no person will demand scrutiny, unless it be some chance tradesman's assistant visiting the building in pursuance of his ordinary work. However, do you feel capable of attending to this part of the programme?"

"Perfectly."

"You will maintain watch until 11.30. If at that hour I have not rejoined you, make your way to the nearest policeman, and tell him that you have good reason to believe that a friend of yours has either been murdered or suffered serious personal injury in a room on the second storey of the house in question. You will then, in company with the policeman, come rapidly to the apartment I have indicated and demand an immediate entrance–if necessary bursting the door open."

"And what then?" gasped the amazed earl.

"I really don't know," said Brett imperturbably. "It is possible you may find my gory corpse in one of the inner rooms. The best I can hope for is that I shall be simply a prisoner, but I fully expect to be seriously injured at the very least."

"But look here, Brett: are you doing the right thing in this matter? Why on earth should you run such an awful risk, and take it alone, too? Isn't it possible to obtain some trustworthy detective to keep watch in the street, and let me go into the place with you? Don't you see, old chap, that two of us might make a reasonable show if violence is attempted? One man hasn't much chance."

The barrister cut short his friend's protestations.

"I sent for you, Lord Fairholme," he said, "because I felt that I could trust you to obey my instructions implicitly. This is a matter in which I do not want the police to interfere. My visit to the Rue Barbette to-morrow morning may end quite satisfactorily. If it does, we shall be in possession of important information leading to the prompt release of Mr. Talbot. If it fails, there will certainly be some shooting or stabbing, or perhaps an attempt may be made to keep me a prisoner. This latter eventuality renders the presence of the police essential. No matter what has happened to me, they will, with your assistance, be able to take up the inquiry exactly where I leave it off. In this note-book here, which I am placing in a locked drawer"–and he suited his action to the words–"you will find details of all that I have done up to the present moment, together with the lines along which future inquiries should proceed. In particular, you will find an elaboration of the theory which I expect to-morrow's visit to confirm. You fully understand me? All this anticipates that after 11.30 to-morrow I shall be personally unable to conduct the investigation further."

"Yes," agreed the earl, with rueful emphasis, "I fully understand the proposition, and I tell you, Brett, I don't like it. There has been enough blood spilt in this beastly business already, and I feel a sort of personal responsibility for you, you know, because I brought you into it."

"Then," said the barrister, with a laugh, "I solemnly acquit you of any such responsibility. I am going into the business with my eyes open. It interests me strangely, and I would not abandon the quest now on any account."

"But can't you explain matters a little more clearly? Is it necessary that I should be kept in the dark as to the circumstances which have led up to this critical movement to-morrow?"

"Not in the least. It is, indeed, very important that you should comprehend all that has gone before; I only started at the end, so to speak, so as to fix accurately in your mind your part of the business, which now stands separate and distinctly outlined in your memory. What I am going to tell you simply leads up to the expected denouement."

He then recited to the wondering earl the whole of the curious events which had happened during the preceding twenty-four hours.

It was late when they got to bed, but they rested well, and, after the manner of their race, fortified themselves with a good breakfast against the trials of the day, whatever these might prove to be. A few minutes before the appointed hour they quitted a *fiacre* in the vicinity of the Rue Barbette, and at eleven o'clock Brett passed the *concierge*, whilst Fairholme took up his stand outside.

The barrister was received with smiling complacence by Hussein-ul-Mulk. On this occasion he was conducted to another room of the flat, and he promptly noted that the windows looked out to the rear of the building, whereas during his previous visit he could survey the street.

"This promises badly," said Brett to himself, but he betrayed not the slightest unwillingness to fall in with the arrangements made for his reception, and lounged back in a comfortable chair so easily that not even the quick-witted Turk suspected that the barrister's hip pocket contained a very serviceable revolver.

Hussein-ul-Mulk commenced the conversation. "I have," he said, "a couple of friends here who are interested in the matter you were good enough to mention to me yesterday. With your permission I will introduce them," and he threw open another door with a single Turkish word which Brett imagined was an invitation to enter.

Two men came from an adjoining room. They were Turks–swarthy, evil-looking customers, but well-dressed, and evidently persons of consequence in their own country. The newcomers eyed the barrister curiously, and with no very friendly intent.

A brief conversation in Turkish resulted in Hussein-ul-Mulk addressing Brett.

"I must apologize for the fact that my friends here only speak their native tongue. Before we proceed to business I wish to ask you a few questions."

"Certainly," said Brett; "go ahead."

"You mentioned to me yesterday that you had no desire to invoke the aid of the police in prosecuting the inquiry which interests you."

"Quite right," said Brett.

"May I ask if you have adhered to that intention?"

"Absolutely."

"Well, Mr.–Mr."–Hussein-ul-Mulk consulted a visiting card–"Mr. Reginald Brett, I think, is your name? It would be idle on my part to compliment you on your bravery, but it would be still more futile to attempt to conceal from you the danger of the position in which you now stand."

"Sit," corrected Brett, still smiling.

"Well," said the Turk, "we will not quibble about words. The fact remains, Mr. Brett, that you have needlessly thrust yourself into an enterprise of such a desperate character that all interlopers can be dealt with only in one way."

"You kill them," said Brett, airily.

"Yes," said the Turk, "I deeply regret to inform you that you have guessed the object of my remarks with the singular skill you have already betrayed in reaching the existing position. I can only add that I am surprised the same skill did not influence you to avoid forcing upon us the only alternative left."

"Am I to be killed at once?" said Brett, speaking with a slight affectation of boredom.

Even the self-possessed Turk could not conceal his amazement at the manner in which his strange visitor conducted himself.

"That is a point we have not yet decided," he said. "We are strangely unwilling to take the life of such a brave man as yourself. If we were assured of your silence, we would even be disposed to permit you to escape this time, with a solemn warning not to cross our path again. But we feel that clemency is out of the question. There is one hope–a slight one, it is true–which may permit us to gag you and tie you securely in this room, where you will be left in peace for at least forty-eight hours, after which time a telegram can be despatched to any address you choose to supply us with. But really, owing to unforeseen circumstances, this chance of a reprieve is remote. It wholly depends upon the arrival, or otherwise, at this house, of a gentleman whom we expect at 11.15."

Brett leaned forward in his chair, and took out his watch. The other misunderstood his movement, and each of the three men promptly produced a revolver.

Brett laughed quite heartily. "Really, gentlemen," he cried, "your nervousness is ludicrous."

He saw that he yet had five minutes' grace before his self-constituted judges would proceed to execute their sentence. As for the Turks, they were manifestly ashamed of having betrayed such trepidation, and they replaced the weapons so readily staged.

"That is a point in my favour," thought Brett. "Next time, if I do wish to reach my revolver, I may be able to get the draw on them first."

"During the interval," said Hussein-ul-Mulk suavely, "is there anything you wish to do—any letters to write, or that sort of thing?"

"No," said Brett, "I do not think so; it seems to me that you have thoroughly misunderstood the purpose of this meeting. I came here in order to obtain from you particulars which will lead to the release of Mr. Talbot and redeem his character in the eyes of his superiors. I did not come here to be killed, Hussein-ul-Mulk. I am not going to be killed. If you touch a hair of my head you will only leave this house for a prison, and subsequently for the gallows. And so, you see, you are talking childishly when you dangle these threats and preliminaries to immediate execution before my eyes. It is not you, but I, who will dictate the terms on which we part. It may perhaps interest you to explain this new phase of the situation to your fellow-countrymen, and the matter will also serve to dissipate the few minutes which yet have to elapse before 11.15."

Hussein-ul-Mulk made no direct reply to this remarkable speech. That it impressed him was quite evident from his manner. Forthwith an animated but subdued conversation took place between the triumvirate.

While it was yet in progress a peculiar knock was heard on the outside door of the apartment.

"Ah! he comes," said Hussein-ul-Mulk in French. He left the room in order to meet the new arrival. He returned without delay, bringing with him a man very different from those whom Brett had encountered thus far in connection with the crime. This was a dapper little Frenchman, wizened, yellow-skinned, black-haired, and dressed almost in the extreme of fashion. He at once addressed himself to the barrister.

"They tell me, my friend," he said, "that you have thrust your finger into the pie which the friends of his Majesty the Sultan are preparing for him. It is a bad business. You are too soon for the banquet. The result is that your poor little finger may get burnt, as the pie is still being cooked."

The man smiled maliciously at his feeble witticism, and Brett instantly took his measure as a member of the gang of flash thieves which infest Paris. He knew that such a ruffian was both pitiless and cowardly. Whatever the outcome of the situation which faced him, he would not stoop to conciliatory methods with this despicable rascal.

"I suppose," he said, "that the only part of the affair which concerns you is the robbery."

"Well, and what if it is?"

"I can only say that your political friends will be well advised to keep a close eye on you, for you would rob them just as soon as the persons against whom they have employed you."

The little thief laughed cynically. "You are right, *mon vieux*. I would be delighted to have the chance. But this time it is impossible. The stones are too big. They are worth–pouf!–millions of francs, so I must be content to receive my pay, which is good."

"Have you entrusted the Sultan's diamonds to the care of a scamp like this?" said Brett, addressing himself to Hussein, and inwardly resolving that unless the conversation by chance took a turn favourable to himself, he would forthwith open fire on the gang and endeavour to escape.

"Yes," cried the conspirator with a savage laugh. "You have never seen them, Mr. Brett? Here they are. To many men the sight would be a pleasant one. To you it should be terrible, for the arrival of these diamonds at this moment means that you must die."

So saying, he produced from an inner pocket of his frock-coat a large, plain morocco case. The pressure of a spring caused the lid to fly back, revealing to the eyes of those in the room a collection of diamonds marvellous by reason of the size and magnificence of each stone.

In the centre reposed the Imperial diamond itself. For an instant Brett reflected that whilst the other men were fascinated by the spectacle, he would have a good opportunity to shoot some of them without mercy and make a dash for liberty.

But at the same moment there came to him an odd thought. His friend the jeweller of the Rue de la Paix had not given him a lesson in vain during the previous afternoon.

The barrister suspected—in fact, he was almost sure— that the gems now flaunting their half-revealed glories in the light of the day—for not one of them had undergone the final process peculiar to the diamond-cutter's trade— were not the real stones stolen from Albert Gate, but well fabricated substitutes.

To his acute brain there came an immediate confirmation of his theory. Evidently the diamonds had not been previously in the Turk's possession. The little Frenchman had just delivered them, and this in itself was a strange circumstance in view of the fact that the genuine stones must have been in Paris at least three days.

Brett concentrated all his dramatic faculties in look, voice, and gesture.

"You fools!" he cried. "You have been swindled by a device which a child might suspect. These are not the Sultan's diamonds. These are frauds–cleverly concocted bits of crystal and alum–intended to keep you happy until you return to Constantinople and discover how thoroughly you were deceived."

"You lie!" roared the little Frenchman. "They are genuine."

Brett wanted to punch the diminutive scoundrel heavily in the face, but he restrained himself. Turning with a magnificent assumption of courteousness to Hussein-ul-Mulk, he said–

"Come, I told you you were acting childishly; this proves it. A most outrageous attempt has been made to swindle you, if I may use such a term to persons who confessedly are plotting to rob another. Surely this will convince you that you have nothing to fear from me. I am here as the agent neither of Sultan nor police. It is a simple matter for you to verify my statement. All that is necessary is for one of your party to take any of these alleged diamonds–I would suggest the smallest one so as not to create suspicion–to any jeweller in the district, and he will test it for you immediately, thus proving the truth of my statement. Look here; I will convince you myself."

He took the monster diamond irreverently in his hand before Hussein-ul-Mulk could prevent him and turned to the window. He pressed the stone against the glass and tried to make it cut. It failed. He placed it against his cheek. It was warm. A pure diamond would be icy cold. More than this, a small portion of the composition of which the imitation had been hastily concocted, broke off in his fingers.

"You see," he laughed. "Do you require further proof?"

Even while he spoke the diminutive little Frenchman turned and bolted. One of the Turks drew a revolver and rushed after him, but Hussein-ul-Mulk uttered some authoritative words which prevented the man from firing. The Frenchman was evidently an adept in the art of dodging pursuit. In the passage he ducked suddenly, and threw the Turk heavily to the ground. Then, without further interference, he slipped the latch of the door and slammed it hastily behind him, leaving Brett silently laughing at Hussein-ul-Mulk and his remaining confederate, whilst the gentleman who had been upset was slowly regaining his disturbed gravity.

"Can it be possible that what you say is true?" said Hussein-ul-Mulk, in such piteous accents that Brett was moved to further mirth.

"Surely you do not doubt the evidence?" he said. "Take any of these stones; they will crumble to pieces on the hearth if struck the slightest blow. See, I will pulverise one with my heel."

And he did so, though the amazed and despairing men whom he addressed would have restrained him, for they still could not bring themselves to believe.

"Come, now," he went on "arouse yourselves; and give me the information I want. That is the only way in which you may attain your ends. Of course I cannot help you. It may be that as you have bungled matters so badly, the authorities will stop you and land you all in prison; but that is no concern of mine. At this moment I simply wish to release my friend and proclaim his innocence. For the rest, you must take care of yourselves. You know best who it is that has so thoroughly outwitted you."

Hussein-ul-Mulk was the first to recover his scattered senses.

"We cannot choose but believe you, Mr. Brett," he said. "We are even indebted to you for making this disastrous discovery at such an early date. We paid our agents so highly that we thought their honesty was assured. We find we are mistaken, and consequently we apologise to you for using threats which were unnecessary. We rely on your honour not to incriminate us with the police. All we can tell you is that your friend is not dead, but we do not know his whereabouts."

"Nonsense," cried Brett angrily. "Why do you seek to mislead me in this fashion?"

"Sir," said the Turk, "I am telling you the truth. We believe that Mr. Talbot is a prisoner in London, but we do not know in what locality. My friends here and myself, as you have already surmised, are merely members of a political organisation. It was necessary for us to secure possession of the Imperial diamond and its companions. We spared no expense, nor hesitated at any means that would accomplish our purpose. We have been foiled for the moment. I can tell you nothing else, and I advise you to leave us and forget that such persons exist, for I swear to you by the beard of the Prophet that had events turned out differently you would now be a lifeless corpse in this room, whilst your body would not be discovered for many weeks, as we intended to leave Paris this afternoon as soon as the diamonds came into our possession."

[Illustration: "The door was thrown bodily from its hinges." –*Page 113.*]

At this moment a thunderous knocking reverberated through the house.

The Turks gazed at each other in affright. None of them moved to open the door. But the knock was not repeated, for the door itself was thrown bodily from its hinges, and the stalwart form of Lord Fairholme, accompanied by two policemen, appeared in the passage.

"Ah," cried Brett, intervening with ready tact, "I had forgotten you, Fairholme. I see you kept your appointment. These are not required," he rattled on pleasantly, turning towards the stern-looking *sergents de ville*; "I am quite alive and uninjured. My friends here and myself had a few earnest words, but we have settled matters satisfactorily."

The suspicious policemen glanced from the smiling Englishman to the perturbed Turks. At the first sound of danger Hussein-ul-Mulk had closed the case in which lay the spurious diamonds, so these pretentious-looking gems did not excite the curiosity of the men of law.

The senior officer demanded from Lord Fairholme an explanation of the exciting statements which induced them to accompany him, but Brett stepped into the breach.

"It is quite true," he said, "that my friend was anxious on my account. It was even possible these Turkish gentlemen here and myself might have proceeded to extremities, but the affair has ended satisfactorily, and if you will allow me—" He put his hand into his pocket and a slight monetary transaction terminated the incident pleasantly for all parties.

Soon Brett and Fairholme found themselves in the street, and again did the barrister draw in deep and invigorating draughts of Paris air.

"Where now?" said Fairholme.

"Tell me," cried Brett eagerly, "did you notice in which direction the little man ran who left No. 11 about ten minutes ago?"

"Better than that, I heard where he was going to. He was in such a fiendish funk that he paid heed to nobody, but flung himself into a passing cab and yelled, 'Take me to the Cabaret Noir, Boulevard Montmartre.'"

"Good. You are a splendid detective. You have saved me hours of search and perhaps days of failure. Come; let us, too, go to the Cabaret Noir."

9
A MONTMARTRE ROMANCE

The exterior of the Cabaret Noir belied its name.

Originally, no doubt, it was one of the vilest dens in a vile locality, but the fairy hand of the brewer had touched the familiar wineshop, and it glistened to-day in much mahogany, more brass, and a dazzling collection of mirrors.

Brett was surprised when the driver of their cab pulled up in front of such an ornate establishment. Somehow, he expected the Cabaret Noir to be a different place. Not so Fairholme, accustomed only to the glaring exterior of London tied houses.

"Here we are," said his lordship cheerfully. "Let's take them by surprise and run over the whole show before any one can stop us."

"No," said Brett; "this is Paris, and the police here have ways even more mysterious than those of Scotland Yard. We will gain nothing by drastic measures. Indeed, had I known the sort of place we were coming to I would have visited it to-night and in disguise. As it is, we have been seen already by any one interested in our movements, and it would be useless to adopt any pretence, so follow me."

He boldly entered through the main door, and found himself in a light, airy room, filled, in three-fourths of its area, with little marble-topped tables surrounded by diminutive chairs, whilst a bar counter was partitioned off in a corner.

The attendant in charge was a dreary-eyed waiter, who seemed to think that the presence of a couple of sight-seeing Englishmen at such an hour was another testimony to the lunatic propensities of the Anglo-Saxon race. He welcomed them volubly, assuring them that the establishment kept the best Scotch whisky in stock, and guaranteed that roast beef would be ready in ten minutes.

"This is the Cabaret Noir?" questioned Brett.

"But yes, monsieur."

"There is no other of the same name in Montmartre?"

"But no, monsieur."

"A gentleman, a friend of mine, came here a few minutes ago in a *fiacre*. He was small, slight, so high"– illustrating the stature by his hand. "He was dressed in dark blue clothes with shiny boots. He was—"

Brett's eager description was cut short by the appearance of a new character. Through a narrow door leading into the bar came a handsome dark-eyed woman, aged perhaps twenty-five, well dressed, shapely, and carrying herself with the easy grace of a born Parisienne.

Her hair was jet black. Her large dark eyes were recessed beneath arched and strongly pencilled eyebrows. Her skin had that peculiar tint of porcelain-white so often seen in women of southern blood.

Yet there was nothing delicate in this lady's appearance or manner. A rich colour suffused her cheeks, and her language was remarkably free both in volume and style. She addressed a few observations to the waiter in the common vernacular of Montmartre, the only translatable portion being the question why he was standing about the floor like the ears of a donkey when there was work to be done.

Her manner changed somewhat as she addressed herself to Brett and his companion. There was sufficient of the landlady in her demeanour when she said, "And what would messieurs be pleased to command?"

Now, if there was one type of femininity more than another which Brett thoroughly understood it was the saucy, quick-witted, handsome adventuress. He knew that the woman scrutinizing him so coolly came well within this category.

He could not tell, of course, in what way she might be associated with the gang whose proceedings contained the explanation of Talbot's fate, but he instantly resolved to adopt a determined position with the lady who half-petulantly, half-curiously, was awaiting his reply.

He came nearer to her.

"I am glad," he said, "that I have met you."

The woman looked him boldly in the eyes. "Was it for the happiness of seeing me that monsieur has visited the house?"

"That might well serve as the reason, but the pleasure is all the greater since it was unexpected."

"You are pleased to be facetious," she replied. "Will you not tell me your business? I have affairs to occupy me."

"Assuredly. I have driven here as quickly as possible from No. 11, Rue Barbette."

This attack, so direct and uncompromising, did not fail to have its effect. A ready mask of suspicion fell across the woman's impudent pretty face.

There was just a tinge of stage laughter in her tone when she cried: "Really, how interesting! And where is the Rue Barbette, monsieur? In what way am I concerned with–No. 11, did you say?"

Brett well knew how to conduct the attack upon this lady. His voice fell to a determined note, his eyes looked gravely into hers as he answered–"It is useless to pretend that you do not understand me. You are losing moments worth gold, perhaps diamonds! Within a few minutes the police will be here, and then it will be too late. Help me first, and I will let the police take care of themselves. Refuse me your assistance, and I will leave you and your friends to the mercy of the district *commissaire*."

A dangerous light leaped into the woman's eyes at this direct challenge.

"Monsieur is pleased to speak in riddles," she said. "This is a restaurant. We can execute your orders, but we are not skilled in acting charades. You will find better performers in the booths out there"; and she swept her hands scornfully towards the boulevard, with its medley of tents, stalls, and merry-go-rounds.

Brett smiled. "You are a stupid woman," he said. "You think you are serving your friends by adopting this tone. In effect you are bringing them to the guillotine. Now listen. If I leave you without further words you do not see me again. You will know nothing of what is going on until the police have lodged you in a cell. Neither you nor your associates can escape. I promise nothing, but perhaps if you tell me what I want to know there may be a chance for you. Otherwise there is none. Shall I go?"

And he turned as if to approach the door.

For an instant the woman hesitated, and Brett thought that he had scored.

"Wait," she said, lowering her voice, though there was still the menace of subdued passion in her accents. "Who is your friend?"

"A gentleman whose identity in no way concerns you. You must deal with me, and it will be better if you ask who I am."

"I know," she said, laconically. "Come this way, both of you."

She raised a flap-door located at one side of the counter. Brett followed her into a passage behind the doorway that led into the bar. Fairholme succeeded him.

The trio passed rapidly through a door at the end of the passage, and quickly found themselves in a long, low room, usually devoted to billiards. The place was dark and smelled evilly of stale tobacco. Daylight penetrated but feebly through the red blinds that blocked up three windows on one side. The woman drew two of these blinds, and thus illuminated the interior. The windows opened on to a yard, and the place was thoroughly shut off from all observation from the street.

"Now," she said, "I will show you something."

She walked towards the fireplace at the end of the room. On the mantelpiece was a square of iron sheeting, painted white and studded with curious-looking spikes in circles, triangles, and straight lines. From a box close at hand she took half a dozen small glass bulbs, red and blue. She placed them in a line on some of the spikes at intervals of two inches. Then she retired to that side of the room where they had entered. The distance was perhaps thirty feet.

Before Brett or Fairholme could vaguely guess her intention she whipped a revolver out of her pocket. It would be idle to deny that they were startled, but the woman paid not the least attention to them.

She steadily levelled the weapon and fired twice, smashing the two outer balls of the six. Then she transferred the pistol to her left hand and smashed another pair. Then she turned her back to the target, adjusted a small mirror attached to the butt of the revolver, and smashed both of the remaining bulbs by firing over her left shoulder. Sweeping round with a triumphant smile towards the barrister, she said, "I can do that in fifty other ways, but six will suffice."

"It is very clever, madame," he said. "May I ask why I am indebted to you for this display?"

She replaced the revolver in her pocket. "It is my answer to your question, monsieur," she said. "That is the way I and my friends often talk to people who annoy us; and now I shall wish you good-day. You will find other sights in Montmartre to interest you."

Brett laughed easily, and bowed low.

"Believe me," he said, "I will find few performers so expert and, may I add, so discreet. We will meet again, and perhaps test your skill."

Without another word the party returned to the front room of the restaurant, and Brett and Fairholme passed into the street where their cab was waiting.

"I suppose she meant," said Fairholme "that if we were not jolly careful she would put a bullet through our hearts as easily as through those glass bulbs."

"Such was her intention," said Brett, dryly. "But women never have true dramatic genius. That was a piece of melodrama which might suffice with many of her class. It amused me, but it was a waste of time on her part."

"Anyhow, we shall not get much out of her in the way of information."

"Oh, yes, we will. She will tell us everything. She has told me a great deal already."

"What?" cried his lordship. "Did that shooting affair convey anything more to you than what I have said?"

"Of course. What need was there for such a trick? In the first place it is very simple. You or I could do it after ten minutes' practice with an expanding charge and a show pistol. Secondly, she admitted that the Cabaret Noir is a centre of operations for the gang in whom we are interested. By the way, I should like to know her name."

He directed the driver to wait for them at a street corner some little distance further on. Close to where they stood an itinerant vendor was selling some mechanical toys.

Brett bought one. The price was twenty sous. He gave the man a two-franc piece and refused the change.

"Do you know," he said, "who is the proprietor of the Cabaret Noir?"

"Certainly, monsieur," replied the gutter-merchant; "it is Gros Jean. His name is Beaucaire."

"Ah! And the lady who lives there, a dark pretty woman with white skin, who is she?"

"That is his daughter," said the man. "She is known as La Belle Chasseuse."

"Why such a name?"

"Because she is clever with firearms. She used to be in a circus, but she left the profession a year ago."

"And does she live here constantly?"

"I cannot say. I think she goes away a great deal. She was travelling recently; she came back–let me see–last Tuesday night."

"Thank you," said Brett. The two re-entered their cab, and Brett told the driver to proceed as rapidly as possible to the Rue St. Honore.

"I hope to goodness," he said to Fairholme, "that Captain Gaultier has not left Paris already; these Foreign Office messengers are liable to be despatched to the other end of the earth at a moment's notice."

"Why do you wish to see him?" said Fairholme.

"Simply to obtain definite confirmation of my theory. La Belle Chasseuse was the woman who accompanied the man made up to look like Jack Talbot during his journey from London. If Gaultier can see her and assure me that I am right I will be convinced concerning that which I already know to be true."

"By Jove!" cried Fairholme, "that never occurred to me. I wonder if it is so?"

"Mademoiselle Beaucaire is quite an adept in two things: she can break tiny glass bulbs and she can flirt. She chose to exhibit the first of these accomplishments to us, and convey what was intended to be a warning; in reality, she gave us some valuable information."

"I suppose," said Fairholme, "that this crowd will watch us pretty closely, won't they?"

Brett leaned back in the cab and laughed heartily.

"We are the most interesting persons in Paris to them at this moment," he said. "That poor fellow who sold us the toys will have to change his position, I am afraid. One of them is following us now. Let's see who it is."

At the next street corner he stopped the cab suddenly, and jumped out, followed by Fairholme. A minute later another vehicle dashed into the street. In it was seated a lady, closely veiled; but a large feather hat and the grotesque pattern of a black veil could not wholly conceal the pretty, determined face of La Belle Chasseuse.

Evidently she had no one at hand to undertake the mission, so she followed Brett in person. He signalled to her and to her driver. Astonished, the man pulled up. Brett instantly advanced and took off his hat with that pleasant smile of his which usually went straight to the female heart, but which now thoroughly lost its effect on the furious young woman who looked at him from the interior of the *voiture*.

"Allow me," he said, "to offer my friendly services. It is a close day and mademoiselle has, I am sure, many other calls on her time. I will save you at least an hour, and myself nearly the same period. I am going to secure the presence of a witness to identify you as the lady who crossed the Channel last Tuesday in company with a gentleman. You both drove to the Grand Hotel, and your companion signed the register there in the names of Mr. and Mrs. Talbot; is it not so?"

She bent forward and looked at him viciously. Her eyes sparkled with annoyance at being caught so easily in her self-imposed piece of espionage.

"Monsieur is clever," she snapped.

"Thank you," he replied, still smiling. "I can occasionally hit the mark with a guess as well as mademoiselle can with her pistol. But, believe me, I only intend at this moment to be polite. Of course, the presence of a witness to identify you is unnecessary. Mademoiselle can now return to the Cabaret Noir, whilst my friend and I will proceed direct to the Grand Hotel. It saves so much trouble, does it not?"

For a moment the woman looked as though she would have liked to produce that infallible revolver and shot him on the spot. Then she angrily commanded her driver to return.

Fairholme surveyed the scene with open-eyed amazement. "Well," he said, "that beats everything. You really have a splendid nerve. The whole business reads like a chapter out of one of Gaboriau's novels."

"That is the way people live in Paris, my dear fellow. Life is an artificial matter here. But all this excitement has made me hungry. Let us have *dejeuner*."

10
ON GUARD

On their way to the hotel, Brett, yielding apparently
to a momentary impulse, stopped the cab at a house in
the Rue du Chaussee d'Antin. Without any explanation to
Lord Fairholme he disappeared into the interior, and did
not rejoin his companion for nearly ten minutes.

"It is perhaps not of much use," he explained on his
return, "but I do not like to leave any stone unturned.
The man I have just called on is a well-known private
detective, and I can trust him to look after my business
without taking the police into his confidence. Two of his
smartest agents will maintain a close watch on both the
Cabaret Noir and No. 11, Rue Barbette, during the
afternoon."

"You do not seem to expect much result?"

"No; we are tracking some of the most expert and
daring criminals in France. It is hopeless to expect them
to provide us with clues; they simply won't do it. No one
but a genius in criminality would have risked such a
dramatic move as the personation of Jack Talbot, or
dared to put in an open appearance at the Grand Hotel.
So my agents here can only hope, at the best, to get sight
of any messenger or assistant scoundrel who may turn up
at either of the places indicated."

"May we expect to be busy to-night?"

Brett did not answer at once. It was evident that
whilst he rattled on in a careless strain his active brain
was busily employed in discounting the future.

"I hope so," he said at last. "Of course I cannot tell.
Our only chance is that we may be able to guess the
course of the hidden trail. If to-night does not yield us
some information, our chances of solving the mystery will

be remote, in which case we may as well abandon the quest."

This faint-hearted reply naturally surprised Lord Fairholme considerably. To his mind, a considerable measure of success had already been achieved, and he utterly failed to understand why his friend should take such a pessimistic view of affairs at the very moment when they appeared to be opening up somewhat. Brett noted the Earl's perplexity, and smiled with genial deprecation.

"Do not be afraid, Fairholme; I will liberate Mr. Talbot and clear his name so effectually that all difficulties will disappear from the path of your marriage."

"Then what is it that makes you so downcast?" cried Fairholme.

"I hate to be beaten at the final stage, and I have a premonition that were I in England–had I but the power to proceed unchecked and unhindered by officialdom–I would soon lay my hands on the man who originated the Albert Gate mystery. But we are in France–in a country of queer legal forms and unusual methods. At home I can always circumvent Scotland Yard; here I am in the midst of strange surroundings, and know not what may happen. Therefore, we must possess our souls in patience and wait developments. The agent I have just employed has promised me to report every two hours at the hotel until eight o'clock. Then I will take personal charge of the Cabaret Noir, and—"

"What about me?" cried Fairholme.

"You, my dear fellow, will remain at the hotel and await orders."

This arrangement did not seem to suit the active young Englishman who had been so suddenly plunged into the excitement of a criminal chase in Paris.

"Really, Brett," he said, "I hate to grumble at anything you propose, because you are always right; but you must pardon me for saying that I do not see what particular value my presence here has been to you."

"What!" laughed Brett; "not after your dramatic appearance in the Rue Barbette this morning?"

"Oh, any one could have done that. All I had to do was to break in a door at a given hour."

"Exactly," said Brett gravely. "I wanted a friend whom I could trust to implicitly obey my orders, and you did it. I am sure you will fall in with my wishes now."

So Fairholme was silenced on this point, but he ventured to put another question.

"How long am I to sit chewing cigars in our rooms, then?"

"All night, if necessary. If I do not appear by seven o'clock to-morrow morning you had better go to the Embassy and tell one of the secretaries everything connected with our visit to Paris. He will then take action through the police in proper form, and after that you must simply await developments."

"Do you mean to say," said Fairholme, anxiously, "that you are contemplating another risky bit of business to-night?"

"Once I take my stand outside the Cabaret Noir about 8.30 I cannot tell where Fate may lead me. If I am lucky I will certainly return, whatever be the personal outcome. If, on the other hand, I learn nothing, you may certainly expect to see me about two in the morning."

At the hotel Brett found awaiting him a letter delivered by the midday post. It was from his elderly assistant in London, whom he had told to make a close scrutiny of all inhabited houses within a certain radius of the Carlton Hotel. The man had done his work systematically, and in only three instances was he called on to report doubtful cases.

Two foreign restaurants in side streets contained a number of residents concerning whom it was difficult to obtain specific information.

One of these establishments he believed to be the resort of Continental gamblers driven from Soho by the too marked attentions of the police. The other was a place of even more questionable repute, and in both instances he had utterly failed to obtain the slightest information from the servants, who apparently "stood in" with the management.

The third dwelling which courted observation was a flat situated above some business premises in another quiet street. So far as he could learn, it was tenanted by an elderly lady who was a helpless invalid, waited on by a somewhat curious couple.

"They are Italians, I think," wrote the ex-policeman, "and very uncommunicative people. I have twice called, on one pretext or another, but when the door is opened it is always kept on the chain, and I cannot see more than the face of a man or woman and a few inches of wall beyond. Still, I have no reason to doubt that the view taken by the milkman and baker is correct, namely, that the owner of the flat is confined to her bed and is suffering from a nervous disease, which renders it imperative she should be shut off from all noise. The landlord informs me that these people have occupied the place for nearly two months. Their rent is paid in advance, and they have not given the slightest cause for complaint. There are, of course, in this district a large number of private hotels and lodging-houses, but they seem to be run on regular lines, and, although some of their patrons might well demand closer observation, I have come across nothing suggestive of any suspicious circumstance whatever with reference to them. I have detained my report until I was able to give details concerning the other houses in the district, and I will now fall back on the second part of your instructions, i.e., to maintain a close watch on the three establishments which I have picked out as being more unusual in their habits than the others."

This was all.

Brett read the concluding portion of the report to Fairholme.

"He is a level-headed, shrewd observer," he said–"one of the few men whom I can trust to do exactly what I want, neither more nor less. I think when we return to London we must endeavour to get that chain taken off the invalid lady's door, or, at any rate, obtain some specific facts concerning her disease from her medical adviser."

Fairholme smiled. "I am glad to hear," he cried, "that you do anticipate our return."

"Oh," said Brett airily, "I never count on failure."

Soon after three o'clock a report arrived from the agent in the Rue du Chaussee d'Antin. It read–

"Nothing unusual has occurred in the vicinity of the Cabaret Noir. The customers frequenting the place are all of the ordinary type and do not call for special comment.

"A Turkish gentleman quitted the house No. 11, Rue Barbette, at 1.15 p.m., but returned shortly before two o'clock. Half an hour later a man, whom my assistant recognized as a member of a well-known gang of flash thieves, entered the place. His name is Charles Petit, but he is generally known to his associates as 'Le Ver.' He is small, well dressed, and of youthful appearance, but really older than he looks. He is still in the house inhabited by the Turks."

"What is the meaning of 'Le Ver'?" said Fairholme.

"It means 'The Worm,'" answered Brett.

"I must say these chaps do find suitable nicknames for one another. I wonder if he is the fellow we followed to Montmartre this morning?"

"Possibly, though I am puzzled to understand why he should trust himself in that hornets' nest again. Most certainly the description covers him, but we shall probably hear more details later. I wonder where the Turkish gentleman went whom 'Le Ver' seems to have followed. He could not have gone to the Cabaret Noir in the time?"

Brett's curiosity was answered to some extent by the next report, delivered about five o'clock. It read as follows—

"Le Ver is still in the house No. 11, Rue Barbette. My agent explains that he did not follow the Turk, who left and returned to the place earlier, because his definite instructions were not to leave the locality, but to report on all persons who entered or left. Absolutely nothing has transpired in this neighbourhood since my first report.

"Gros Jean, the father of La Belle Chasseuse, arrived at the Cabaret Noir soon after four o'clock. My agent ascertained from the cabman who drove him that Gros Jean had hired the vehicle outside the Gare de Lyon. Otherwise nothing stirring."

At seven o'clock came developments.

"Three Turkish gentlemen have quitted No. 11, Rue Barbette, but the Frenchman is still there. As it might be necessary to follow another person leaving this house, I stationed another watcher with my assistant, and this second man followed the Turks to a restaurant in the Grand Boulevard. So far as he could judge, they seemed to be excited and apprehensive. They drank some wine and conversed together in low tones. At 6.15 they quitted the cafe and rapidly jumped into an empty fiacre, being driven off in the direction of the Opera. So unexpectedly did they leave their seats that before my agent could hire another cab they had disappeared in the traffic, and although he drove after them as rapidly as possible, he failed to again catch sight of them. I have reprimanded him for his negligence, although he did right in coming at once to me to report his failure. In accordance with your instructions, I have ordered the watchers at the Cafe Noir and in the Rue Barbette to be in this office at 8.15 p.m."

"Now I wonder," said Brett, "why the Turks left the Frenchman alone in No. 11. It is odd, to say the least of it. Since the dramatic discovery of the spurious diamonds this morning they must be even more in the dark than I am. It must be looked into, but I cannot attend to it now.

At this moment, if I am not mistaken, the centre of interest is the Cafe Noir."

The two men occupied a sitting-room on the first floor of the hotel, and their respective bedrooms flanked it on each side. Brett explained that he could not tackle the table d'hote dinner, so he made a hasty meal in their sitting-room and then excused himself whilst he retired to his bedroom to change his clothing.

He was absent some twenty minutes, and Fairholme amused himself by glancing over the copies of the day's London newspapers which had recently arrived. Suddenly the door of Brett's bedroom opened, and a decrepit elderly man appeared, a shabby-genteel individual, disfigured by drink and crumpled up by rheumatism.

"Who the devil—" began Fairholme.

But he was amazed to hear Brett's familiar voice asking–

"Do you think the disguise sufficiently complete?"

"Complete!" shouted Fairholme, "why, your own mother would not know you, and your father would probably punch me for suggesting that it could be you."

"That is all right," said the barrister cheerfully. "I will now proceed to get quietly drunk at the Cafe Noir. Goodbye until seven o'clock to-morrow morning–perhaps earlier, and perhaps–well, no–until seven o'clock!"

They shook hands and parted, and not even Brett, the cleverest amateur detective of his day, could have remotely guessed where and how they would meet next.

Montmartre by day and Montmartre by night are two very different places. This Parisian playground, perched high on the eminence that overlooks the Ville Lumiere, does not wake to its real life until its repose is disturbed by the lamplighter. Then the Moulin Rouge, festooned with lamps of gorgeous red, flares forth upon an expectant world. The Cafe de l'Enfers opens its demoniac mouth to swallow ten minutes' audiences and vomit them forth again, amused or bored, as the case may be, by the delusions provided in the interior, whilst other questionable resorts shout forth their attractions and seek to beguile a certain number of sous from the pockets of sightseers.

The whole district is a place of light and shade. It is artificial in every brick and stone, in the pose of every stall, the lettering of every advertisement. And it flourishes by gaslight; by day it is garish and forlorn.

Prominent among the regular houses of entertainment was the Cabaret Noir, which, between the hours of 9 p.m. and 1 a.m., usually drove a roaring trade. Situated in the heart of a mountebank district, its patrons embraced all classes of society, from the American tourist with his quick eyes noting the vagaries of demi-mondaines, to the sharp-witted Parisian idler, on the alert for any easy and dishonest method of obtaining money which might present itself.

Among such a crowd a wine-sodden and decrepit old man was not likely to attract particular attention.

He sprawled over the table close to one of the windows which commanded a view of the side passage leading to the rear of the building. Although none of the noisy crowd in the cafe could suspect the fact, the half-closed eyes of this elderly drunkard noted the form and features of every individual who entered or left by the main door, whilst at the same time he paid the utmost possible attention to the comings and goings of any person who used the passage by the window.

To facilitate his observations in this direction he querulously complained to the waiter that the atmosphere was stuffy, and prevailed on the man to raise the window a few inches, thus admitting a breath of clear cold air.

Brett had previously ascertained from his agent that Gros Jean and his daughter were still in the private part of the building. No other visitor had put in an appearance, and so the time passed, until the clock in the cafe marked eleven, without any incident occurring which could be construed as having even a remote bearing upon his quest.

Brett began to feel that his diligence that night would not be rewarded.

At five minutes past eleven, however, a pink-and-white Frenchman, neatly attired, unobtrusive both in manner and deportment, entered the cafe and seated himself quietly near the door. He ordered some coffee and cognac, and lighted a cigarette.

The barrister, of course, took heed of him as of all others, and he would soon have placed him in the general category that merited no special attention had he not noticed that the newcomer more than once glanced at the clock and then towards the corner bar, whence, it will be remembered, a small door led towards the billiard saloon in which La Belle Chasseuse had displayed her prowess with the pistol.

In such a community the stranger's self-possession and reticence were distinguishable characteristics. So Brett watched him, largely for want of better occupation.

"That is a man of unusual power," was his summing up. "He is elegant, fascinating, unscrupulous. Although apparently out of his natural element in this neighbourhood, he has some purpose in putting in an appearance in such a place as this at a late hour. Perhaps he is one of mademoiselle's lovers, though he looks the sort of person who would be singularly cool in conducting affairs of the heart, and most unlikely to wait many minutes beyond the time fixed for an appointment. His hands are large and sinewy, his wrists square, and, although slight in physique, I should credit him with possessing considerable strength. Being a Frenchman, he should be an expert with the foils. The effeminate aspect given to his face by his remarkable complexion might easily deceive one as to his real character. As a matter of fact, he is the only unusual man I have seen during my two hours' lounge in this corner."

Brett had hardly concluded this casual analysis of the person who had enlisted his close observation, when the private door into the bar opened and Mlle. Beaucaire entered.

Without taking the least notice of any of the numerous occupants of the cafe she turned her back on them, and apparently busied herself in checking the contents of the cash register. Beyond this useful instrument was a mirror, and Brett at once perceived that from the point where she stood she could command a distinct reflection of the pink-and-white Frenchman.

The latter was gazing at the clock, and whilst doing so stroked his chin three times with his right hand. Immediately afterwards La Belle Chasseuse three times rang the bell of the register, and then, having apparently concluded her inspection, quitted the bar as unceremoniously as she had entered. Half a minute later the Frenchman finished the remains of his cognac, lit another cigarette, and passed into the street.

It was with difficulty that Brett restrained himself from following him, but he was certain that no one could leave the residential portion of the building without using the passage—a view of which he commanded from his window—and he resolutely resolved to devote himself for that night to shadowing the movements of the ex-circus lady.

His patience and self-denial were soon rewarded. A light quick step sounded in the passage, and a shrouded female form shot past the open window.

Then the inebriated individual, now hopelessly muddled by drink, staggered towards the door and lurched wildly round the corner, just in time to see mademoiselle cross the Boulevard and daintily make her way between the rows of stalls.

The air seemed, however, to have a surprising effect on the old reprobate, for the simple reason that to simulate drunkenness and at the same time keep pace with the lady's rapid strides was out of the question.

La Belle Chasseuse was evidently in a hurry. She sped along at a surprising pace, until she reached a crossing where the rows of stalls and booths were temporarily suspended. At one corner stood a cab, and towards this vehicle she directed her steps. Before Brett quite realized what was happening, the door of the cab opened, mademoiselle jumped inside, and, as if he were waiting for her appearance, the driver whipped up his horse and drove off at a furious pace.

At that instant a small victoria with a sturdy pony in the shafts, which had just deposited a lively fare in the vicinity of the Moulin Rouge, drove along the street.

Brett sprang into it and said eagerly to the driver—

"Keep that cab in sight! I will pay you double fare!"

The man tightened his reins and raised his whip in prompt obedience to the order, when suddenly two men jumped into the vehicle from opposite sides, seized Brett and forced him down on to the seat, whilst one of them said in stern tones to the astonished cabby—

"Take us at once to the Central Prefecture of Police."

The man recognized that these newcomers were not to be trifled with. Without a word or a question, he rattled his horse across the stone pavement, and Brett, choking with rage at this interference at a supreme moment, realized that for some extraordinary reason he was a prisoner, and in the hands of a couple of detectives.

By this time the cab containing the lady had vanished, but the barrister made one despairing effort.

"For heaven's sake," he said to his captors, "take me where you will, but first follow that cab and ascertain its destination."

"What cab?" demanded one of his guards sarcastically.

"The cab which I wished our driver to overtake at the moment when you pounced on me."

"This is a mere trick," broke in the other. "Don't bother about his cab. We have got him safe enough, and let the *commissaire* deal with him now."

"Listen to me," cried Brett. "You are making a frightful mistake. Your action at this moment may cause irretrievable delay and loss. If you will only do as I tell you—"

"Shut up," growled the first man, "or it will be worse for you. Your best plan, my good fellow, is to keep a quiet tongue in your head."

It was not often that Brett lost his temper, but most certainly he lost it on this occasion. He was endowed with no small share of physical strength, and for an instant the wild notion came into his head that he might perhaps succeed in throwing the two detectives into the roadway and then overpower the driver, taking charge of the vehicle himself and trusting to luck to again catch sight of the vanished lady and her companion, who, he doubted not, had awaited her arrival at the quiet corner where she joined him.

Unconsciously he must have given some premonition of this desperate scheme, for the two policemen tightened their grasp, forced his hands higher up his back, and bent his head forward until he was in danger of having either his neck or his shoulder dislocated.

"Will you keep quiet?" murmured the chief detective. "You cannot escape, and you are only making the affair more disastrous to yourself."

Then Brett realized that further resistance was hopeless. He managed to gurgle out that if they would allow him to assume a more comfortable attitude he would not trouble them any further.

Gingerly and cautiously the two men somewhat relaxed the strain, and he was able to breathe freely once more.

Then he laughed, almost hysterically, but he could not help saying in English–

"The shadow of Scotland Yard falls on me even here. Poor old Winter, how I will roast him over this adventure!"

"What are you talking about?" demanded one of the men.

"I was only thinking aloud," replied Brett.

"And what were your thoughts?"

11

A DISCONCERTED COMMISSARY

The journey across Paris proceeded without further incident, until they reached the prefecture.

The two detectives hurried their prisoner into a large general office, where he was surveyed with some curiosity by the subordinates lounging near a huge fire, whilst one of their number reported his arrival. After a brief interval he was taken into an inner office. Behind a green baize-covered table was seated a sharp-looking man, whose face was chiefly composed of eyebrows, pince-nez, a hooked nose, and a furious imperiale.

This individual turned the shade of the lamp so that the light fell in its full radiance on the face and figure of the prisoner. He produced a huge volume, and thumbed over its leaves until he reached the first vacant place, ruled and numbered for the description of all persons brought before him.

"Your name?" he said sharply.

"Reginald Brett," was the reply.

The Frenchman required this to be spelt for him.

"Age?"

"Thirty-seven."

"Nationality?"

"English."

"Profession?"

"Barrister-at-law."

The official consulted a type-written document, which he selected from a mass of papers fastened by an indiarubber band. Then he looked curiously at the prisoner.

"Are you sure this is the man?" he said to the senior detective.

"Quite positive, monsieur."

"Then take off his wig and get a towel, so that he may remove some of his make-up. The rascal should be an actor. I never saw a better disguise in my life."

Brett knew it was hopeless to attempt explanations at this stage. He readily fell in with their directions, and in a few seconds he stood revealed in something akin to his ordinary appearance.

Now, the French Commissary of Police was no fool. He was an adept at reading character, but he was certainly puzzled after a sharp scrutiny of Brett's clear-cut, intelligent features. Nevertheless, he knew that the criminal instinct is often allied with the most deceptive external appearances. So he turned to the detective, and said—

"Tell me, briefly, what happened?"

"In accordance with instructions, monsieur," the man replied, "Philippe and I ascertained the movements of the prisoner at the Grand Hotel. During the afternoon he received messages from London and from some persons in Paris, which documents are now probably in his possession. He quitted the hotel at eight o'clock, disguised as you have seen. He called for a moment at a house in the Rue du Chaussee d'Antin, the number of which we noted, and then made his way to the Cafe Noir in Montmartre. There we watched him from the door for nearly three hours. He feigned drunkenness, but held communication with no person."

"Ha!" cried the commissary. This struck him as an important point. He made a memorandum of it.

"Soon after eleven o'clock he rose hastily and quitted the cafe, crossed the Boulevard, and hailed a cab. We would have followed him, but there was no other vehicle in sight. As our instructions were to arrest him at any moment he seemed likely to elude us, we seized him. He struggled violently, and told us some story about his desire to follow another cab, which he said had disappeared. We saw no cab such as he described, and we treated his words as a mere device to abstract attention. We were right. A moment later he made an attempt to escape, and we were compelled to use considerable force to prevent him from being successful."

The commissary turned his eyes to the prisoner and was seemingly about to question him, when Brett said with a smile–

"Perhaps, monsieur, you will allow me to say a word or two."

"Certainly." The official knew that criminals generally implicated themselves when they commenced explaining matters.

"You are acting, I presume," said the barrister, "in obedience to reports received from the London police with reference to the murder of four Turkish subjects at Albert Gate, and the theft of some valuable diamonds belonging to the Sultan?"

This calm summary of the facts seemed to disconcert the Frenchman. It astonished him considerably to find his prisoner thus indicating so clearly the nature of the charge to be brought against him.

"That may be so," he admitted.

"It is so," went on Brett; "and in this matter you are even more hopelessly idiotic than I took you to be. I have told you my name and profession. I am a friend of Mr. Talbot, the English gentleman who has been spirited away in connection with this crime, and I have in my pocket at this moment a letter from the British Under-Secretary of State for Foreign Affairs, authorising me to use my best efforts towards elucidating the mystery and tracking the real criminals. Here is the letter," he continued, producing a document and laying it before the amazed official.

"I was on the point of making an important discovery with reference to this case when these too zealous agents of yours seized me and absolutely refused, even whilst I was a prisoner in their hands, to follow up the definite clue I had obtained. It is an easy matter to verify my statements. The authenticity of this letter will be proved at the British Embassy, whilst a telegram to Scotland Yard will place beyond doubt not only my identity, but my bona fides in acting for Mr. Talbot's relatives and the Foreign Office. Further, an inquiry made at the Grand Hotel will produce unquestionable testimony from the manager, who knows me, and from my friend, Lord Fairholme, who occupies rooms there at this moment."

"Lord Fairholme!" stuttered the official. "Why, that is the name given by the other prisoner."

"Do you mean to say you have arrested the Earl of Fairholme?" gasped Brett, struggling with an irresistible desire to laugh.

The Frenchman covered his confusion by growling an unintelligible order, and bent over the letter which Brett had given to him. In half a minute one of the detectives returned, and with him was Fairholme, on whose honest face indignation and astonishment struggled for mastery.

"Oh, surely that cannot be you, Brett!" cried his lordship, the moment he entered the room. "Well, of all the — fools that ever lived, these French Johnnies take the cake. I suppose that they have spoiled the whole business! If the brutes had not taken me by surprise I would have knocked over a dozen of them before they arrested me."

"Silence!" shrieked the commissary, into whose mind was intruding the consciousness that he had committed an outrageous blunder.

"What did you say your name was?" he demanded fiercely.

"I told you my name an hour ago," said his lordship haughtily, "and if you had not been so beastly clever you would have believed me. I am the Earl of Fairholme, a fact that can be readily substantiated by dozens of people here in Paris, and this is Mr. Reginald Brett, a friend of mine, who would have probably discovered the mystery of my friend's disappearance and the whereabouts of those diamonds by this time if you had not interfered."

His lordship was hardly coherent with annoyance, but the acute official had now convinced himself that a stupid mistake had been committed by his department.

He became apologetic and suave. He explained that their mysterious proceedings had to some extent committed them in the eyes of the police to secret knowledge of the crime which had so thoroughly aroused the detective departments in both London and Paris.

Evidently Scotland Yard had not advised the French police of Mr. Brett's official connection with the hunt for the murderers. The agents of the Paris Bureau had watched Brett's comings and goings during the day, and the detectives' suspicions, once aroused, were intensified when his friend, Lord Fairholme, sought the aid of two uniformed policemen to break in the door of the Turkish residents in the Rue Barbette.

Even now, politely concluded the commissary, he would regretfully be compelled to detain them for a little while, until he verified their statements. Meanwhile, they would not be subject to any further indignities, and might procure such refreshments as they desired. They would probably be set at liberty within a couple of hours.

At 1.30 a.m. Brett and Fairholme were ushered forth from the doors of the prefecture and stood in freedom in the street.

"Where now?" said Fairholme.

"To the hotel," replied Brett, wearily. "I must have sleep, so I consign the Turks, and the Sultan's diamonds, and every one concerned with the Albert Gate mystery, to perdition for the next eight hours."

Notwithstanding his weariness, Brett rose early next morning. His companion slept like a top, and the barrister had to shake the earl soundly by the shoulder before the latter woke into conscious existence and sat up in bed sleepily demanding–

"What's up? Where's the fire?"

"I want you to dress at once," said Brett cheerily, "and join me at breakfast. You must leave for London by the 11.50 train."

"Am I such a nuisance then that I have to be packed off at a moment's notice?" said the earl.

"By no means. Decidedly the contrary, in fact. As matters in France evidently require persistent attention on my part for many days, perhaps weeks, I think it is hardly fair to leave Talbot in confinement any longer. Your mission is to restore your prospective brother-in-law to the bosom of his family, and I regret that it is impossible for me to accompany you."

"Are you serious, old chap?" was the startled answer. "What has happened since one o'clock this morning to make you so confident?"

"Nothing that is not already known to you. Had I succeeded last night in following Mlle. Beaucaire to her destination, I might have been able to accompany you to London this morning. As it is, Heaven alone knows what sort of dance she may lead me. However, you complete your toilette, my dear fellow. I have ordered breakfast to be served in a quarter of an hour. Then you can eat and listen."

During the first portion of the repast Brett seemed too busily engaged to unburden his mind. It was not until he had lit a cigarette and pushed his chair away from the table, so that he could assume a posture of complete ease, that he commenced–

"You slept so soundly, Fairholme, that you have not had time to review all the circumstances of yesterday's adventures. Otherwise I am sure you would have reached the same conclusions as suggest themselves to me. Curiously enough, although dog-tired when I went to bed, I woke about seven o'clock feeling thoroughly rested both in mind and body. I procured some coffee, took a bath, and went out for a stroll, with the result that I returned and aroused you after reaching finality in some of my conclusions, and deciding on a definite plan of action for both of us."

"It is really very decent of you, Brett, to constantly assume that I can see as far through a brick wall as you can, especially as you know quite well that, although I am fairly well acquainted with all that happened yesterday, the only tangible opinion I can offer is that the Paris police interfered with you at a most inopportune moment."

Brett smiled. "That is because you have not accustomed yourself to analysis," he said. "However, I will summarise my views, and if you can find any flaws in my reasoning I will be glad. The first thing to observe is that the diminutive Frenchman drew on himself the special vengeance of the Turks when I exposed the attempt to foist on them a collection of dummy diamonds. Yet he actually had the nerve to return to the Rue Barbette later in the day. He has not been seen since, so the little scoundrel is either dead or a prisoner in Hussein ul-Mulk's flat. As I cannot permit myself to participate in a murder or even in an illegal imprisonment, I am regretfully compelled this morning to take the police into my confidence and inform them of an obvious fact which escaped their penetration yesterday."

Fairholme whistled.

"I must say," he cried, "I gave a passing thought to the incident myself last evening when your spy reported that the Frenchman remained in No. 11 after the Turks had quitted it."

"Yes," said Brett. "You see, all you need to cultivate is the habit of deduction, and you will soon become a capital detective."

The earl laughed. "I hope you will tell that to Edith," he said, "and perhaps you may change her opinion concerning my reasoning capacities. She thinks I am an awfully stupid chap as a rule."

"That is because she is in love with you," said Brett.

"Well, now, that remark puzzles me more than anything else you have said." His lordship darted a quick look at the barrister in the endeavour to learn whether or not he was in a chaffing mood.

"Why should a woman seek to depreciate anything she values?"

"Simply because it denotes a secure sense of complete ownership. Miss Talbot would never hold such a view of your intellectual powers if you were merely a friend."

"Well," said the earl dubiously, "that is a new point of view for me at any rate."

"It is a fact nevertheless. But we have not much time, so we must reserve any further consideration of feminine inconsistency. The fate of the Frenchman must be determined to-day, and to decide the question I must act through the police, so a conversation with our friend the commissary becomes inevitable. And now to return to the hypothetical part of my conclusions. I began by assuming that the individual who planned the Albert Gate outrage and subsequently sought to bamboozle his employers by palming off on them a set of spurious diamonds, is far too acute to attempt to dispose of the real gems for many months yet to come. He obtained sufficient funds from the Turks, in pursuance of what may be termed the legitimate part of his contract, to enable him to live for a considerable period without further excitement. Closely associated with him in the present adventure is La Belle Chasseuse. Neither would endeavour to procure safety by flight to a foreign country. They will seek insignificance by living in a normal and commonplace manner. What more easy, for instance, for Mademoiselle than to return to the life of the circus, whilst her lover—granted that he wished to remain in her company—will obtain some suitable employment in the same circle. There is a suspicion of a joke in the statement, but I am quite serious. The mere consciousness that they have in their possession a vast fortune, which time alone will enable them to realize, will serve as an inducement to undergo the period of hard work which means safety. You remember that the lady's father, Gros Jean, visited the Gare de Lyon yesterday?"

Fairholme nodded.

"I think you will find that he was depositing there the necessary luggage for a contemplated trip into the interior, so that Mademoiselle might slip out late at night quietly and unnoticed and join her lover at some preconcerted rendezvous, a thing which we now know she did. I cannot, of course, be certain whether the Frenchman who signalled to her in the Cafe Noir was himself the favoured individual. It is possible. By the way, what height is Talbot?"

"About five feet nine."

Brett pondered for a little while.

"Yes," he communed aloud, "I think I am right. That pink-and-white Frenchman is the master mind in this conspiracy. And to think that the unintelligent muscles of a couple of thick-headed French policemen should have crudely interfered with me at such a moment!" He sighed deeply.

"Never mind," he went on, "it cannot be helped. I must keep to the thread of my story. Mademoiselle Beaucaire left the Cabaret shortly after eleven o'clock. We cannot be certain that she went to the Gare de Lyon, but the cab unquestionably set off in that direction. It is a long drive from Montmartre to the Lyons station. We will give her, say, until twelve o'clock to reach there. Now, unless she was journeying to some suburban district—a contingency which upsets the whole of my theory—there was no main line train leaving for the south until 1.5 a.m., and that is a slow train, stopping at nearly every station south of Melun. Let us suppose that they guard against every contingency. She and her companion wish to escape the scrutiny of detectives. It will at once occur to you that they run far more risk of observation if travelling by a fast express than if they elect to journey by the commonplace trains which only serve the needs of country districts."

"It did not occur to me," said Fairholme candidly. "Still, there is a lot in the idea all the same."

"Very well. To sum up, I imagine that the pair, providing the two travelled together, would break their journey south at some quiet town in the interior early in the morning, and subsequently proceed to their destination by easy stages."

"I am still fogged as to what you mean by their destination?" said Fairholme.

"I mean the circus, the music-hall, the cafe chantant, or whatever place mademoiselle and her astute adviser may select as a safe haven wherein to avoid police espionage during the many months which must ensue before they dare to make the slightest effort to dispose of the purloined diamonds."

"And how do you propose to follow them up?"

"I cannot tell at present. My movements depend upon the results of the inquiries I shall make to-day in theatrical circles, and particularly at the Gare de Lyon, where I shall not meet with success in any event until the night staff comes on duty.

"The third item," continued Brett, "which demands attention in Paris is the whereabouts of the Turks. They must be found and observed. My chief difficulty will be to keep that delightful commissary from imprisoning them, if, as I imagine, we find the little thief a captive in the Rue Barbette. So you see my actions are speculative. Yours, on the other hand, will be definite."

"Ah!" said Fairholme, "I am glad to hear that. If you expect me to analyse and deduce and find out the probable movements of intelligent rascals, I am sure I shall make a mess of things."

"You will reach London," said Brett, "at 7.30 p.m. I suppose you have in your service a reliable servant, endowed with a fair amount of physical strength?"

"Rather," cried the earl. "My butler is a splendid chap. He has been fined half a dozen times for his exceeding willingness to settle disputes with his fists."

"Telegraph to him to meet you at Charing Cross Station. I can depend upon my man Smith to use his nerve and discretion. Moreover, he knows Inspector Winter, of Scotland Yard, and should trouble arise, which I do not anticipate, this acquaintance may be useful to you. The third person who will meet you will be the ex-sergeant of police, whose report to me you heard yesterday. He will point out to you the flat tenanted by the invalid lady. You speak French well, and after a few questions you should be able to satisfy yourself whether or not the person who opens the door to you when you visit that flat is acting a genuine part. You can pretend what you like, but if admission is denied to you I want you to force your way inside and see that invalid lady at all costs. In the event of a gross mistake having been committed you must apologize most abjectly and assuage the wounded feelings of the servants with a liberal donation, whilst the ex-sergeant of police will advise you as to any other place which may demand personal inspection. I do not conceal from you the difficulties of your task, or the chance that you may get into trouble with the police. But the fact remains that Talbot, alive or dead, is concealed somewhere in the neighbourhood of the Carlton Hotel, and it is high time that this portion of the mystery attending his disappearance should be made clear. Do you follow me?"

"Precisely," said Fairholme. "My programme appears to be very simple. I am to kick down any door that is pointed out by the ex-policeman, provided I am refused admission by fair means."

Brett laughed. "I think," he cried, "you have put my instructions in very direct and succinct form. All I hope is that the invalid lady may prove to be an elderly fraud. It only remains for me to give you my blessing and say good-bye."

"But what about you?" said the earl anxiously. "Suppose we come across Talbot to-night, as you anticipate, where shall I find you to-morrow?"

"You must telegraph to me here," was the answer, "and you must possess your soul in patience until you hear from me.

"No, don't protest," he went on, as Fairholme gave indications of impatience. "You need not fear that you will be left out of the denouement, whatever it be. I am sure to need your help before long, and I will cable you at the first possible moment. For that reason, should you leave your house for more than hour or so, I hope you will make special arrangements for telegrams to reach you without delay."

"You may rely on that," was the hearty answer. "But look here, Brett. It is 10.45 a.m. now. If I have to catch that 11.50 train from the Gare du Nord I have no time to lose. By the way," he added, turning at the door, "is there any reason why I should not wire to Edith to expect me to-night?"

"Not the slightest," said Brett, smiling, "except perhaps this, that instead of calling on Miss Talbot this evening you may be locked up on the charge of housebreaking."

"Um," said the earl, thoughtfully, "I had not thought of that. It will be more fun to take her by surprise. So here goes to get my traps packed."

After Lord Fairholme's departure, Brett took matters easily. He did not put in an appearance at the Prefecture until late in the afternoon, and, as he surmised, the commissary whom he encountered the previous night had even then only just arrived at his office. Without any difficulty, the barrister was introduced to the official, who evidently awaited an explanation of the visit with great curiosity.

Brett's ill-humour at the uncalled-for interference of the police was now quite dispelled, and he greeted the commissary with the genial affability which so quickly won him the friendship of casual acquaintances.

"I think," he began, "that your agents, monsieur, were watching me throughout the whole of yesterday."

"That is so," nodded the other, wondering what pitfall lay behind this leading question.

"Do I take it that after my departure from No. 11, Rue Barbette about midday they maintained no further guard over that house?"

"Assuredly. It was monsieur's personal movements which called for observation."

"Then you do not know that an individual whose identity may be much more important than mine is an inmate of the apartment at this moment–probably a captive against his will, possibly a corpse?"

The Frenchman's huge moustache bristled with alarm and annoyance.

"It is a strange thing, monsieur," he cried, "that an English gentleman should come to Paris and know more about the movements and haunts of criminals than the French police."

It was no part of Brett's design to rub the official the wrong way, so he said gently–

"Your remark is quite justifiable, and under ordinary circumstances any such pretence on my part would be ridiculous. But you must remember, monsieur, that I came here from London possessed of special information which was not known even to the police authorities in that city. I am working solely in the private interest of persons high in English Society, and it would not serve the purposes of any of the Governments concerned were too much stress publicly laid on their connexion with this mystery. If I can succeed in elucidating the problem it will be a comparatively easy matter for the police to bring the real criminals to justice. As a step towards that end I have come to you now to place you in possession of a clue which may reveal itself in the Rue Barbette. All I ask is, in the first instance, that the affair may be conducted with the utmost secrecy, and, secondly, that you will permit me to be present when you examine the person whom I expect to find there. I may be able to help you very materially in your questions, provided the man is alive and well."

The commissary was soothed. The barrister's judicial reference to the importance and confidential nature of the inquiry raised in his mind a dazzling vision of personal distinction and preferment.

"The matter shall be conducted with the utmost discretion," he cried. "What force does monsieur consider to be requisite in order to examine this house thoroughly, and prevent the attempted escape of others whom we may find there in addition to the man described?"

Brett with difficulty repressed a smile. "I do not think that a large force of police will be necessary. If you yourself, monsieur, and another officer will accompany me in a cab, I am sure we will be able to deal with all possible opposition. There is no exit from the flat save through the main door, and the apartment is situated on the second storey. Escape by way of the windows is practically impossible if we act with promptitude."

The commissary could not reach the Rue Barbette too rapidly. He bundled a subordinate into a *fiacre*, and the three were driven off at breakneck speed.

They stopped the vehicle at the corner of the street and walked quietly to the house, attracting no attention, as neither of the Frenchmen were in uniform.

Inquiry from the *concierge* elicited the information that none of the occupants of the flat tenanted by the Turkish gentlemen had put in an appearance since the previous afternoon. So the trio mounted the staircase, and without any preliminary summons the junior official applied his shoulder to the door.

The lock yielded quite readily. Indeed, the damage done by Lord Fairholme was but temporarily repaired, and no special precaution had been taken to fasten the place. All was quiet within. The first room they searched was empty. So was the second; but in a bedroom, the door of which was locked and required forcible treatment, an extraordinary sight met their eyes.

Stretched on the bed, gagged and securely tied, was the figure of the diminutive Frenchman, who, little more than twenty-four hours earlier, had so coolly suggested that Brett should be murdered.

Stout leather thongs were fastened to his wrists and ankles and then tied to the four uprights of the bed. His arms and legs were consequently stretched widely apart, and the only sign of vitality about the man was the terrible expression of fear and hate in his eyes as he looked at them.

The gag stuffed in his mouth prevented him from uttering the slightest coherent sound, whilst the agony of his frame owing to the position in which he lay, joined to the exhaustion induced by terror and want of food, rendered him a pitiable object.

They removed the gag and cut the bonds. The poor wretch remained on his back unable to move, though he flinched somewhat when the police, as gently as possible, loosened the leather straps from his wrists and ankles, for his useless struggles had caused the thongs to cut deeply into his skin.

Brett was the first to realize the unfortunate wretch's chief requirement. He procured some water, raised the man's head, and allowed him to take a deep and invigorating draught.

"Why, it is 'The Worm!'" said the junior policeman. "I know him well. He is a pick-pocket, an expert rascal in his line, but hardly up to the standard of great events."

At the sound of his nickname a flicker of intelligence came into the little thief's eyes, but he was still dazed, and did not recognize his rescuers.

"I don't care what you do with me," he murmured at last, in a weak and cracked voice. "Kill me quietly if you want to, but don't tie me up again. I have done nothing to deserve it. I really haven't. I have been acting quite square in this business." And then he broke down and whimpered further protestations of innocence.

"He is weak from want of food, and dazed with terror," said Brett quietly. "I suggest that one of you should get him some meat and wine, whilst the others remain here and endeavour to reassure him. In half an hour he will be greatly recovered. Meanwhile we might examine the place."

The commissary thought Brett's suggestion a good one. His assistant summoned the *concierge* and attended to the wants of "The Worm," whilst Brett and the commissary conducted a careful scrutiny of the premises.

They found little, however, beyond a considerable accumulation of dirt; for the ways of Turks are primitive and their habits unpleasant in European households. If was evident that before taking their departure the occupants of the flat had carefully removed or destroyed all documents or other articles which might throw light on their proceedings.

The leather thongs which bound the prisoner evoked some comment from the barrister.

"These are somewhat unusual articles," he said to the commissary. "You will notice that they are cut from raw cowhide and well stretched. In other words, they are the familiar 'bow-strings' of Constantinople, and warranted not to yield if twisted round the neck. I think they will answer for other purposes than tying people to beds."

"We must find these Turks," said the commissary. "They are desperate characters."

"Find them by all means," said Brett earnestly, "but on no account arrest them."

"And why, monsieur?" cried the other, with elevated eyebrows.

"Because if you do you will paralyse our future actions. When all is said and done, the only charge you can bring against them is a trivial one. It is evident they merely tied up this man, either with the object of frightening him into a confession, or to leave their hands free whilst they dealt with his employers. Perhaps they had both objects in view. In either event the appearance of the police on the scene would close their mouths more tightly than an oyster. As it is, I expect they will return, and, if possible, you must compel the *concierge* to conceal the fact that you have visited the house. Let him put all the blame on me. They know that I am mixed up in the inquiry, and fear me far less than the recognized authorities. Oblige me in this respect and you will not regret it."

The policeman was wise enough to fall in with the suggestion.

An hour later "The Worm" was taken in a cab to the Prefecture, as his condition was yet so hopeless that little real benefit could ensue from a searching cross-examination.

So Brett parted company with the officials, having made an appointment with the commissary for the next day at noon, when they assumed that the prisoner would be considerably recovered from his weakness and fright.

The barrister subsequently made a round of the minor cafes in the neighbourhood of the Cirque d'Hiver. After much casual questioning, he elicited the information that a well-known circus, of which Mlle. Beaucaire was at one time a shining light, was performing at that moment at Marseilles. He ascertained that during the winter season this class of entertainment perambulated the South of France and Northern Italy.

The actor from whom he gleaned these important facts said that he had a trustworthy friend in Marseilles who would easily be able to ascertain whether or not La Belle Chasseuse intended to rejoin her former profession. Brett secured his hearty co-operation by a liberal donation for expenses.

The barrister resolved to pay another visit to the Cabaret Noir late that evening, but he waited in the hotel until nearly ten o'clock in anxious expectation of a telegram from Fairholme.

At last the message arrived. Its contents were laconic.

"Right first time," it ran. "Invalid lady's name 'Jack.' Somewhat exhausted, after long confinement. Edith delighted. Jack visits Under-Secretary to-night. We all purpose joining you in Paris to-morrow. Do you approve?"

Brett promptly wired, "Yes," and then set out for Montmartre, dressing himself in the height of fashion so far as his wardrobe would permit, and donning a fierce moustache and wig, which completely altered his appearance. He looked like a successful impressario or popular Italian tenor.

12
THE INNKEEPER

The fair-ground of Montmartre was in full swing when Brett arrived there. The Cabaret Noir was in charge of his former acquaintance, the weary-eyed waiter, and other assistants.

The barrister wondered whether Mlle. Beaucaire had taken her father completely into her confidence. To make certain he questioned the waiter.

"Is Monsieur Beaucaire in?" he said.

"But yes, monsieur. You will find him in the billiard-room."

This time Brett was not conducted through the private passage that led through the rear of the bar. The man politely indicated another entrance, and brought him to the proprietor with the introductory remark—

"A gentleman who wishes to see you."

The room was tenanted by a nondescript crowd, whose attention was promptly attracted by the appearance of a stranger, and a well-dressed one at that.

The games in progress at the two tables were momentarily suspended, whilst Gros Jean, a corpulent man above the middle height, whose legs seemed to be too frail to support his rotund body, advanced, peering curiously beneath his bushy eyebrows to get a glimpse of the newcomer, for the shaded light did not fall on Brett's features, and M. Beaucaire wondered who the stranger could be. The barrister almost started when he recognized his fellow-passenger, the man who travelled to Paris with Gaultier and himself. Gros Jean bowed politely enough, and murmured something about being at Brett's service.

"Oh, it is nothing of great importance," said Brett airily, as he was not anxious to attract too much

observation from the unwashed humanity who took such
interest in him. "I merely wish to know when it will be
convenient for me to have some conversation with
mademoiselle, your charming daughter?"

"May I inquire the reason, monsieur?" said the other.

"Certainly. I have heard of her skill as an artist, and
it is possible I may be able to arrange a London
engagement for her."

"Ah," said the landlord deprecatingly, "what a pity!
Had monsieur called here yesterday he could have seen
mademoiselle. She has now left Paris for some weeks."

"Perhaps," said Brett, "I may have the pleasure of
meeting her elsewhere. I myself depart to-morrow on a
tour in the South of France. It is possible that
mademoiselle may be employed in some of the southern
cities. If so I will certainly make it my business to call on
her."

Beaucaire came a step nearer. Clearly he did not
recall the barrister's face. He knew well that his
daughter's attainments were not such as to command the
eager search of London theatrical managers, yet he was
assured that the individual who now addressed him was
not an ordinary music-hall agent, hunting up fees.

He lowered his voice, after an angry glance at the
loungers in the room, which caused them to turn to the
tables with redoubled interest.

"I regret," he said, "that mademoiselle is not
professionally engaged at this moment. Indeed, she has
not appeared in public for some months. May I ask how
monsieur came to hear of her name?"

"It is the easiest matter in the world," said Brett with
his ready smile, producing his note-book and rapidly
turning over the leaves. "I have here the names and
addresses of a large number of artists whom I was
recommended to visit. Mademoiselle's name was given to
me among others at the Cirque d'Hiver, where I heard
most encouraging accounts of her skill. You see,
monsieur," he went on, "that in England the public are

not acquainted with any other language than their own, and when Continental artists are engaged we prefer those whose performance consists chiefly of acrobatic or other feats in which dialogue is unnecessary."

The barrister's ready explanation was sufficient. Nevertheless Beaucaire was puzzled. But even the most vulgar or brutal Frenchman is endowed with a certain amount of politeness, and in this instance Gros Jean felt that his visitor should be treated deferentially.

"I am most sorry," he cried, "to be unable to assist monsieur any further. If, however, you leave me your address I will communicate with you after I have heard from my daughter. I have no doubt that she will readily come to terms."

"I think you said that mademoiselle was in the South of France?" observed Brett casually.

Instantly Beaucaire became suspicious again.

"No," he replied shortly; "I do not think I said so."

"Of course not," laughed Brett. "How foolish of me! It was I who mentioned the South of France, was it not? You see that French is a foreign language to me, and I do not express myself very easily."

Beaucaire grinned politely again: "Permit me to congratulate monsieur upon both his pronunciation and facility. Not many Englishmen speak French as he does."

The barrister was determined not to allow the conversation to end too rapidly. He wished to note more carefully the details of this interesting household. Pulling out his cigar-case, he offered it to Gros Jean with the remark: "Your small French tables seem curious to my eyes after long acquaintance with English billiards. Are any of these gentlemen here skilled players in your fashion?"

"Oh, yes," said the innkeeper. "Andre there, for instance, can make big breaks. I have seen him make forty consecutive coups. Will you not take a seat for a little while and observe the play?"

"With pleasure." And Brett confirmed the favourable opinion formed of him by ordering refreshments for Beaucaire and himself and inviting the redoubtable Andre to join them.

He apparently took a keen interest in the game, and applauded the manner in which the Frenchman scored a series of difficult cannons.

Meanwhile he noted that between the private passage from the bar and the public one that led from the cafe was a room into which the light of day could not possibly penetrate. He was certain that no door communicated with it from the public passage, and he could not remember having passed one that first afternoon when La Belle Chasseuse brought him and Fairholme into the billiard-room to display her prowess as a markswoman.

It was certainly a curious apartment, and for some undefinable reason he could not prevent his mind from dwelling upon its possible uses.

Probably the Cafe Noir had no cellars. The place might serve as a store room. This natural hypothesis was upset by the appearance of the waiter, who passed through the billiard-room and opened another door at the further end, through which he soon emerged, carrying a fresh supply of bottles.

"It is obvious," said Brett to himself, "that if there is no door communicating with the private passage, then the only way in which that room can be reached is by a ladder from the top. Now I wonder why that should be necessary?"

He remained in the billiard-room some twenty minutes. When Gros Jean was called on some momentary errand to the front of the house he took his departure, purposely making the mistake of quitting the room by the wrong exit. At the same instant he struck a match to relight his cigar, and while the expert billiard player, Andre, ran after him to direct him as to the right way he rapidly surveyed the passage. The plaster walls were

smooth and unbroken on their inner side, affording no
doorway exit.

Apologising to Andre with a laugh, he then sauntered
towards the front cafe, where he purchased another drink
at the counter. He assured himself that he had not been
mistaken. The only private door out of the bar led into the
passage, so that the room beyond could only be reached
by a staircase or through a trap-door.

"I have learned something, at any rate," he murmured
as he passed out into the Boulevard, "and I imagine that
my knowledge is not shared by the Paris police.
Mademoiselle would have acted more wisely had she not
yielded to impulse, and reserved her shooting display for
a more dramatic occasion."

Brett kept his appointment with the commissary next
morning. That worthy official set himself to the congenial
task of examining a prisoner with the air of one who said:
"Now you will see what manner of man I am. Here I am
on my native heath."

He consulted bulky volumes, made notes, fussily
called up various subordinates, both in person and by
speaking-tube, and generally conducted himself with a
business-like air that much amused the barrister, who,
however, for his own purposes took care to appear greatly
impressed.

At last all was ready, and the captive of the Rue
Barbette was introduced.

This precocious personage had recovered his self-
possession and natural impudence during the night. By
the commissary's instructions he had been well supplied
with eatables, and the restrictions as to persons under
detention were relaxed, to permit him to enjoy a supply of
his much-loved cigarettes. Consequently, the little thief
was restored to his usual state of jaunty cheekiness.

The first part of the interrogation, which promptly
ensued, was not strange to him.

"Your name?" said the commissary.

"Charles Petit."

"Age?"

"Believed to be twenty-seven, but as no record was kept of my birth I cannot be certain."

"Abode?"

"Changeable. Of late I have dwelt in the Cabaret Noir, Boulevard de Montmartre."

"You are generally known as 'The Worm?'"

"That is so."

"You have served several periods of imprisonment, and have paid over 400 francs in fines?"

"I have not kept count, but I suppose it is all written down there." And he jerked his thumb towards the conviction book on the commissary's desk.

"You are a noted thief, and you obtained your nickname by reason of your dexterity in picking locks and climbing through scullery windows?"

"If you say so, monsieur, your words cannot be disputed."

"Very well." The commissary scratched a few lines on a memorandum tablet. Then he suddenly raised his quick eyes and fastened them on the prisoner with the direct question—

"How came you to be detained in such an extraordinary manner in the house, No. 11, Rue Barbette, yesterday?"

A vacant and stolid expression intended to convey an idea of utter innocence came over "The Worm's" face.

"Believe me, monsieur," he said, "I cannot give you the slightest explanation of that extraordinary incident."

"Indeed! You surprise me. I suppose you wish me to understand that you casually strolled in out of the street and were set upon by three Turks, who gagged you and bound you with leather thongs, leaving you to starve quietly to death if you had not been rescued by reason of a chance visit paid to the place by myself and others?"

"I assure you, monsieur, that, strange as it may seem, you have almost related the facts. I went to the place in question with a very ordinary message from a Turkish gentleman with whom I have a slight acquaintance. The other Turks listened to me with the gravity peculiar to their nation, and then, before I could offer a word of remonstrance, treated me exactly as you saw."

"At what time did you go there?"

"It must have been nearly three o'clock, the day before yesterday," was the answer.

"And what message did you bring?"

"I was told to ask the Turkish gentlemen to be good enough to cross the Pont Neuf exactly at half-past six, when they would meet a friend who desired to give some information to them."

"Oh! come now," said the commissary, with a knowing smile, "that will not do, Petit. You are far too old a hand to convey such a childish message as that. What reason can you have for seeking to shield these men who treated you in a barbarous way and left you to die a cruel death?"

"On my honour—" began the thief melodramatically, but Brett here interrupted the conversation.

"Will you allow me," he said to the commissary, "to put a few questions to this man?"

"Certainly," was the answer.

"Now listen," said Brett, sternly gazing at the truculent little rascal with those searching eyes of his, which seemed to reach to the very spine. "It is useless for you to attempt any further prevarication. We know exactly who are your confederates. We are acquainted with a large number of the gang that frequents the Cafe Noir. Do not forget that I was present when you tried to palm off on Hussein-ul-Mulk the false diamonds, which your confederates hoped he would accept. For you to attempt now to escape from the law is hopeless. The sole chance you have of remitting a punishment which may even lead you beneath the guillotine is to confess fully and freely all that you know concerning the outrage which has been committed.

"No, don't interrupt me," he continued with even greater emphasis, when "Le Ver" tried to break in. "You will tell me that you merely acted as the agent of others, and that you yourself are not conscious of the nature of any crime that has been committed. I know that to be so. You have been made a mere tool. You are the cat, simply employed by the monkey to pull the chestnuts out of the fire, and you have only succeeded in getting your own paws burnt. Your sole chance of safety now is to inform the commissary and me exactly how you came to be mixed up with this affair."

The Frenchman's truculency seemed to vanish under Brett's cutting words. His wizened face even manifested a faint flush of anger as the barrister pointed out how he had been duped by his employers and made to run risks which they avoided.

Yet the order of his craft was strong in its influence, and he commenced another series of protestations.

"I assure you, gentlemen," he cried, "that with respect to the Turks I have no knowledge whatever of their pursuits or motives. I was present when this English gentleman here was debating with them, and I understood that they even went so far as to use threats against him. My mission was to give to the leaders of the Turks a package which I did not even know contained diamonds, either genuine or false. No one could be more surprised than myself when the Turkish gentleman produced them."

"Who sent you there with the diamonds?" said Brett.

"Even that I cannot tell you," said Petit. "It was a mere chance affair. I was seated in a cafe sipping some absinthe when a man asked me if I would execute a small commission for him. He explained that it was to deliver a parcel at a house not five minutes distant, and—"

"I see," interrupted Brett, with the cynical smile which so often disconcerted glib liars like Petit. "It is hopeless to expect you to tell the truth. However, I think I know a way to clear your wits. You must be brought face to face with La Belle Chasseuse. Perhaps when you are confronted with that lady in the room between the cafe and the billiard saloon of the Cabaret Noir—"

"The Worm" gasped out brokenly–

"Pardon, monsieur! I will tell you everything!"

The man's face had absolutely become livid as he listened to the barrister's words.

The commissary was vastly surprised at the turn taken by the conversation. He could not guess what deep significance lay behind the Englishman's threat, and, to tell the truth, Brett himself was considerably astonished at the effect of his vague insinuations, but he lost not a moment in following up the advantage thus gained.

"Well," he said, "tell us now who it was that sent you to the Turks with the diamonds?"

"It was Le Jongleur, Henri Dubois."

"What?" cried the commissary, starting violently. "Henri Dubois! The most expert thief in France! A scoundrel against whom the police have vainly tried for years to secure evidence."

"I know nothing of that, monsieur," said the little man, who seemed to be strangely crestfallen, "but I am telling you the truth this time. It was he who sent me the day before yesterday to the Rue Barbette, and again yesterday, although I was very unwilling to go the second time, because, as this gentleman will tell you, they looked very like murdering me on the first occasion."

"What was the object of your visit yesterday?" said Brett.

"There, monsieur, I have told you the truth, although monsieur the commissary here thinks it was childish. My instructions really were to ask them to meet him on the Pont Neuf at 6.30 p.m., when he said he would explain everything to their satisfaction. But, above all, I was to warn them to beware of the Englishman."

"Then, why should they seize and gag you for conveying such a simple message?" demanded the commissary.

"I cannot tell. I have done them no harm. Believe me, gentlemen both, I have not the slightest idea how these diamonds were obtained, or why there should be such a fuss about them. All I know is that these Turks are desperate fellows, and you won't catch me going near them again, I swear."

"How long have you known Dubois?" said Brett.

"Oh, two years more or less."

"Have you ever been associated with him before?"

"Never, monsieur. My record is there." And he again jerked his thumb towards the volume on the table. "It will tell you that I deal in small affairs. Dubois is an artist. If he found a woman's purse in the street he would return it to her with a bow, if she were rich and handsome—and with some francs added, if she were poor."

"I know little about him," he continued, "except that he is a great man. They say that he once robbed the Bank of France of 200,000 francs!"

And the little wretch's voice became tremulous with admiration as he recounted the legend.

"He is a favoured lover of La Belle Chasseuse?" demanded Brett sharply.

"The Worm" recovered his equanimity somewhat at this question. He softly drew his hand over his chin as he replied with a smirk: "There are others!"

"I think not," came the quick retort. "No; there are none on whom mademoiselle bestows such favours. She left Paris with him last night."

"The devil!" ejaculated the little man.

"Oh, yes; and she has just passed a fortnight with him in London."

"A thousand thunders!" screamed Petit. "Her father told me she was performing in a music-hall at Marseilles."

The barrister had evidently touched a sore point, and "The Worm" was more ready than ever to tell all that he knew about Le Jongleur. But his information amounted to little more of importance. The chief fact had been ascertained, its predominant interest was the identity of the man who had planned and carried out the "Albert Gate outrage."

Brett quickly realized that to question him further was useless. Petit evidently expected to be set at liberty at once. In this, however, he was disappointed, for the commissary curtly remanded him to the cells.

Brett, on the other hand, made up his mind that "The Worm" at liberty might be more valuable to him than "The Worm" in gaol. So he asked the commissary, as a favour to himself, to set Petit free, first giving the thief to understand that he owed his release to the barrister's intervention.

This was done, and "Le Ver" was voluble in his expressions of gratitude. Brett soon cut him short.

"Here," he said, "are a couple of louis for your immediate necessities. I am living at the Grand Hotel, and I want you to call there each morning at ten o'clock. You will inquire at the office if Mr. Brett has left any message for you. Then, if I need your services, I will be able to reach you early."

Petit protested that he would serve monsieur most willingly, and soon afterwards the barrister took leave of the commissary, promising to keep him fully posted as to further developments, and secure for him, and him only, the ultimate credit of capturing such a noted thief as Dubois. Fate settled matters differently.

The French official was already much impressed by Brett's method of handling this difficult inquiry, and he consented readily enough not only to assist him in every possible way, but to restrain the police from further active interference in the case until matters had developed from their present stage.

During the afternoon Brett received a visit from his actor acquaintance, who brought him a telegram from Marseilles. It read–

"Mlle. Beauclaire has obtained an engagement here at the Palais de Glace. She makes her first appearance on Monday evening."

Brett smiled as he realized how accurately he had interpreted the actions of La Belle Chasseuse and her companion.

"This is certain," he said to himself. "They left Paris on Thursday night and they probably will not reach Marseilles until Monday. I have plenty of time to hear Talbot's story from his own lips before I take my departure for the South."

An hour later he was seated in his room smoking and reading a magazine when the waiter appeared.

"A lady and three gentlemen wish to see monsieur," he explained.

He rose promptly, and accompanied the man to the foot of the staircase. There, near the elevator, he saw Edith Talbot, Lord Fairholme, and Sir Hubert Fitzjames, whilst with them was a tall, handsome young man, in whom the fair outlines of the girl's face were repeated in sterner and bolder characteristics.

Edith was the first to catch sight of him. She sprang forward and cried with an impulsiveness that showed how deeply her quiet nature had been stirred.

"Oh, Mr. Brett, I cannot tell you how grateful I am to you! Here is my brother!"

The two men shook hands and looked at each other with a natural curiosity, for seldom had an acquaintance been made after more exciting preliminaries.

"I am indeed glad to see you," said Brett, shaking Talbot's hand with more demonstrativeness than was usual to one of his quiet temperament.

"Then how shall I find words to express myself?" was the reply, "for in my case there is joined to the pleasure of making a much-desired acquaintance the knowledge that to your efforts I am indebted for my liberty and possibly for my reputation."

"We have much to say to each other," said the barrister. "I suppose you have secured rooms in the hotel?" he continued, turning to Miss Talbot.

"Oh, yes, everything is settled," she cried. "The servants are looking after our trunks. I simply would not wait a moment until I had seen you. Please take us all somewhere at once where we can talk quietly."

Brett answered with a smile: "Lord Fairholme and I have a sitting-room which we use in common, and which has already been the scene of many earnest conferences. Let us go there."

13
THE RELEASE

"Now, who talks first?" Brett cried, once the door was fairly closed behind them.

"I do," burst forth Fairholme. "My story will not take long to tell, and if I do not get it off my chest, I shall simply explode."

"We must not have any more tragedies," said Brett, "so proceed."

"Well, thanks to your foresight, I found the two servants and your ex-policeman waiting for me on the platform at Charing Cross. As I only carried a handbag, I had no trouble with the Customs, and we walked straight out of the station. In less than five minutes we were standing outside the building which contained the invalid lady's flat. Your agent told me that, so far as he knew, there were no other persons in the place except the tenant and her two servants, an elderly French or Italian married couple. Our collective wits could not devise a plausible pretext for gaining access to the lady, so I determined to settle the business in the brutal British fashion. We marched quietly up the stairs to the second storey, and your assistant pointed out the right door. There were only two flats on that landing, and the other one was apparently empty. Your man had made a somewhat important discovery since he wrote to you. This empty flat had been taken by the agent who acted for the parties opposite, and although the place was not tenanted, the landlord was, of course, satisfied, as the rent had been paid in advance. This seemed to indicate that the place was left vacant simply to prevent the others from being overlooked."

Brett marked his appreciation of Fairholme's sagacity by a nod, and the earl continued–

"I rang the bell and promptly put my ear to the keyhole. It seemed to me that a couple of doors were hastily closed, and then someone slowly approached. The outer door was opened and a man's head appeared. I could only see his face and a portion of his left shoulder, because the chain was on the door, and the opening was not more than eight or ten inches. Speaking in broken English he said–'Vat you vant?' His accent showed that he was a Frenchman.

"I answered in my best French, 'I wish to see madame, your mistress, at once.'

"'It is impossible,' he said in the same language, and simultaneously he tried to shut the door in my face. I shoved my foot against the jamb and prevented him. At the same instant my own servant and I–as, if there was to be trouble, I thought it best to keep the others out of it–applied our utmost force to the door and succeeded in snapping the chain. It might have been a tough job, as you know that to force a way through anything that yields slightly and yet holds fast is much more difficult than to smash a lock or a couple of bolts. Luckily the flats were jerry built, so the chain broke, and so suddenly that the Frenchman was pitched violently backwards. We nearly fell after him. The ex-policeman was a splendid chap. His first idea was to jump towards the switch of the electric lights and turn on every lamp in the place.

"I shouted, 'Talbot, are you there? It is I, Fairholme.'

"I got no answer, but a woman darted out of a room which proved to be the kitchen, screamed something which I could not catch, and handed a revolver to the Frenchman, who was just struggling to his feet. That was where my prize-fighting butler came in useful. Before you could say 'Wink' he gave the man an upper-cut that settled him effectually for the next minute. Almost with the same movement he caught the woman a slap over the ear that upset her nerves considerably. She had a revolver in her hand too. It fell to the floor, and Smith, your servant, seized both weapons.

"The ex-policeman called out–'I do not think we are making any mistake, sir. They would not act after this manner if they were on the square.'

"I must say it seemed to me that so far it was we who had been acting in an extraordinary way, but there was no time to discuss the ethics of the case then. Whilst my butler and Smith took care of the couple, your assistant and I hastily examined three rooms. They were empty, save for a small quantity of furniture. The fourth door resisted our efforts, so, of course, we burst it open. And the first thing that met our eyes was poor old Jack lying on his back on the bed, and glaring at us in a way that made me think at first he was mad."

"I should think so," interrupted Talbot. "I would like to see your face if you were trussed up as I was–not able to speak a word–and a fiendish row going on in the passage outside."

"You were gagged," questioned Brett, "and your wrists and ankles were secured to the four corners of the bed, your limbs being distended in the form of an X?"

Fairholme glanced round admiringly. "Of course," he cried delightedly, "I knew you would guess it. That is the pleasant way these Turks have of securing their prisoners."

"It is an awfully uncomfortable one," said Talbot. "My joints are still stiff at the mere recollection of it. I have lain in that way, Mr. Brett, for countless hours. Occasionally the brutes would allow me to change my posture, but the moment anyone came to the door I was strapped up in an instant and a gag slipped into my mouth. What used to make me so furious was the knowledge that if only I got the chance of a second I could have broken that Frenchman's neck and escaped, but he and his wife always took such precautions that I never had the liberty to do more than reach with some difficulty the food that they gave me. However, I must not interrupt."

"I really have not much more to say," went on Fairholme. "You may be sure it did not take me long to release Talbot, and what do you think his first words were when he slowly sat up in bed and tried if his legs would bend?"

"I cannot guess," said Brett.

"He said: 'Have they got the diamonds?'

"I answered 'Yes.'

"'But it was impossible,' he said. 'They could not have mastered all those policemen.'

"'But they did,' I replied, and then and there, before he would budge an inch, he made me tell him the whole story. Just as I had ended we heard a scuffle in the passage. We went out, though Jack was hardly able to walk at first. It was Smith wrestling with the woman, who was a regular wild cat, and who would, even then, have done us any mischief in her power. There was nothing for it but to tie her hands behind her back, and then fasten her securely in a chair. After this was done we took counsel as to our next movements."

"Wait a little," said Brett. "How many rooms were there in the flat? You have accounted for four."

"I forgot," said Fairholme. "The place had six rooms. The small apartment in which Jack was confined was a sort of dressing-room, and the bedroom beyond looked out into the well of the block of flats. They had carefully nailed the blind of this dressing-room, so that not even a chance puff of wind could blow it aside and reveal its secret to anyone in the flats on the opposite storey or higher. The remaining room was empty. Your friend the policeman subsequently searched the place from top to toe, but he found nothing. The only document of any importance was an address on a card which he discovered in the Frenchman's pocket."

"Ah," said Brett, "what was that address?"

"Here it is."

The earl produced a small piece of pasteboard on which was scribbled, "Monsieur Jean Beaujolais, chez Monsieur Henri de Lisle, 41, Rue Bonnerie, Paris."

"That is important," said the barrister. "Why did you not wire it to me last night?"

"I had a reason," said the earl eagerly, "but that comes in with Jack's part of the story." And he turned towards Talbot, who, thus summoned to the stage, began to explain matters.

"I understand, Mr. Brett," he said, "that you are accurately acquainted with all that transpired until the moment when I entered the Albert Gate mansion on that remarkable night?"

"That is so," said Brett.

"Well, when Inspector Sharpe met me at the door on my arrival he told me that his Excellency Mehemet Ali, with three strange gentlemen and the junior members of the commission, awaited me in the dining-room. I went in and was surprised to find the three visitors, for during the preceding month not a single stranger had entered the house save a member of the Government and one or two important officials of the Foreign Office, who came with me out of sheer curiosity to see a collection of remarkable diamonds.

"The strangers bowed politely when I was introduced. Two of them spoke neither French nor English, but the third man spoke French fluently. He had, by the way, a somewhat peculiar accent, different from that to which I was accustomed in the Turks. It was softer, more sibilant, and impressed me as that of a man who was accustomed to speak Italian. He was a good-looking chap, about my height and build, and were it not for his brown skin, one would not have regarded him as a Turk. One side of his face was deeply scarred with a sword-cut, but, if anything, this did not detract from his appearance, and it gave a manly aspect to an otherwise effeminate face."

Brett could not help smiling involuntarily.

"Are you sure it was a sword-cut?"

"It certainly looked like one."

"And his skin was very brown?"

"Oh, quite. Indeed it was a shade deeper than that of most Turks. I have seen very many of them. Although dark-featured, they are often pallid enough in reality, and their deep-hued complexion is due more to their black hair and eyebrows than to the mere colour of the skin."

Brett smiled again.

"I think," he said, "I will show you the same gentleman in a somewhat different aspect. But proceed."

"The explanation given to me by Mehemet Ali was both extraordinary and disconcerting, especially at such a late hour. He told me that the three gentlemen to whom I had been introduced–I am sorry, by the way, that I cannot remember their names, as they were all Mohammeds, or Rasuls, or Ibrahims, and the dramatic events of the night subsequently drove them from my mind–had been sent post haste from Constantinople on a special mission. They had only reached London that night, and they bore with them a special mandate, signed by the Sultan himself, directing Mehemet Ali to hand over the diamonds to their charge, and to at once return with his assistants to Yildiz Kiosk.

"There could be no questioning the authenticity of the Sultan's instructions. The document was in his own handwriting, was endorsed with his private seal, and conveyed other distinguishing marks which rendered his Excellency assured on this important point. He told me that he was compelled to obey implicitly, and were it possible he would have started from London that night. This, however, was out of the question, but he had not lost a moment in sending for me and acquainting me with his Majesty's wishes.

"You will readily perceive that the affair placed me in an awkward predicament. I was, so to speak, representing the British Government in the matter, and the Foreign Office had pledged itself, through our

Ambassador at Constantinople, to undertake all the precautions for safeguarding the diamonds with which you are acquainted. It seemed to me that notwithstanding the urgency of the Sultan's order, I should not be doing my duty to permit the transfer to be made in such an irregular manner. So I said quite plainly that the matter could not be settled that night. They must all wait until the morning, when I would consult my Department, and Mehemet Ali, together with his aides, could leave for Constantinople by the evening train, after my superiors had been acquainted with the Sultan's wishes.

"Turks are difficult people to understand. It seemed to me that my decision gave some satisfaction to Mehemet Ali, who was undoubtedly very much upset by the queer manner in which he had been deposed from his important trust. At once an animated discussion took place."

"In French?" interrupted Brett.

"No; in Turkish."

"Did the gentleman with the sabre-cut on his face take any part therein?"

"Not in the least. He sat and smoked cigarettes in the most unconscious manner possible, leaving his two associates to carry on the conversation."

As the barrister appeared to have no further question to ask at the moment, Talbot continued–

"Several times Mehemet Ali appealed to me to change my mind and formally ratify the transfer at once. I was quite firm in my refusal, and did not hesitate to describe the Sultan's demands as ridiculous. I was rendered more determined, if anything, in this attitude by a growing certainty in my mind that his Excellency himself approved of my attitude. Ultimately, it seems, they hit upon a compromise. The whole party would remain together all night in a sort of dual control, and then the change of guardianship would take place next day in accordance with my views as to what was right and proper. I must admit I was intensely relieved when this decision was arrived at. Looking back now over the events of the night, I can perceive that from that moment the gang who effected the murders and the robbery had me in their power, for they had completely succeeded in allaying my suspicions, and I can only plead in extenuation of my shortsightedness that Mehemet Ali himself, and the other gentlemen with whom I had been acquainted during the past month, were willing accessories to the arrangement."

"I do not see," said Brett, "that you have the slightest cause to reproach yourself. You acted quite properly throughout, and I am sure that when all the facts are known your status at the Foreign Office will be improved rather than diminished by this incident."

The other man's face flushed with pleasure as he heard these words.

"Thank you," he replied simply. "I certainly took every precaution that suggested itself to me. Subsequently I was the victim of circumstances. The French-speaking Turk, as I have told you, took no part whatever in the negotiations, and when he became aware of the *modus operandi* determined upon—"

"By the way," said Brett, "how did he become aware of it?"

"Oh, Mehemet Ali told him in French."

"Didn't that strike you as curious?"

"Most certainly it did. But the scoundrel explained it afterwards by telling me that although a Turkish subject, he had lived in Algiers and France since he was a child, and had quite forgotten his mother tongue. But he was employed in a confidential position in the Turkish Embassy at Paris, owing not only to family influence, but to his intimate acquaintance with the French language."

"Ah!" said Brett, "Monsieur Henri Dubois has a ready wit."

"What!" cried Edith, who naturally enough was following each word with the utmost interest, "do you already know his name?"

"Not only his name," replied Brett, "but his identity, Miss Talbot. You shall see him in another skin and without the sword-cut. It is possible, however, that before we meet, this distinguishing mark may be replaced by a fractured skull or a bullet wound."

Fairholme suddenly clenched his right fist and examined his knuckles, his unconscious action causing the others to laugh.

"Is he a Frenchman, then?" said Talbot.

"Unquestionably–a most modern product."

"And his name is Dubois?"

"Yes."

"All right. In future I will allude to him by his proper title. Well, Monsieur Dubois strolled towards me with the easy confidence of a man who was sure of himself.

"'This affair bores me,' he said. 'I see no reason why I, who am in no way concerned with the Sultan's collection of precious stones, should sit up all night keeping guard over them with these very earnest gentlemen here. I am going to my hotel. I have sent my portmanteau to the Carlton. Will you honour me by driving there and telling me something about your wonderful London as we go?'

"The man looked at me with a meaning in his eyes that conveyed quite plainly the intimation–

"'We can talk quietly in the cab, and I can explain much that is at present hidden.' Unfortunately I fell in with his suggestions.

"We crossed the dining-room together. We were searched by the police in the hall, much to his apparent surprise, and then we drove off through St. George's Place.

"He at once aroused my curiosity by telling me sensational details of a widespread plot to dethrone the Sultan. An essential part of the conspiracy was to obtain possession of the diamonds before they had been cut, as they were an heirloom from the Prophet, and it would be a terrible thing in the eyes of the more fanatical section of the Mohammedans if they were tampered with in any way.

"This sounded reasonable enough, as the same story had been dinned in my ears for several weeks.

"He made out that for reasons of State the Sultan had decided to change the Minister Plenipotentiary charged with secret mission to London.

"Altogether he talked so candidly, and with such an air of treating the whole business as the bugbear of a timid monarch, that I really believed him.

"At last we reached the Carlton. We got out and he paid the cabman, who drove off round the corner; then my new acquaintance explained to me that he placed no greater trust in his fellow-countrymen than did their ruler. Therefore he had led them to believe he was staying at that hotel, whereas he had in reality taken up his abode in the flat of a French family with whom he was acquainted. If I would come with him for a moment he promised to place me in possession of certain documents which would render easy my explanations to the Foreign Office next morning.

"I accompanied him without hesitation, secure in the knowledge that a strong force of police guarded my charge at Albert Gate, both inside and outside the house. We went to the mansions where he said he lived. The place had a perfectly respectable exterior, and is situated, as you know, in a reputable thoroughfare. We ascended to the second floor, entered the flat, and were ushered by a middle-aged Frenchwoman into a sort of sitting-room.

"Dubois turned to a writing-desk and unlocked a drawer.

"'Here are the documents I promised you, Mr. Talbot,' he said; but, to my amazement, he whipped out a revolver and held it within two feet of my breast.

"'If you move, or attempt to cry out, you are a dead man!' he cried.

"At the same instant a door behind me opened and some three or four persons entered. I was so furious at the trick that had been played upon me that I disregarded his threat and sprang at him, but he did not fire. Flinging the revolver behind him on the writing-table he closed with me. Before I well knew what had happened I was tied hand and foot, gagged, and placed helpless in a chair. A few minutes later, after a muttered consultation between my captors, I was taken to the room in which Fairholme found me, and I never left the place until nearly nine o'clock last night.

"It was a most ghastly experience. I would sooner die than go through it again.

"If ever I get within measurable distance of Monsieur Henri Dubois I promise you that I will repay him with interest some of the agony he inflicted on me. I never thought I should hate a man as I hate that Frenchman. I do not want to kill him. I want to torture him!"

This was the first sign that Talbot had given of the anger that filled his soul. For a moment no one spoke. Edith stifled a sob, and Sir Hubert Fitzjames broke the tension by swearing as vehemently as ever did the army in Flanders.

"You have suffered," said Brett quietly, "but not in vain. It is only by the manner in which these blackguards treated you that we have obtained so much knowledge. Your capture was a necessary part of their scheme. I wonder now that after you had served their purpose they did not kill you. It was not out of pity, believe me. The fact that you were spared confirms me in the opinion that the Albert Gate murders were a gigantic blunder, never contemplated by the expert criminal who planned the theft. But continue. What happened afterwards?"

Talbot almost summoned up a smile as he said—
"Really, the next thing was so grotesque that were not the

whole business so serious a one you would be compelled to laugh at it.

"Looking back now to those first ghastly hours when I laid on the bed tied hand and foot, I find it difficult to recall any definite impressions. It would be absurd to say that I suffered, either mentally or physically. I was sunk in a sort of stupor of rage, and my bonds did not hurt me so long as I kept quiet. Curiously enough, my thoughts were somewhat altruistic. Instead of speculating as to my own fate I rather wondered what would be the outcome of the whole mysterious business. I could not bring myself to believe that, cleverly as the rogues had outwitted me, they would be able to similarly dupe a strong body of Metropolitan police, not to mention Mehemet Ali and his assistants.

"At last I fell asleep, dozing fitfully at first, but finally giving way to the deep slumber of exhaustion.

"I was awakened by someone shaking me, though not roughly. It took me some time to recover my scattered senses, and at first I was almost unable to move, owing to the constrained position of my limbs. As well as I could judge it was not yet daylight, for the electric lamps were turned on, and I subsequently found that such rays of natural light as penetrated into my room during the day did not arrive for a considerable time.

"Thenceforth, of course, my sole method of judging the progress of time was by the alternation of meals and the difference of light between day and night.

"Someone assisted me to assume a sitting posture, the cords attached to my wrists were relaxed, and I was firmly held by two men—one a Turk whom I had not seen before, the other a Frenchman whom you found in the flat.

"At the foot of the bed were standing Dubois and a closely-veiled female—a young woman, as well as I could judge, and a person of tall and elegant stature, who, it would appear, spoke only French.

"Dubois addressed me calmly.

"'I hope,' he said, 'you are in a better temper, my dear Talbot?'

"'It does not appear to me that the state of my temper is of any material significance,' I answered.

"'No,' he replied nonchalantly. 'The game is in my hands, and will probably remain there for a considerable period. But I do not wish to be unkind. You have, I am given to understand, a highly respectable uncle and a very charming sister, who will no doubt suffer much perturbation owing to your mysterious disappearance. Now, you may not think it, but I am a very humane sort of fellow. Consequently, I am quite agreeable that you should write them a brief note, omitting of course all superfluous information, such as dates, addresses, and other embarrassing facts, but simply telling them that you are well. I will guarantee its safe delivery.'

"Naturally, I jumped at the offer. The veiled lady supplied me with a sheet of notepaper and an envelope, and I scribbled the unfortunate letter which was subsequently posted in Paris and caused such a sensation. I had only one hand at liberty, so Dubois politely offered to seal the envelope for me, first, however, reading carefully what I had written.

"'That is quite correct,' he said; 'it will relieve their feelings and prove at the same time highly serviceable to me, as the letter will be posted in Paris and not in London. You see, my dear Talbot, how readily you fall in with my plans. You are as putty in my hands. Now, I suppose, being a brave Englishman, you would sooner have died than written this letter if you had guessed it would prove of material assistance to me?'

"I fear I used some very bad language to Dubois, notwithstanding the presence of the lady, but he paid little heed to me, and the pair at once undertook the most curious proceedings I have ever witnessed.

"They had before them a table set out with all sorts of paint, paste, and powders, such as one might expect to find in an actor's dressing-room.

"Sitting himself astride a chair so that the light fell on his face, Dubois submitted himself to the skilful hands of the woman, who forthwith began to make him up in an exact resemblance to me. The right side of his face was towards me, but when, in obedience to her requirements, he turned somewhat, I noticed to my astonishment that the scar which I have mentioned had completely disappeared, and then I saw that his Turkish complexion had also vanished, leaving him a particularly white-skinned Frenchman, with a high colour."

"Ah!" said Brett, leaning back in his chair and attentively surveying the ceiling.

"You must remember," went on Talbot, "that my wits were somewhat confused by the extraordinary circumstances of the hour. Having been so suddenly awakened from a sound sleep, and subsequently annoyed by the incident of the letter, it took me some moments to recognize these discrepancies in his appearance. At first, so to speak, I knew him immediately as Dubois, but the more I looked at him the less confident I would have been were it not that his voice and manner supplied unerring indications of his identity.

"The lady proceeded with her work in the most business-like fashion, and to my intense amazement he quickly assumed a marked resemblance to myself. Not such, perhaps, as would bear close scrutiny, but rather the effect attained by a skilful artist in a rapid sketch, or caught by a fleeting glance whilst passing a mirror.

"'What is the game now?' I cried, when the true nature of their purpose dawned upon me.

"'Oh, just the same,' replied Dubois, grinning, 'I merely wish to puzzle the thick-headed brains of you Englishmen a little more. That is all.'

"'Halloa!' I cried, 'you understand English?'

"'Yes,' he answered coolly. 'It is frequently necessary in my business.'

"'Well,' I said, 'there can be no doubt that you are an accomplished villain. What you intend to achieve by masquerading in this fashion I utterly fail to understand. You can never be such a fool as to think that you will be able to gain admittance to Albert Gate by impersonating me. Were you even to succeed you would still be as far off as ever from securing your booty, which, I suppose, is the Imperial diamond and its companions.'

"'Really,' he said, with a sneer, 'I thought that you, Mr. Talbot, were endowed with a little more intelligence than the average. Pardon, Mignon, *pour un moment.*'

"He rose from his chair, unfastened a case which he took from the breast-pocket of his overcoat, and showed me the diamonds which had been the object of so much care and solicitude on my part during many weeks.

"'You see,' he continued, seating himself again, whilst the lady resumed her task without a word, 'the business has been satisfactorily accomplished, Mr. Talbot. The diamonds are here; so are you. Unfortunately his Excellency and the secretaries are with the Prophet. You will, I am sure, express my regrets to the police, to the Foreign Office, and to all concerned, that the Sultan's commissionaries should have been so unceremoniously despatched to Paradise. It was not my fault, believe me, nor was it altogether necessary. I am in no way responsible for the bungling measures adopted by my Turkish assistants. You see, in Constantinople they are accustomed to these drastic means of settling disputes.'

"He rattled on so pleasantly that I hardly grasped the true significance of his words, so I replied with almost equal flippancy–

"'I will be most pleased to convey your regrets to the proper authorities. May I ask when I shall be at liberty to do so?'

"'Ah,' he said, 'there you puzzle even my intelligence. It will certainly be days, it may be weeks, before you can communicate with your friends.'"

"A sudden frenzy seized me at those words, and I endeavoured to smash the heads of my two gaolers together by throwing them off their balance outwards, and then rapidly contracting my arms. Thereupon I made another discovery. A cord lying loosely round my neck was suddenly tightened, and I was thrown back choking. A fourth man, of whose presence I was unconscious, was stationed behind me and held the noose in his hands.

"It was some time before I recovered my breath or my speech.

"At last I was allowed to rise again, and Dubois said with a quiet smile which was intensely irritating—

"'By this time, Mr. Talbot, you should have realized that you have not fallen into the hands of children. We do not wish to do you a mischief. Indeed, it would not suit our purpose. It is far from our desire to quarrel with the British Government or to take the life of one of its rising young diplomatists. The dispute in which you are unfortunately involved is between a certain section of the Sultan's subjects and that potentate himself. But really you must recognize the absolute helplessness of your position. You have just received a stern reminder. Let it be the last, for if you give us any more trouble we may end a difficult situation by effectively cutting your throat. Such an operation would be distasteful to us and most distressing to you. So please do not compel us to perform it.'

"I glared at him viciously. Speak I could not, but he paid no further attention to me, and his make-up was now pronounced to be perfect by his critical companion.

"'*Vous etes un tres bel Anglais, mon vieux,*' she cried, coquettishly setting her head on one side and glancing first at him and then at me."

"The cat!" cried Edith. "She evidently thought you good-looking, Jack."

Talbot blushed and laughed at the involuntary slip. "I am not responsible for her opinions," he said. "I am simply telling you what happened.

"Dubois left the room," he continued, "and returned in a few moments, dressed in an English tweed suit, with my overcoat and a deerstalker cap. Upon my honour, he was so like me that, notwithstanding my rage, I was compelled to smile at him. He caught my transient mood for an instant.

"'*Tiens!*' he cried, 'that is better. The surgical operation is beginning to take effect. You see the joke?'

"'It is a somewhat bitter species of humour,' I replied. 'Perhaps in the future it may have a sequel.'

"'Life is made up of sequels,' was the airy answer. 'Events generally turn out to be so completely opposite to that which I anticipated that I no longer give them a thought. I live only for the present, and at this moment I am victorious. But now, Mr. Talbot, I purpose taking a little trip to the Continent on your account. I hope, therefore, for your sake, that the Channel will be smooth.'

"With a mock bow of much politeness he took his leave, carrying with him the case of diamonds. I have never seen him since. Last night in the Foreign Office I met Captain Gaultier, who told me of the *rencontre* on the steamer. I readily forgave him for the mistake he had made with reference to my appearance, but it was too bad that he should imagine I would bolt to Paris with a lady of theatrical appearance in broad daylight."

"Yes," cried Fairholme, "if it had been the night steamer—"

"Bobby!" exclaimed Edith.

"Oh, I meant, of course," stammered Fairholme, "that by night Gaultier might have been more easily mistaken."

"Well, and what happened at the Foreign Office?"

Brett's question recalled the younger people to the gravity of the conclave.

"First of all," said Talbot, "Fairholme drove me straight home, where it was necessary to give some slight preliminary explanation before I made a too sudden appearance, so I remained in the cab outside whilst Fairholme went in and found Edith."

"Ah!" said Brett, still surveying the ceiling; but there was so much meaning in his voice that this time it was the turn of the young couple to blush.

"We did not take long to explain matters," continued Talbot. "I sent off messengers post-haste to the Under-Secretary and others suggesting that if possible we should meet at the Foreign Office. Within an hour my chiefs were good enough to fall in with my views, and therefore I had an opportunity to tell them my story exactly as I have repeated it to you. The result is that I carry with me a letter from the Under-Secretary in which he explains his views. I am already acquainted with his reasons, but I have no doubt that he puts them before you quite clearly."

He handed a letter to Brett. Its contents were laconic, but unmistakable—

"The inquiry in which you are engaged," it read, "must be conducted with the utmost secrecy and discretion. The gravest political importance is attached to its outcome. No trouble or expense should be allowed to interfere with the restoration of the diamonds to their rightful owner. The British Government will regard this as a most valuable service to the State, and Mr. Talbot is commissioned to place at your disposal the full resources of the Foreign Office. You will also find that his Majesty's Ministers throughout Europe have been advised to give you every assistance, whilst there is little reason to doubt that the various European Governments will be ready to offer you all possible support. The first consideration is the restoration of the gems intact to the Sultan; the second, absolute secrecy as to the whole of the circumstances."

"Whew!" whistled Brett. "Read between the lines, this communication shows the serious nature of our quest. If those diamonds are not recovered, a revolution in Turkey is the almost certain outcome, and Heaven alone knows what that means to the European Powers most concerned."

"If you succeed," said Sir Hubert Fitzjames, "the Government will make you a baronet."

"If you succeed," growled Talbot, "I will get even with that Frenchman."

"And when you succeed," said Fairholme, in a matter-of-fact tone that indicated the wild improbability of any other outcome, "Edith and I will get married!"

14
"TOUT VA BIEN"

Brett now deemed it advisable to take the commissary of police fully into his confidence. The official promptly suggested that every personage in Paris connected even remotely with the mystery–Gros Jean, the Turks, the waiter at the Cafe Noir, and even the little thief "Le Ver"–should be arrested and subjected to a *proces verbal*. But Brett would not hear of this proceeding.

He quite firmly reminded the commissary that the wishes of the British Government must be respected in this matter, and the proposed wholesale arrests of persons, some of whom were in no way cognisant of the crime, would assuredly lead to publicity and the appearance of sensational statements in the Press.

"But, monsieur," cried the Frenchman, "something must be done. Even you, I presume, intend to lay hands on the principal men. While they are wandering about the country each hour makes it easier for them to secrete the diamonds so effectually that no matter what may be the result the Sultan will never recover his property."

"Calm yourself, I beg," said the barrister, with difficulty compelling himself to reason with this excitable policeman. "You speak as though we had in our hands every jot of evidence to secure the conviction of Dubois and his associates before a judge."

"But is it not so?" screamed the other.

"No; it is very far from being so. Let us look at the facts. In the first place the Turks will not speak. They are political fanatics. The moment a policeman arrests them they become dumb. Torture would bring nothing from them but lies. Then we have the two people who acted as Mr. Talbot's gaolers. What charge can we prefer against them? Merely one of illegal detention, whilst they would probably defend themselves by saying that Talbot was represented to them as a lunatic whose restraint was necessary for family reasons. Then we come to Dubois himself and the fair Mlle. Beaucaire. In the first place, you may be certain that they have provided a strong alibi to prove that they were in Paris on the days when we are certain they were in London. Who can identify either of them? The lady we rule out of court at once. The only persons who saw her were Mr. Talbot and Captain Gaultier, the latter of whom has already placed on record the statement that he would not recognize her again. Talbot's evidence is stronger, but I would not like to hear him subjected to the merciless cross-examination of an able counsel. As for Dubois, there are two inspectors of police and a dozen intelligent Metropolitan constables who would be forced to swear that he was not the man who entered Albert Gate on the night of the murder in company with the other Turks. I tell you candidly, monsieur, that in my opinion the case would not only break down very badly, but Mr. Talbot would leave the court under grave suspicion, whilst I would be regarded by the public as a meddlesome idiot."

"Then what are we to do?" said the commissary, piteously throwing out his hands and shrugging his shoulders with the eloquent French gesture that betokens utter bewilderment.

"Difficult though it may be, we must first accomplish the main part of our work. In other words, we must secure the diamonds before we collar the murderers."

The Frenchman was silent for a moment. At last he said submissively—

"In what way can I help?"

"By procuring for me from the chief of your department an authorization to call in the aid of the police when and where I may desire their assistance. This, of course, will render necessary on his part some inquiry before I am entrusted with such an important document. The British Embassy in Paris and your own Foreign Office will quickly supply you with the reasons why this power should be given to me."

"But what of the house of the Rue Bonbonnerie?"

"You anticipated my next request. Whilst you are looking to that letter you must place at my disposal two of your most trusty agents. In their company Lord Fairholme and I purpose visiting the house to-night."

They were conversing in the commissary's office at a late hour after Brett had quitted his friend in the Grand Hotel.

[Illustration: Reginald Brett. –*Page 200.*]

Within a few minutes the two Englishmen and their French companions were standing outside No. 41, Rue Bonbonnerie, and they found that Monsieur de Lisle kept a small shop, whose only significant feature was a placard announcing that letters might be addressed there.

"Oh," said Brett, when he noticed this legend, "this is simple. We need not waste much time here."

The four men walked inside, crowding the narrow space before a diminutive counter. The proprietor was supping in style, as they could perceive through the glass top of the door which communicated with the sitting-room at the back. His feast consisted of a tankard of thin wine, half a loaf of black bread, and two herrings.

The man was surprised by the sudden incursion of customers. He came out looking puzzled and alarmed.

"Have you any letters here for Monsieur Jean Beaujolais?" said Brett.

"No, monsieur."

"Have you received any letters for a person of that name?"

"No, monsieur."

"I suppose you never heard the name of Jean Beaujolais before in your life?"

"I think not, monsieur."

"Then," exclaimed Brett, turning quietly away, "I fear you must be arrested. These two gentlemen"–and he nodded towards the detectives–"will take you to the Prefecture, where perhaps your memory may improve."

The man blanched visibly. His teeth chattered, and his hands shook as if with ague, whilst he nervously arranged some small objects on the counter.

"I cry your pardon, monsieur," he stammered, "but you will understand that I receive letters at my shop for a small fee, and I cannot remember the names of all my customers. I will search with pleasure among those now in my possession to see if there are any for M. Beaujolais."

"You are simply incriminating yourself," said Brett sternly. "If your excuse were a genuine one you would first have looked among your letters before answering so glibly that the name of Beaujolais was unfamiliar."

"I beg of you to listen," cried the dismayed shopkeeper. "I had no idea you were from the Prefecture, otherwise I would have answered you in the first instance. There have been letters here for Monsieur Beaujolais. They came from London. He called for them three or four times. The last letter arrived yesterday morning. It is here now. I have not seen Monsieur Beaujolais since the previous evening."

He took from a drawer a packet of letters tied together with string, and the handwriting betrayed the contents of most of them. They evidently dealt with that species of the tender passion which finds its outlet in the agony column or in fictitious addresses.

One of the detectives did not trust to Monsieur de Lisle's examination. He seized the bundle and went through its contents carefully, but this time Monsieur de Lisle was speaking the truth.

There was only one letter addressed to Beaujolais, and it bore a foreign postmark. Brett tore it open. It contained a single sheet of notepaper, without a date or address, or any words save these, scrawled across the centre—

"Tout va bien."

He placed the document and its envelope in his pocket-book, and then fixed his keen glance on the shopkeeper's pallid face.

"What sort of a person is Monsieur Beaujolais?"

The man was still so nervous that he could hardly speak.

"I am not good at descriptions," he began.

So Brett helped.

"Was he a Frenchman, about my height, elegant in appearance, well built, with long thin hands and straight tapering fingers, with very fair skin and high colour, dark hair and large eyes set deeply beneath well-marked eyebrows?"

"That is he to the life," cried the shopkeeper. "Monsieur must know him well. I recall him now exactly, but I could not for a hundred francs have described him so accurately."

"How long have you known him?" broke in Brett.

"Let me think," mused the man, who had now somewhat recovered from his alarm. "He came here one day last week–I think it was Thursday, because that day my daughter Marie–no matter what Marie did, I remember the date quite well now. He came in and asked me if I did not receive letters for a fee. I said 'Yes,' and told him that I charged ten centimes per letter. He gave me his name, and thereafter called regularly to obtain the enclosure from London. He always handed me half a franc and would never take any change."

"Was he alone?"

"Invariably, monsieur."

"Thank you. You will not be arrested to-night. I think you have told the truth."

The shopkeeper's protestations that he had given every assistance in his power followed them into the street.

Brett dismissed the two detectives and returned to the hotel, where he and Fairholme found Edith and her brother sitting up for them. When Talbot heard the contents of the letter he remarked: "I suppose that 'All goes well' means that I am still a prisoner?"

"Undoubtedly," said the barrister. "The letter was posted in the Haymarket. It came from your French host. I wonder what he will write now? By the way, where is he? Did you lose sight of the couple after your escape?"

"I did," laughed Talbot. "But Inspector Winter did not. By some mysterious means he learnt all about Fairholme's action in smashing in the door. Whilst I was at the Foreign Office that night he arrested both the man and the woman."

"Winter is a perfect terror," said Brett. "He dreams of handcuffs and penal servitude. I hope this couple will not be brought to trial, or at any rate that your name will not be mixed up in it."

"Oh, no. As soon as I heard the Under-Secretary's wishes, I promptly communicated with Scotland Yard. The Frenchman and his wife will be remanded on a mysterious charge of abetting a felony and held in durance vile until their testimony is wanted, should we ever capture Dubois."

At Brett's request, detectives were hunting through Paris all that night and the next day for a sign of Hussein-ul-Mulk and his Turkish friends. But these gentlemen had vanished as completely as if the earth had swallowed them up.

This was a strange thing. Although Paris is a cosmopolitan city, a party of Turks, only one of whom could speak French, should be discovered with tolerable rapidity in view of the fact that the French police maintain such a watch upon the inhabitants.

It was not until Brett and his four companions quitted the train at Marseilles late at night and the barrister received a telegram from the commissary announcing that the search made by the police had yielded no results, that he suddenly recalled the existence of a doorless and windowless room in the Cafe Noir.

Curiously enough, he had omitted to make any mention of this strange apartment in his recital to the official. He would not trust to the discretion of the Telegraph Department, so on reaching the Hotel du Louvre et de la Paix he succeeded, after some difficulty, in ringing up the commissary on the long-distance telephone.

Having acquainted the police officer with the exact position of the hidden apartment, he ended by saying—

"Continue inquiries throughout Paris during the whole of to-morrow. Do not visit the Cabaret Noir for the purpose of police inspection until a late hour—long after midnight—when the cafe is empty and the Boulevard comparatively deserted. It is only a mere guess on my part. The Turks may not be there. If they are, they should be set at liberty and not questioned. Tell them they owe their escape to me. If you do not find them you may make other discoveries of general interest to the police. But above all things, I do not wish you to interfere with Gros Jean or his house until the next twenty-four hours have elapsed."

The commissary assured him that his desires would be respected, and soon afterwards Brett went upstairs with the full determination to secure a long and uninterrupted night's sleep, of which he stood much in need.

He had reached the sitting-room reserved for the use of the party when Talbot and Lord Fairholme burst in excitedly.

"We have seen her!" gasped the earl.

"Seen whom?" demanded the barrister.

"Mademoiselle Beaucaire," cried Talbot; "the woman who accompanied Dubois in his flight from London. I recognized her instantly. I could pick her out among a million as the same person who so coolly made up Dubois to represent me, whilst I was lying tied on the bed in that flat."

In their eagerness the two men had forgotten to close the door. Brett ran to it, and looked out into the passage to learn if their words had perchance been overheard. No one was in sight. He closed the door behind him when he re-entered the room, and said quietly–

"How did you happen to meet her?"

"Whilst you were wrestling with the telephone," said Fairholme, "Edith and Jack and I went to the door of the hotel to have a look at the people passing in the Cannebiere. None of us have ever been in Marseilles before, you know. We were gazing at the crowd, when suddenly Jack gripped my arm and said: 'There she is! Look at that woman, quick!' He pointed to a tall, well-dressed female, wrapped up in a fur cloak, and wearing a large feather hat. Luckily her veil was up, and the electric light fell fully on her as she passed. She was undoubtedly La Belle Chasseuse, and I bet you anything you like she had just come away from the music-hall where she is performing."

"Did she see you?" demanded Brett excitedly.

"Not a bit; she was gazing at the passing tramcars, and evidently on the look-out for some particular line."

"What happened next?" demanded the barrister. "Where is Miss Talbot?"

"Edith has gone after her," said Fairholme.

"What!" cried Brett, more startled than he cared to own.

"Yes," broke in Talbot eagerly. "She heard my words and instantly decided to follow her. She said that the woman knew both of us, and might easily detect us, but she, Edith, was unknown to her, and would never be suspected. She simply forced us to come and tell you, and then darted off like a greyhound before we could stop her."

Brett forced himself to say calmly—

"I always knew that Miss Talbot had brains, but still I wish she had not taken this risk. Nevertheless, your chance discovery and her prompt action may be invaluable to us."

"But what must we do?" exclaimed the impetuous Fairholme. "We cannot allow Edith to go wandering around Marseilles by herself at this hour of the night. I have always heard that this town is a perfectly damnable place. What a fool I was not to follow her at once."

"Miss Talbot has acted quite rightly," said Brett decisively. "We must simply remain here until she returns. There is not the slightest ground for alarm. A woman who could act with such ready judgment is well able to take care of herself. Unless I am much mistaken, we shall see her within the hour."

It was well for the peace of mind of the younger men that Sir Hubert Fitzjames had gone to his room soon after the party reached the hotel. Had the irascible baronet known of his niece's mission, no power on earth could have restrained him from setting every policeman in Marseilles on her track forthwith.

And so they kept their vigil, striving to talk unconcernedly, but watching the clock with feverish impatience until Edith should return.

15
"MARIE"

Marseilles is one of the most picturesque cities in the world. Its streets cluster round an ancient harbour, famous before history was writ, or climb the sides of steep hills enclosing a land-locked bay. In the suburbs Marseilles is modern enough, but the chief thoroughfare, known to all who read, the famous and ever busy Cannebiere, plunges rapidly downhill until it empties itself on the crowded quays that surround the old port.

With the newer Marseilles of the Joliette–well found in wharfs and warehouses, steam cranes and railway lines–the town beloved of the Phoenicians has no concern. There is no touch of modern ugliness in the tiny maritime refuge which is barely half the size of the Serpentine. Lofty, old-fashioned, half-ruined houses throng close to its rugged quays.

At night this quarter of the turbulent city wears an air of intense mystery. The side streets are narrow and tortuous. Dark courts and alleys twist in every conceivable direction, while the brightness of the many wine shops facing each other across the tideless harbour only serves to enhance the squalid gloom that forms the most marked characteristic of the buildings clustered behind them.

Edith Talbot, intent on the pursuit of a woman so dramatically bound up with the mystery affecting her brother, paid heed to no consideration save the paramount one, that the hurrying figure in front must be kept in sight.

Contrary to the opinions expressed by the two men, Mlle. Beaucaire did not board a passing tramcar. To Edith's eyes she seemed to be eagerly watching for some person who might pass in one of the small open carriages which in Marseilles take the place of the London hansom. Even as she rapidly walked down the crowded street mademoiselle closely scrutinised each vehicle that overtook her, and once, at a busy crossing, she deliberately stopped. Edith, of course, slackened her pace, and simultaneously she became aware how incongruous was her appearance at such an hour in such a thoroughfare.

Much taller than the average Frenchwoman, neatly dressed in an English tailor-made costume, with her smart straw hat and well-gloved hands, Miss Talbot naturally attracted the curious gaze of the passers by.

Instantly it occurred to her that some disguise was absolutely necessary if she would not court an attention fatal to her enterprise. It chanced that where she stood for a moment a fruit-seller occupied a tiny shop, squeezed tightly between a church and a restaurant. The interior was dark enough, for a couple of flaring naphtha lamps were so disposed as to cast their flickering brilliancy over the baskets of fruits and vegetables displayed in the window or crowded together on the pavement.

The woman inside had a kindly and contented face, cherry ripe in cheek and lips, and from a pair of deep-set blue eyes she looked out quizzically at the hurrying crowd.

Assuring herself with one fleeting glance that La Belle Chasseuse still remained motionless and intent at the crossing, Edith darted into the shop. She produced a sovereign.

"I have not much French money," she said hurriedly, "but this is worth twenty-five francs. Can you let me have a large dark shawl? I do not care whether or not it is old or worn. It is necessary that I should remain out for some few minutes longer, and I do not wish to court observation."

Even as she spoke she removed her straw hat and eagerly tore off her gloves. The Frenchwoman saw that one of her own sex, English, and consequently mad, desired to screen her appearance from too inquisitive eyes.

It was sufficient for her that there should be a spice of romance in the request. With one hand she pocketed the sovereign; with the other she dived into a recess beneath the counter and produced the very article Edith wanted.

"But certainly, mademoiselle," she cried. "See. It will cover you to the waist."

Edith advanced another pace into the darkest corner of the shop, quickly arranged the shawl over her head and shoulders, and, hastily murmuring her thanks, rushed forth into the street again, leaving hat and gloves behind in her haste.

The fruit-seller was far too wise a woman to call after the other and apprise her of the loss.

"It must be serious, this adventure," she mused. "And yet the novelists say that the English are cold! For me, now, I think that women are very much alike all over the world."

And with this bit of Provencal philosophy she picked up the discarded articles and discovered, to her joy, that they must be worth at least ten francs.

"Thirty-five francs for an old shawl is a good night's work," she murmured. "Who could dream of such fortune at this hour? To-morrow I will buy a candle and place it in the church of Notre Dame de la Garde."

Meanwhile Edith was just in time to see Mlle. Beaucaire either abandon her search or resolve it in some manner, for the lady once more resumed her progress towards the old harbour, in whose placid bosom could be seen the reflections of numberless lights from the small promontory beyond, crowned with the Fort St. Nicholas and the Chateau du Phare.

Looking neither right nor left, but hastening onwards with rapid strides, mademoiselle crossed the rough pavement of the Quai de la Fraternite, bearing away diagonally towards the left.

But if the Frenchwoman was a good walker, Edith Talbot was a better one, and now that she no longer feared notice–for she draped the large shawl as elegantly about her shoulders as any woman in Marseilles–she decided to adopt a little strategy. Instead of keeping directly behind mademoiselle she broke into a run under the shadow of the houses. By thus making up ground she approached the narrow street towards which the Frenchwoman was heading almost simultaneously with her quarry, but apparently from an opposite direction. The aspect of the thoroughfare through which the two women sped was forbidding in the extreme. The houses were many storeys in height, of disreputable appearance, and so close together on both sides that, were other conditions equal, an active man might easily spring from one room into another across the street.

The walls appeared to be honeycombed with doors and windows, while an indescribable number of shutters, balconies, projecting poles and clothes-lines created such a medley in the darkness, which was only made visible by a solitary bracket lamp, that Edith felt some anxiety as to whether or not she would be able to recognize the house into which mademoiselle disappeared, should her destination be close at hand.

There were, of course, many other people in the street besides themselves, else Edith's self-imposed piece of espionage would have been rendered difficult, if not impossible.

Men, women, and children lounged about the doorways and kept up a constant cackle of conversation in a mysterious *patois* which Miss Talbot, though an excellent French scholar, could make nothing of. The presence of these people naturally shielded her from the direct observation of La Belle Chasseuse, but nevertheless threatened a slight danger should it be necessary for her to stand still, for she well understood that in such a locality each person was known to the other, and the loitering of a stranger could not fail to arouse curiosity.

Soon after passing beneath the lamp mademoiselle vanished into a doorway. Edith perceived to her joy that at this point there was no group of loungers. Indeed, for a few yards the street was empty. Keeping her eyes sedulously fixed upon the exact spot where the Frenchwoman disappeared, she reached the door, and, after a moment's hesitation, stepped lightly into the interior darkness.

The narrow entrance was at once lessened to half its width by a staircase. She listened intently, and could hear the other woman ascending the second flight of stairs.

At the next landing mademoiselle paused and knocked three times. Presumably in reply to a question within, she murmured something which Edith could not catch, and was at once admitted. The shooting of a rusty bolt supplied further evidence that the door was locked behind her.

Edith's next task was to identify the house. She stepped out into the street again and crossed to the opposite pavement. She looked up to the second storey, but, owing to the short distance–barely fourteen feet–that separated her from the house–she could discern nothing, save that the windows on that floor were closely shuttered.

She rapidly noted that the door was the third removed from the lamp.

Whilst wondering what to do next, a couple of girls approached her. They were young and of course inquisitive. Without any dissimulation, they stood in front of her and scrutinized her face, wondering, no doubt, who this tall and graceful newcomer could be.

"What is your name?" said one. "Where do you live? Have you just come here? Are you staying with old Mother Peter?"

With difficulty Edith caught the drift of their questions. But she answered smilingly–

"No, I do not live here, and I do not know Mother Peter. But I want you to tell me who lives in the house opposite?"

Her Parisian French greatly surprised the two girls, who giggled at each other, and one of them cried–

"Oh, here's a lark!"

But they scented an intrigue, and were quite ready to give all the information in their power.

"A lot of people live there," said the elder one, trying, with the ready tact of her nation, to accommodate her words to the understanding of the stranger. "It all depends who you want to know about. On the ground floor is Josef the barber and his wife, with three little ones. It cannot be them, I am sure, and it cannot be Monsieur Ducrot, who is their lodger, for he is seventy years old and a sacristan in the Church of the Sacred Heart. Then on the first floor there are three men, not a woman amongst them. One is a bill-sticker, another a fisherman, and the third a waiter in the Cafe du Midi. I do not know their proper names. We call the bill-sticker 'Paste-pot,' and the fisherman 'Crab.' The waiter is called 'Thomas' in the cafe, but when a letter comes for him it is in another name. Then, on the second floor–by the way, Marie, who is it that lives on the second floor?"

Edith with difficulty restrained her excitement. She felt that if only these youngsters rattled on a little longer she might gain some valuable information.

Marie, thus appealed to, was evidently of a more cautious temperament than her companion.

"If the young lady will tell us why she wants to know, we may be able to help her?" she stipulated.

"Certainly," cried Edith, instantly resolving to pursue the tactics of the penny novelette. "I have been deserted. My lover has been taken away from me by another woman–at least, that is what I am informed. I do not wish to make any trouble about it. There are plenty as good men as he left in the world; but, on the other hand, I must not act unjustly. I have been told that he lives in this house–that he is living with her here at this moment, in fact. If I can make sure of it, I will go away and never set eyes on him again unless by chance, and then you may be sure I will take no notice of him. I am not one of those silly girls who break their hearts over a faithless sweetheart."

Marie was reassured.

"I should think not," she said, with a sympathetic and defiant sniff. "I had the very same experience last Sunday, when Phillippe–the grocer's boy at the corner, you know–walked along the Corniche Road with a chit of a girl out of a shop. She thinks herself better than we are because she stands behind a counter, and I am sure she made eyes at Phillippe one day when his master sent him there on an errand."

"Phillippe must have bad taste," broke in Edith. "But I am sorry I must hasten away. If you girls will tell me quickly all the other people that live in that house I will give you two francs each. That is all the money I have got."

She produced the coins, which she easily distinguished from the gold in her pocket by their size. She knew that to appear too well supplied with money in that neighbourhood was to court danger, if not disaster, to her undertaking.

Both girls eagerly seized the forty-sous pieces.

"Oh, on the second floor," said Marie, "I am afraid you will find your young man. They are a funny couple that live there. They only came here on Monday. When did your young man leave you?"

"I saw him on Saturday."

"Where?"

This was a poser, but Miss Talbot answered desperately:

"At Lyon."

"What is he like?"

Another haphazard shot.

"He is tall and dark, and, oh! so good-looking, with a beautifully white skin and a pink complexion."

"That is he!" cried both girls together.

"The scoundrel! But tell me," went on Edith, whose excitement was readily construed as the pangs of jealousy, "who is the creature that lives with him?"

"We think she is a music-hall artiste," replied Marie. "At least, that is what the people say. I have not heard yet what hall she appears in. They say she is very pretty. Are you going to throw vitriol over her?"

"Not I," said Edith, with a fine scorn. "Do they live there alone?"

"Yes, quite alone. They rent the place from Pere Didon. He owns most of the houses in this street, you know, and is a regular skinflint. He won't let any one get behind with their rent for an hour. He is old, so old that you would not think that he could live another week, yet he is that keen after his francs you would imagine he was a young man anxious to get money for a gay life. You ought to have heard the row here last Saturday when he turned the people out from their rooms where your lover now lives with his mistress. It was terrible. There was a poor woman with two sick children."

How much further the revelations as to Pere Didon's iniquity might have gone, Miss Talbot could not say, but at that moment there came an interruption.

From the opposite doorway appeared the figure of Mlle. Beaucaire, carrying a small bag. She was followed by a man, tall, slight, and closely muffled up, who shouldered a larger portmanteau. Edith grabbed both the girls, and pulled them close to her against the closed door behind them.

"It is he!" she whispered tragically. "Silence! Let us watch them!"

The man darted a suspicious glance up and down the street. There was no one whom even the clever Henri Dubois could construe as an enemy—no one save some chattering Marseillais loitering around their doorsteps, and three girls huddled together in close conclave directly opposite.

Thus reassured, he strode after La Belle Chasseuse, who cried out impatiently:

"Come quick, Henri; what are you waiting for?"

"Is his name Henri?" whispered the awe-stricken Marie.

"Yes. Isn't he a villain? I wonder where they are going now!"

"Let us follow them and see," suggested Marie.

"Yes, let us follow them and see," chimed in the other one, who delighted in this nocturnal romance. It was a veritable page out of one of Paul de Kock's novels.

The programme suited Miss Talbot exceedingly well.

They strolled off down the street, nestling together, Edith in the centre, and keeping the shrouded couple in front well in sight. This time, when Mademoiselle Beaucaire and her companion reached the point where the street emerged on to the harbour, they did not cross over towards the broad and brilliantly-lighted Cannebiere, but hurried on through the darkness in the direction of a cluster of fishing smacks that lay alongside the Quai de Rive Neuve.

"My faith, Eugenie!" cried Marie, "they must be going on board one of the vessels."

"What a lark!" was the answer. "I suppose they fear you," she added, turning her sharp eyes on Edith. "What is your name?"

"Lucille," came the answer on the spur of the moment.

"Lucille what?"

"Lucille Beauharnais."

"My gracious!" cried Eugenie, "what a swell name!"

"Oh, let us hurry," interrupted Miss Talbot desperately. "You girls know everybody. You must know all the vessels. If they are going on a boat and you find out the name and number for me I will give each of you a whole louis. I will give them to you now—I mean, that is, if you will walk with me afterwards to my lodgings."

Even amidst the exciting circumstances surrounding her, Edith recognized the absolute necessity there was to maintain the credibility of her previous narrative.

Unquestionably Dubois and the lady intended to embark on one of the fishing boats. They hastened to the further end of the harbour, through whose tiny entrance Edith could now see the dark waters of the bay beyond, for the night was beautifully clear and fine, and the bright stars of the south lent some radiance to the scene, when the girls quitted the deep shadow of the houses.

A solitary boat, a decked fishing-smack of some forty tons, was lying by the side of the quay, apart from the others. Edith, who knew something about yachting, recognized that her gearing was not fastened in the trim manner suggestive of a craft laid by for the night. At the same instant, too, she caught sight of a third form—that of a man who had been seated on a fixed capstan, and who now strode forward to peer at the newcomers.

Some few words passed between the three, but it was impossible for the girls to hear a syllable. Instantly the sailor assisted Dubois and Mademoiselle Beaucaire to step down from the quay on board the smack. He followed them, and three other men, who appeared out of the chaos of sails and ropes, commenced to labour with a large pole in order to shove the sturdy vessel out into the harbour.

"Quick!" murmured Edith, in an agony lest the opportunity should slip. "Tell me what vessel it is."

"I think," said Marie, "it is the *Belles Soeurs*. Anyhow, we can easily make certain. All we have to do is to go back around the top of the harbour, walk down the Quai du Port, and watch her as she passes under the lighthouse of the Fort St. Jean. They will hoist her sail then and we shall see her number."

"Oh, come," cried Edith, "let us run!"

"We can run if you like," replied Marie coolly, "but there is no need. They have to get out by using the sweeps, and we will be underneath the lighthouse at least a minute or two before they pass, even if we walk slowly."

Whilst they were talking the three girls put their words into practice, and Edith found herself battling with a logical dilemma. Dubois was evidently escaping from France–making out from Marseilles at this late hour on a vessel capable of sailing to almost any point of the Mediterranean.

What could she do? Was it possible to invoke the aid of a policeman and get some authority to hail the craft and order her to return, or was there time to take a cab in the Cannebiere and drive furiously to the hotel, where Brett, Fairholme, and her brother must be anxiously awaiting her return?

Rapidly as these alternatives suggested themselves, she dismissed them. It was best to fall in with Marie's suggestion and ascertain beyond doubt the identity of the fishing smack. Then, at any rate, Brett would have a tangible and definite clue.

So she hastened with her companions along the three sides of the now almost deserted quay, and, in accordance with the prediction of her youthful guides, she reached the promenade beyond the small lighthouse of the inner port before the vessel had quitted the harbour. To move a forty-ton boat with oars is a slow matter at the best.

As the craft came creeping steadily through the narrow channel Edith saw, to her great relief, that two of the men drew in their sweeps, and commenced to haul upon ropes whilst the clanking and groaning of pulleys heralded the slow rising of the mainsail.

She thought the sail would never climb up in time, but as it began to yield to the steady pull of the men it mounted more and more rapidly, and at last, feeling the influence of a gentle breeze blowing off the land, it shook out its cumbrous folds and the number stood clearly revealed in huge white letters on the dark brown canvas.

At first, in her eagerness, she could hardly discern it, save a big "M" and an "R."

"There!" cried Eugenie, bubbling over with excitement. "There it is! 'M.R. 107,' Marseilles, No. 107, you know. Why, isn't that Jacques le Bon's boat?" she demanded from her companion.

"Yes, it is," said Marie; "and there is Jacques himself standing by the tiller."

Edith's eyes were now becoming accustomed to the night and the dancing water.

"Where are the others?" she said. "I cannot see them. There is no one standing on the deck but the sailors."

"Oh, they have gone below, I expect," said the practical Marie. "They will be in the way of the sails, you know. There is not much room for people who don't work on the deck of a small ship like that. Besides, they don't want to be seen. If a customs officer or a harbour official were to notice the boat now he would think that Le Bon was going out fishing for the night, but he would be sure to wonder what was happening if he caught sight of a woman on board. Funny, isn't it," she rattled on, "that Jacques should be called 'Le Bon,' for he is the worst man in Marseilles? They say that his ugly grin when he draws a knife would frighten anybody!"

16
THE HALL-PORTER'S DOUBTS

When one o'clock came and Edith had not arrived, the three men waiting in the hotel made no further effort to conceal their anxiety. The impetuous Fairholme was eager to commence an immediate search of Marseilles, but Brett steadily adhered to his resolution not to stir from their sitting-room until either Miss Talbot came back in person or it became quite certain that she was detained by some other influence than her own unfettered volition.

"It may be," he argued, "that she will require some action on our part the moment we see her, and nothing could be more stupid than for the three of us to be wandering about this great city hopelessly inquiring for a missing English lady, whilst she was impatiently awaiting our return in the knowledge that valuable time was being lost to no purpose. What is there to fear? Miss Talbot is absolutely unknown to all the parties concerned in the affair. Even if she attracted their attention, which is improbable, it is almost inconceivable that they should connect her with the search being made for them. The only risk she runs is that of insult by some semi-intoxicated reveller, and even in a rowdy city like this, it must indeed be a strange locality in which she would be denied some protection. Of course I will be much relieved when Miss Talbot returns, but up to the present I see no reason for undue anxiety on our part. Indeed, we ought to congratulate ourselves on the fact that she deems it necessary to leave us for such a long period. The probability is that she is making highly important discoveries which may tend materially to reduce the area of inquiry."

With this view Talbot could not help concurring, so Fairholme had to content himself by smoking many cigarettes and walking uneasily about the room. Sit down he could not, whilst any casual ring at the hotel door found him leaning over the balustrade of the inner court and listening intently for the first words of the new arrival.

But the Englishmen were not the only persons in the hotel that night whose composure was disturbed. Their extraordinary behaviour caused uneasiness to the manager and those members of his staff who remained on duty. The facts disclosed by the hall-porter were certainly remarkable. Only one member of the party had behaved in a normal manner. Sir Hubert Fitzjames, soon after his arrival, went quietly to bed, but the hall-porter's report as to the conduct of the others was passing strange.

One of them, to his surprise, had rung up the Prefecture of Police in Paris on the telephone. The others were standing at the hotel door, gazing quietly enough at the passers-by, when suddenly about midnight much excitement rose amongst them. They conversed eagerly in their own tongue for a few moments, and the lady had rushed off down the street by herself, whilst her two companions ran with equal precipitancy to join the third in the sitting-room they had engaged, and there they were still seated in moody expectancy, apparently watching for some dramatic event to happen.

It was time that all good people were in bed. But it was hopeless to approach such lunatics with questions, for they were English, and no decent Frenchman could possibly hope to understand their actions or motives. It was satisfactory that they could speak French well; therefore the manager counselled the hall-porter to exhibit patience and prudence. Moreover, milords upstairs would be sure to recompense him for an enforced vigil by a liberal *pourboire*.

At last, when even the Cannebiere was empty, and when the latest cafe had closed its doors and the final tramcar had wearily jingled its way up the hill towards a distant suburb, the electric bell jangled a noisy summons to the front door. It produced the hall-porter and Fairholme with remarkable celerity.

The Frenchman cautiously opened the door and saw outside a muffled-up female who eagerly demanded admittance. He knew by her accent that she was not a Marseillaise, but the shawl that covered her head and shoulders showed that she belonged to the working classes.

"Whom do you wish to see at this hour?" he gruffly demanded.

"I live here," said Edith. "I came here to-night with my brother from Paris. Please let me in at once."

In her excitement and breathlessness, for she had hurried at top speed from the harbour, Edith forgot that the homely garment she adopted as a disguise effectually cloaked her from the recognition of the hall-porter as from all others.

Moreover, her French accent was too good. It deceived the man even more thoroughly than did the shawl.

"Oh, really now," he said, "this is for laughter! A woman like you staying at the hotel! Be off, or I will call a gendarme."

In his amazement at her demand he had not heard Fairholme's rapid approach behind him. He was now swung unceremoniously out of the way and the earl jumped forward to seize Edith in his arms.

"My darling girl," he cried, "where have you been? We almost gave you up for lost. Where is your hat? Where did you get that shawl?" And all the time he was hugging her so fiercely that it was absolutely impossible for her to say a single word. At length she disengaged herself.

"Don't be so ridiculous," she said, "but let me come in and close the door. The hall-porter will think we are cracked."

She summarised the hall-porter's sentiments most accurately. He explained the transaction to the manager with most eloquent pantomime, and the two marvelled greatly at the weird proceedings of their strange guests.

"Ah," said the manager at length, "now that mademoiselle has returned, perhaps they will go to bed."

At that instant Brett's voice was heard upon the stairs. He wanted the telephone again.

Edith had rapidly detailed her adventures to her astonished auditors, and Brett seemed to resolve on some plan of action with the lightning rapidity peculiar to him.

Owing to the late hour he got through to Paris without much difficulty, and then he returned to the sitting-room, where Edith was rehearsing in greater detail all that had happened since she left them at the hotel door. Brett explained to his companions the motives of his second telephonic message.

"I am convinced," he said, "that Gros Jean is in communication with his daughter. For this reason I did not wish the police to put in an appearance at the Cafe Noir until to-morrow night, or rather to-night, for we have long entered upon another day. I wished to have a reasonable time for quiet inquiry at Marseilles before mademoiselle could be apprised of our presence here. Miss Talbot's remarkable discovery has, however, wholly changed my plans. Mlle. Beaucaire and her lover have set off for some unknown destination, and the best chance we have of discovering it is to secure the immediate arrest of her father. Possibly, being taken by surprise at this hour of the morning, some document may be found on him which will reveal his daughter's destination. It occurs to me that she half expected him to arrive by a late train. Again, when the fishing-smack puts into port, the girl will probably adopt some method of communicating with him, and that communication must come into our hands, not into his. So I have telephoned the police officials in Paris to raid the Cabaret Noir forthwith, and it is possible that they may report developments within the next two or three hours."

"Is there no chance of your discovering the whereabouts of that fishing-smack?" said Fairholme.

"In what way?" demanded Brett.

"Well, this is a big port, you know, and there are always tugs knocking about with steam up, on the off-chance of their services being required. Isn't it possible to charter a steamboat and set off after the smack?"

"I do not think so," said Brett. "I imagine it would be wasted effort. By this time the *Belles Soeurs* is well out to sea. She can go in a dozen different directions. She may beat along the coast towards Toulon and the Riviera. She can make towards Corsica, Sardinia, the Balearic Islands, Spain, or the mouth of the Rhone. She will certainly not show any lights, and I personally feel that although there is, perhaps, a thousand to one chance we might fall in with her, it will be far better for our purpose to remain quietly here and await developments in Paris."

"Anyhow," remarked Fairholme, convinced that his proposal was impracticable, "it will be an easy matter for the authorities to ascertain the port that she arrives at."

Brett shook his head dubiously.

"I have my doubts on that point," he said. "The man who has thus far kept himself so easily ahead of all pursuers, and exhibited such a wealth of resource in his methods, may well be trusted to cover up his tracks effectually. There is even a possibility that the *Belles Soeurs* will never be seen again, and that her number will long remain vacant on the shipping register of Marseilles. However, we shall see."

"Then, Mr. Brett," put in Edith quietly, with a tired smile, "I suppose we may go to bed?"

"Most certainly, Miss Talbot. You have earned your rest more than any of us to-night," he answered.

He held out his hand to wish her good-night, but she demanded with some surprise, "What are you going to do? Surely you want some sleep?"

"I will remain here," he said. "I have bribed the hall-porter to keep awake, and I may be wanted on the telephone at any moment."

"Then I will stop with you," cried Fairholme.

"And I too," chimed in Talbot.

"You will do nothing of the sort," he answered with pleasant insistence. "You will just be off, both of you, and get some hours of sound sleep. You may need all your energy to-morrow. Do not be afraid. I will arouse you if anything dramatic should happen."

Left to himself, Brett again interviewed the hall-porter and returned to the sitting-room, where he disposed himself for a nap on the sofa. Like all men who possess the faculty of concentrated thought, he also cultivated the power of dismissing a perplexing problem from his mind until it became necessary to consider it afresh in the light of further knowledge.

Within five minutes he was sound asleep.

At length he woke with a start. He was stiff with cold, for the fire had gone out, and the tiny gas jet he had left burning was not sufficient to warm the room. He sprang to his feet and looked at his watch. It was half-past six.

"Surely," he cried, "there must have been a message from Paris long before this!"

He ran downstairs, encountering on his way some of the hotel servants, who even thus early had commenced work, for your industrious Frenchman is no laggard in the morning. Going to the hall-porter's office he found that functionary snoring peacefully. The poor fellow was evidently tired out, and twenty telephone bells might have jangled in his ears without waking him.

So, for the third time, Brett rang up the exchange to get in touch with Paris. As he had anticipated, he quickly learnt that the Prefecture had endeavoured to get through to him about 4.30 a.m., but the operators were unable to obtain any answer.

"I can hardly blame the man," said he to himself, "for I was just as tired as he."

The intimation he received from the Prefecture was startling enough. In accordance with his instructions a number of detectives had raided the Cabaret Noir soon after three o'clock. They found the place in possession of a waiter and a couple of female servants. Gros Jean had quitted the house the previous evening, and, most astounding fact of all, with him were three Turks.

Neither the waiter nor the domestics could give any information whatever concerning the hidden room. They knew of its existence, but none of them had ever seen it, and the place was generally regarded as a sort of cellar for the reception of lumber.

The police forced a padlock which guarded its trap-door, and found to their surprise that the place was much more spacious than they anticipated. It really contained two apartments, one of which was so firmly secured that it had hitherto resisted all their efforts to open it. The other was a sort of bed-sitting-room, and it had recently been occupied. From various indications they came to the conclusion that its latest tenants were Hussein-ul-Mulk and his confederates.

Judging from the fact that these gentry had quietly left the cafe in Gros Jean's company about half-past seven the previous evening, they were not in confinement against their will. In fact, the police theory was that this secret chamber provided a safe retreat for any person who desired complete seclusion other than that provided by the authorities.

"It is assumed," said the officer who communicated this bewildering information to Brett, "that the locked room contains a quantity of stolen goods. The police remain in charge of the cafe, and when the necessary workmen have been obtained this morning the door will be forced. We will at once let you know the result of our further investigations."

"But what about Gros Jean and the Turks? Surely Paris cannot again have swallowed them up?" inquired Brett.

"Every effort is being made to trace their whereabouts," was the reply, "but you must remember, monsieur, that they had many hours' start of the police, and that this period of the day is the most difficult of the twenty-four hours in which to make successful inquiries. You must rest assured that the moment we receive even the slightest clue we will ring you up, provided, that is, you arrange for someone at your end to answer the telephone."

"Oh," said Brett with a laugh, "there is little fear of further delay in that respect. It will be daylight in another hour, and the servants are already busy about the place."

He rang off and then darted back to his sitting-room to consult a time-table, for the thought came to him that Gros Jean and the Turks had quitted the cafe in order to reach Marseilles.

He could not yet explain this strange alliance. It was impossible to believe that the innkeeper would betray his daughter to serve the ends of a political party. No; there must be some other explanation which the future alone could reveal.

He well knew that the last thought likely to occur to the Paris police would be to suspect the missing men of any desire to reach the south coast. It was with an almost feverish anxiety that he scrutinized the pages of the *indicateur des chemins de fer*, and he heaved a sigh of profound relief when he discovered that the first train Gros Jean and the Turks could travel by left Paris the previous evening at 8.40 p.m., and was not due at Marseilles until 8.59 that morning.

It was now close on seven o'clock, so he went to his bedroom, effected some much-needed changes in his personal appearance, and then consumed an early breakfast of coffee and rolls. At half-past eight he called a carriage and was driven to the railway station, where, punctually to the minute, the Paris train arrived. Brett managed to secure a favourable point whence he could observe the passengers without being seen, for on the platform were stacked hundreds of baskets of fruit and vegetables which had arrived by a local train.

There were not many passengers in the express, and among the first to alight were Gros Jean and the three Turks–Hussein-ul-Mulk and the two others he had seen in the Rue Barbette.

It would be idle to deny that the barrister experienced a thrill of satisfaction at his own shrewdness, and he smiled as he realized the consternation of the Paris commissary when informed that he had so easily allowed the rogues to slip out of the net.

The travellers were evidently tired after a sleepless journey. Gros Jean, being a fat man, had wobbled about a great deal during the night. He much needed the restorative effect of a comfortable bed; whilst the Turks, though younger and more active, also showed signs of fatigue, for this long journey, in their case, was a sequel to many hours of detention in an ill-ventilated apartment.

So they paid not the slightest heed to their whereabouts, save in so far as to eye with suspicion a harmless gendarme who happened to be on the platform.

The policeman, of course, took no notice of them whatever. Gros Jean was to him merely a typical Frenchman, whilst persons of dark complexion and Moorish appearance are everyday sights in the streets of Marseilles.

A diminutive railway porter loitered near Brett in the conceit that perhaps this well-dressed stranger might have felonious designs on the oranges and cabbages. His intense joy may therefore be pictured when the barrister beckoned to him, placed a gold piece in his hand, and said–

"You see those Turks there. Go after them and find out where they are going to. They are sure to take a carriage, as their luggage appears to be somewhat heavy."

The man darted off, secure in the belief that no one who could afford to give away twenty francs for such trivial information would be likely to pocket a cauliflower. In half a minute he returned.

"They have all driven off together, monsieur," he announced eagerly, "and the French gentleman first of all inquired of the driver how much he would charge to take them to the Jolies Femmes. Two francs was the fare, and this was agreeable, so they have gone there."

"I hope, in this instance," said Brett gravely, "that the Jolies Femmes is the name of a hotel."

"But certainly," replied the porter, elevating his eyebrows; "what else could it be?"

He meditated on this question for five minutes after Brett's departure, and then an idea struck him.

"Ah," he cried, slapping his thigh with a grin, "he is a droll dog, that Englishman."

Brett, secure in the knowledge that his quarry had been located, drove back to his hostelry. He found Edith, Fairholme, and Talbot just sitting down to breakfast. He joined them, and had barely communicated his startling intelligence when Sir Hubert Fitzjames put in an appearance.

"Dear me," said the genial old soldier, smiling pleasantly at the assembled party. "I see you are all nearly as lazy as I have been myself. I hope you slept well, and enjoyed a quiet night."

The burst of merriment which greeted this remark not only amazed the worthy baronet, but startled the other guests in the dining-room.

"That is a strange thing," whispered a Frenchman to his wife. "I thought the English never laughed!"

17
THE YACHT "BLUE-BELL

After breakfast the party adjourned to their sitting-room, and there Brett detailed his immediate plan of action.

"The first point to determine is an important one," he said. "Which of you three–Sir Hubert Fitzjames, Talbot, or Fairholme–looks most like a Frenchman?"

The trio at once began to scrutinize each other carefully, to Edith's intense amusement.

"I am afraid, uncle," she laughed, "we must rule you out at once. You have 'British Major-General, late Indian Army' stamped so plainly on you that here in Marseilles, a port accustomed to the weekly transit of P. and O. passengers, the smallest child could not fail to identify you. And as for you, Bobby! Good gracious! You are painfully Anglo-Saxon. I am afraid, Jack, that we must decide against you. That is to say, I suppose it hurts your vanity to be taken for a Frenchman; but you must not forget that Mademoiselle Beaucaire thought you were good-looking, and I suppose she adopts Parisian standards."

Jack was amused by his sister's raillery.

"It is gratifying to find," he said, "that there are some handsome Frenchmen. But may I ask, Brett, why you wish one of us to haul down the British flag?"

"Because it is necessary that someone should keep a close eye on Gros Jean and the Turks. As a matter of fact, Miss Talbot is doubly right. Sir Hubert Fitzjames might possibly be made up to represent *un vieux moustache*, but it is essential that he should speak French well."

"Then," cried Sir Hubert decisively, "I am out of court, because my French is weak, and I always want to go off into Hindustani whenever I open my mouth. Why, even this morning, when I rang for my hot water, I said to the waiter, '*Gurrum pani lao.*' I am sure he thought I was swearing at him."

"Very well," concurred the barrister, "it comes back to you, Talbot, and I regret to inform you that for the next few hours you must be content with the inferior cooking and accommodation of the Jolies Femmes Hotel. If you will come out with me now I will get you rigged up in a cheap French suit. That, and a supply of bad cigarettes, will provide a sufficient disguise for your purpose. You must pack a few belongings in a green tin box and betake yourself to the Jolies Femmes. Do not make any inquiries about Gros Jean. Simply watch him."

"But what about the Turks?" said Talbot. "Perhaps two of these scoundrels may be the identical pair who accompanied Dubois to Albert Gate. It is possible that they may recognize me at once."

"No," said Brett decisively. "This is a different gang. The two men who committed the murders never came to Paris. Dubois would not hear of it, I am certain. If you act with discretion, I am sure they will never suspect you."

"Can't you find me a job?" demanded Fairholme.

"Yes, a most pleasant one. It will be your duty to accompany Miss Talbot and Sir Hubert, and show them the sights of Marseilles. I will meet you here at luncheon, but we probably cannot see Mr. Talbot again until late to-night, when he will have an opportunity to come here quietly and detail the results of his observations. Of course," he added, addressing the young man directly, "if anything important happens during the day you know where to find me, either personally or by messenger."

It was natural that Edith's first steps with her lover and uncle would tend towards the scene of her overnight adventure. But Miss Talbot was a clearheaded girl and took no risks. She knew well that in a chance encounter the sharp eyes of Marie and Eugenie might pick her out unless she was to some extent shrouded from observation.

So she donned a large Paris hat and a smart costume, which, with the addition of a thick veil, rendered her very unlike the girl who twelve hours earlier was pursuing a recalcitrant lover.

Secure in the changed appearance effected by these garments, and especially in the escort of two such English-looking persons as Lord Fairholme and Sir Hubert Fitzjames, she walked with them down the Cannebiere and on the quay. She showed them the street up which she pursued Mlle. Beaucaire, and the point on the wharf whence the fishing smack took her departure into the unknown.

Then they strolled back around the harbour, still pursuing the track of Edith's midnight wanderings, when Fairholme suddenly whistled with amazement.

"By Jove, look there!" he cried. "That's a piece of luck."

He pointed to the upper part of the basin, in which a number of smart yachts were anchored side by side. Marseilles is a natural point of departure for Mediterranean tours, and many yacht-owners send their vessels there to be coaled and stored for projected trips.

"What is it?" queried Edith, when she could see nothing in the locality indicated save the vessels and the small expanse of water dancing in the rays of a bright sun.

"The very best thing that could have happened. There is Daubeney's yacht, the *Blue-Bell*."

"Yes. So I see. It would be charming if we had time to go for a run along the Riviera, but I am afraid, whilst Mr. Brett controls our energies, amusement of that sort will be out of our reach."

"Not a bit of it. You do not see my point, Edith. Daubeney is a first-rate chap, and a thorough sportsman. Suppose it becomes necessary for us to follow up Dubois and his fishing-smack, and we let Daubeney into the know. The *Blue-Bell* would pursue the *Belles Soeurs* to

China. He would ask no better fun. I tell you that Brett
will be delighted when he hears of it."

"Yes, dear, but we do not even know that Mr.
Daubeney is in Marseilles."

"Let us go and see. It doesn't matter a pin anyhow,
because a telegram from me to him would place the yacht
at our disposal, and he would join us by express at the
first possible stopping-place. You do not know what a
good chap Daubeney is."

"No," said Edith shortly. "He is evidently a most
useful acquaintance."

It is a most curious fact that young ladies in the
engaged stage regard their *fiance's* male friends with
extreme suspicion; the more enthusiastic the man, the
more suspicious the woman.

Fairholme, sublimely unconscious of this feminine
weakness, continued to dilate upon the superlative
excellences of Daubeney until they reached the yacht
itself.

A smartly-attired sailor was pretending to find some
work in carefully uncoiling a rope which did not satisfy
his critical eye. Before Fairholme could hail the man, a
rotund form, encased in many yards of blue serge,
surmounted by a jolly-looking face on top of which was
perched an absurdly small yachting cap, emerged from
the companion.

"Why, there he is," shouted the earl. "Halloa,
Daubeney! Yoicks! Tally-ho!"

The person addressed in this startling manner
stopped as though he had been shot. He gazed at the sky
and then gravely surveyed the gilded statue that
surmounts the picturesque church of Notre Dame de la
Garde.

"Here I am, you idiot," continued Fairholme. "I am not
in a balloon. I am on the quay. Come here quick. I want to
introduce you to Edith and Sir Hubert."

Luckily Miss Talbot's dark doubts had vanished after
one keen glance at Daubeney. He was eminently a safe

friend for her future husband. Such a fat and hail-fellow-well-met individual could not possibly harbour guile. So she passed over without reference the extent of Daubeney's acquaintance concerning herself, implied by the use of her Christian name. Indeed, was there not a compliment in Fairholme's unconscious outspokenness? If he only discussed her charms with Daubeney then Daubeney was a man to be cultivated.

The meeting on the quay was hearty in the extreme, and the Honourable James Daubeney further ingratiated himself by saying: "Even if Lord Fairholme had not told me who you were, Miss Talbot, I should have known you at once."

"That would be very clever of you," purred Edith.

"Oh, no, there is nothing remarkable in the fact, I assure you. He always sat in his chambers so that he could look at your photograph, and as, in addition to that speaking likeness, I know the colour of your hair, your eyes, your teeth even, I could not be mistaken."

Miss Talbot thought Mr. Daubeney rather curious. But still he was very nice, and unquestionably the services of the *Blue-Bell* might be more than useful.

So she was graciousness personified in her manner, and promptly determined to invite him to luncheon, thinking that the chance direction of their conversation with Mr. Brett might lead towards the use of the yacht being hinted at.

She counted without Fairholme. The latter slapped his heavy friend on the back.

"Look here, old chap, are you fixed up for a cruise? Plenty of coal, champagne, and all that sort of thing?"

"Loaded to the gunwales."

"That's all right, because we may want the *Blue-Bell* for a month or so."

"There she is," said Daubeney; "fit to go anywhere and do anything."

Miss Talbot had never heard such extraordinary conduct in her life. She wondered how two women would have conducted the negotiations. The question was too abstruse, so she gave it up and contented herself instead with accepting Daubeney's hearty request that they should inspect the yacht.

The *Blue-Bell* was an extremely smart little ship of 250 tons register, and an ordinary speed of twelve knots. Incidentally Miss Talbot discovered that the owner made the vessel his home. He was never happy away from her, and the *Blue-Bell* was known to every yachtsman from the Hebrides to the Golden Horn.

To eke out her coal supply she was fitted with sails, and Daubeney assured his fair visitor that the *Blue-Bell* could ride out a gale as comfortably and safely as any craft afloat. Altogether Miss Talbot congratulated herself on Fairholme's discovery, and she could not help hoping that their strange errand to Marseilles might eventuate in a Mediterranean chase.

When the tour of inspection had ended Daubeney suggested an excursion.

"I understand you have never been to Marseilles before, Miss Talbot. In that case, what do you say if we run over and see the Chateau d'If–the place that Dumas made famous, you know?"

"Is it far?" said Edith.

"Oh, not very; about a mile across the harbour. Monte Cristo swam the distance, you know, after his escape."

"Shall we go in the yacht?"

Daubeney bubbled with laughter.

"Well, not exactly, Miss Talbot. You cannot swing a ship of this size about so easily as all that, you know. I have another craft alongside that will suit our purpose."

He whistled to a tiny steam launch which Edith had not noticed before, and without further ado the party seated themselves. They sped rapidly down the harbour and out through the narrow entrance between the lighthouses.

No sooner did Edith behold the splendid panorama of rocky coast that encloses the great outer bay, with its blue waters studded with delightful little islands, through which fishing boats and small steam tugs threaded their way towards different points on the coast, than she clapped her hands with schoolgirl delight.

"I had no idea," she cried, "that Marseilles was half so beautiful. Why, it is a wonderful place. I have always read about it being hot and dirty. It certainly is untidy, but to wash its citizens would take away all the romance! As for the climate being hot, just imagine a day like this in the middle of November. Can you possibly think what the sensation would be if you were plunged into a London fog at this moment, Mr. Daubeney?"

"I have hardly ever seen one," he replied. "I take mighty good care to be far removed from my beloved country during the fog season."

She sighed. "What it is to be a man and to be able to roam about the world unfettered."

"It all depends upon the meaning of the word 'unfettered,'" said Daubeney. "Have you got any sisters, Miss Talbot?"

They all laughed at this inconsequent question. It was impossible to resist Daubeney's buoyant good nature, and Edith felt certain that in half an hour she would be calling him "Jimmy."

They sped across the waves towards the Chateau d'If, and drew up alongside its small landing-stage.

The island supplies an all-the-year-round resort for the townspeople. Every fine day a steamer runs at intervals to and fro between it and the inner harbour. The good folk of the south of France, whether Marseillais or visitors to the city, find a constant delight in taking the short marine excursion and wandering for half an hour about the rocky pathways and steep turrets of the famous prison, whilst they listen with silent awe to the words of the guide when he tells them how the Abbe died, and shows them the hole between the two walls excavated by Monte Cristo. So the English visitors found themselves in the midst of a number of laughing, light-hearted French sightseers.

They wandered round with the crowd until Edith looked at her watch.

"It is past twelve o'clock," she said. "Should we not be going back to the hotel to lunch? You will come with us, of course, Mr. Daubeney?"

"I am famished with expectation," answered the irrepressible Jimmy, "but before we go away you certainly ought to climb to the leads and get the panoramic view of the harbour which the tower affords on a clear day. It is a sight to be remembered, I promise you."

So they made the ascent, Daubeney leading in his capacity of guide, though he was quite breathless when they reached the top of the steps.

Edith followed him, and to her alarm perceived that he was purple in the face. He tried to smile, and indicated by a gesture that he would recover in a minute. Meanwhile he was speechless.

Fairholme was the next up. He had hardly set foot on the roof before he exclaimed—

"Well, I'm d—d!"

Edith turned round quickly.

"What on earth is the matter?" she cried. "Why are you using such horrid language? Mr. Daubeney only hurried a little too fast, that is all."

Fairholme dropped his voice to a whisper.

"Look," he said, indicating with his eyes a distant corner.

Edith followed his glance, and instantly comprehended the cause of his startled exclamation. For in that quiet spot, far removed from watchful police or inquisitive hotel servants, stood four men, whom she could not fail to recognize as Gros Jean, Hussein-ul-Mulk, and the other two Turks, although, of course, until this moment she had never previously set eyes on them.

She instantly understood that they must continue to talk and act in the guise of ordinary tourists. In this respect the presence of Daubeney was invaluable, for he naturally could not guess the community of interest between his aristocratic friends and the motley group in the corner.

As soon as he regained his breath, Edith and he commenced a lively conversation. Sir Hubert joined them, and in the course of their casual stroll round the tower they passed close to the Frenchman and his companions, attracting a casual glance from the former, who instantly set them down as English people bound for the East, and whiling away a few hours in Marseilles prior to the departure of their steamer.

But another surprise awaited them.

A small staircase led to the top of the turret, which, as already described, formed part of the angle that sheltered the group of men.

When Edith and the others strolled past the door they glanced inside and caught sight of a shabby-looking Frenchman, who had paused halfway up the stairs, and was leaning eagerly forward through an embrazured loophole, obviously intent on hearing every word uttered by the quartette beneath.

Fortunately Edith, who was nearest to the door, was completely shrouded from Gros Jean's observation. Else that astute gentleman might have noticed her involuntary start of surprise. For the shabby-looking Frenchman was her brother.

The instant Talbot heard footsteps he naturally turned to see who it was that approached, and he also was amazed to find Edith's wondering eyes fixed upon him at a distance of only a few feet.

She nodded her head and placed a warning finger upon her lips. As it happened, Daubeney caught her in the act, and for the next few moments that gentleman's emotions were intense, not to say painful.

"Who would have thought it?" he muttered to himself. "A girl like her making secret signs to a dirty scoundrel of that sort. The beggar was good-looking, of course; but what–well, I give it up. Poor old Fairholme! What funny creatures women are, to be sure!"

How much further this soliloquy might have proceeded he knew not, for Edith sharply interrupted his thoughts.

"You seem to be preoccupied, Mr. Daubeney. What has happened?" she inquired.

"I–I–really don't know."

His distress was so unmistakable that her quick woman's wit divined the true cause. They had now sauntered some distance away from the part of the tower that might be marked "dangerous," so she grasped Jimmy's ponderous arm, and whispered with a delightful smile–

"You saw me make signs to that Frenchman, didn't you?"

"Well–er–I–er—"

"Oh, yes, I understand. Of course you were surprised. But don't jump now, or say anything; he is my brother!"

She need not have warned Daubeney as to any remarks he might feel inclined to make, for her announcement again rendered him speechless.

"It is a mystery," she whispered, "a deep secret. We will tell you all about it at lunch."

18
TALBOT'S ADVENTURES

Although Miss Talbot spoke so confidently of revelations to accompany the expected meal, it is idle to pretend that any of the three people who were cognizant of Talbot's mysterious appearance on the island betrayed undue haste to return to the waiting lunch. Sublimely unconscious of the excitement raging in their breasts, Sir Hubert Fitzjames could not understand why they each and all answered him in such a flurried manner when he dilated upon the beauties of the bay. Finally he turned to Edith with an air of apprehension.

"I fear," he said, "that your expedition of last night has upset you. Have you a headache?"

Then she could contain her news no longer. Drawing him close to the rampart, and bending down so as to apparently take a deep interest in the laughing excursionists beneath, she murmured—

"Listen to me carefully, uncle. Don't look around. Have you noticed the party of Turks and a Frenchman grouped together in the opposite corner?"

"Yes," he said. "You do not mean to tell me that they are the people whom Mr. Brett met this morning at the station?"

"Yes, unquestionably they are. Had your attention not been otherwise taken up you must have recognized them from their description. But the most marvellous thing remains. You know the little turret close to which they are standing?"

"Yes."

"Well, in the staircase leading to the top, and leaning out through a window, trying to hear what they are saying, is Jack!"

"What an extraordinary thing," said the major-general, who was really very annoyed that such a meeting should have taken place under his very nose and its significance remain hidden from him.

"Can we do anything?" he added.

"Nothing save to remain here a little longer and be most careful not to appear to have the least knowledge of their identity. I have told you lest we might chance to meet Jack face to face, and you should be taken by surprise if you recognized him."

"Is he in disguise, then?" gasped her uncle.

"Yes, in a sense. Mr. Talbot has put him into a sort of French working-man's holiday suit. He looks so odd, but it is evident that neither Gros Jean nor the Turks have the least suspicion of his presence. It was very clever of Jack to get into that turret without alarming them."

They were joined by Daubeney and Fairholme, and Edith knew by a single glance at the expressive expanse of the former's face that should he be again brought into close proximity to the Turks and her brother it was quite possible the quick-witted Gros Jean might detect the look of interested amazement which must inevitably appear upon his honest British countenance.

"Bobby," she said at once, "I want you and Mr. Daubeney to go down to the launch and await us there. We will join you in a few minutes."

"Certainly," was the reply, for Fairholme knew that some motive lay behind the request. "You cannot do much by remaining here, can you, so I suppose you will not be long?"

"No; uncle and I will survey the view until it is firmly fixed in our minds. After that it is full steam ahead for the Hotel du Louvre."

The two young men disappeared down the stairs leading to the courtyard. On their way they encountered a number of holiday makers, climbing to the top of the tower. In they came, twenty or more of them, and promptly spread themselves around the walls, the

Marseillais amongst them indicating to their country cousins points of interest in the city and along the coast.

At this moment, too, the siren of the small pleasure steamer at the quay announced she was about to make her hourly trip back to the town. Whereupon Gros Jean and the Turks, having apparently ended their consultation, crossed the roof and disappeared down the staircase.

Instantly Jack Talbot strolled after them, but no sooner had the bulky form of Gros Jean—who was the last of his party—vanished than Talbot ran towards his uncle and sister, and said rapidly—

"Dubois and the girl have gone to Palermo. Gros Jean and the Turks have been in communication with the Sultan, and there is a movement on foot to buy back the diamonds. That is all that I can tell you now, but let Mr. Brett know. When I have seen these chaps safely home, I will at once come to the hotel."

Then he, too, vanished.

Edith felt a thrill of elation that her good judgment should have led her to remain sufficiently long on the tower to glean such important information.

When Brett heard the news it seemed to annoy him.

"I feared as much," he said. "I had not much faith in the patriotism of the Young Turks. I wonder how much the Sultan has offered. It must be a severe wrench for him to dip his hands into his money-bags, and Dubois will certainly demand a handsome figure before he disgorges his booty. However, we must possess our souls in peace until Talbot comes here and tells us all what he has learnt. At this moment I cannot help marvelling at the strange coincidence which should have led the Turks and yourself to select the Chateau d'If for a morning stroll. I fully expected that Gros Jean would be in bed. He must have received some startling intelligence to keep him away from his rest after a long journey. Meanwhile, I have not been idle."

Everyone awaited with interest his next words, for Brett seldom made such a remark without having something out of the common to communicate.

"I telephoned to Paris," he explained, "to tell the Prefecture that Gros Jean and the Turks had arrived at Marseilles. The police were surprised, and perhaps a little sore, that they had not discovered the fact for themselves, but when I soothed them down they informed me that 'Le Ver'–the diminutive scoundrel whom we rescued from the Rue Barbette–had faithfully kept his appointment with me at the Grand Hotel yesterday.

"It seems that he was much upset when he learnt that I had left. He went straight to the commissary to inform him that, contrary to expectations, the Turks were acting in complete accord with mademoiselle's father. This naturally puzzled the commissary a good deal, and the affair became still stranger when an attache from the Turkish Embassy called a little later and urged the police to do all in their power to discover the whereabouts of Hussein-ul-Mulk, as he was particularly anxious to have a friendly talk with him.

"Close on the heels of the Turk came a confidential messenger from the British Embassy, requesting the latest details, and, when questioned by the commissary, this man admitted that he had in the first instance called to see me at the Grand Hotel.

"In a word, Miss Talbot, I had suspected the existence of the negotiations, which your brother's smart piece of work this morning has confirmed."

Whilst they were talking Fairholme took Daubeney on one side, and with Brett's permission gave him a detailed account of the whole affair.

The Honourable James Daubeney was delighted to be mixed up in this international imbroglio. He told the earl that the *Blue-Bell* was at his disposal at any moment of the day or night she might be required. Indeed, he forthwith excused himself on the ground that certain little formalities were requisite before he could clear the harbour, and he must hurry off to attend to these immediately.

"I tell you what," he added, with his hand on the door, "I will come back and dine with you, if I may, at half-past seven, because I shall not sleep to-night until I hear how things are going on. But I promise you, if I meet a single Turk between here and the harbour, I will cross over to the other side of the street."

No one quite knew what he meant by this portentous guarantee, but it was evident that Daubeney, if nothing else, was a man of action, and his yacht might become very useful.

He had hardly quitted the hotel when a waiter announced that a *jeune Francais* wished to see Mr. Brett.

"Show him up," said the barrister, and a moment later Talbot entered. He stood near the door twiddling his hat in his hand until the waiter had gone. Then he told them what had happened since he took up his quarters at the Hotel des Jolies Femmes.

"When I reached there," he said, "I was under the impression that Gros Jean and the Turks were in bed. I hired my room; sent my tin box there, and then settled myself in the cafe to smoke cigarettes and read these vile Marseilles newspapers until lunch time. You may judge my surprise when I saw the three Turks and Gros Jean come out into the street and ask a waiter the way to the post-office.

"They set off, and, being sure of their destination, I did not quit the cafe myself until they were well out of sight. Then I walked away in the same direction, inquired of a policeman the quickest way to reach the post-office, and stepped out rapidly.

"I had not gone far when I overtook them. They reached the building. The Turks remained in the street and Gros Jean went inside, so I followed him, and found him inquiring for letters at the Poste Restante department. Whereupon I sent a telegram to London."

"Who on earth did you telegraph to, Jack?" broke in Edith.

"To my shirt-maker, telling him to put a couple of dozens in hand at once."

This unexpected answer evoked a general titter.

"The funny thing to me," said Talbot, "was the effect of the message on the telegraph clerk. He could evidently read English, and he surveyed me curiously, for in my present appearance I looked a most unlikely person to order shirts by telegram from a well-known London house. However, I achieved my purpose, which was to overhear Gros Jean's request. He asked if there were any letters for M. Isidor de Rion."

"Good gracious," cried Edith, "what an aristocratic name for that fat man."

"Anyhow, it was effective. There was a letter for him, and he evidently only expected one, for, before the clerk who handed it to him was able to examine the remainder of the packet, he tore it open, glanced briefly at its contents, and then hurried out to join his friends to the street. After a short conclave they entered a cafe and procured a railway guide. I tried hard to find out what section of the book Gros Jean was looking at, but failed, for the double reason that he did not consult the Turks, nor did he seem to make up his mind, for he looked through the book, sighed impatiently and suggested to the others that they should go out again. I followed them into the Cannebiere, and thence down towards the harbour. When we reached the quay a small pleasure steamer was whistling for passengers, and a placard announced a fifty-centimes return trip to the Chateau d'If.

"Seemingly on the spur of the moment, Gros Jean invited the others to accompany him. It probably occurred to him that the island would supply a safe nook in which they could talk without fear of observation, as their presence on board the steamer would stamp them as excursionists. So, of course, I followed them. When we reached the island, I quickly perceived that the castle filled the whole of it. Therefore, in place of keeping behind them I went in front. We all passed on with the stream of sightseers until we reached the courtyard. I had never been in the place before, but Gros Jean seemed to know it well. Owing to my policy of preceding them I found myself halted for a moment at the foot of the stairs leading to the tower. It struck me that the Frenchman was making in this direction, so I took the chance and ran up. I reached the top and looked over before the party had entered the doorway at the bottom. They came in. Thus far I was right. I looked around, and found, as you know, the square roof surrounded by bare battlements with a turret in one corner. I decided instantly that it would be hopeless to try to get close to them if they halted at any other point save in the vicinity of the turret. Elsewhere I must remain too far away to catch any portion of their conversation. So I darted across and entered the turret, noting on my way up the stairs the existence of the loopholed window where you finally saw me. It would never do to be caught there, so I went to the top and peeped over. You can guess how delighted I was when they came straight across and settled themselves in the angle beneath. Then I crept halfway down the stairs and leaned as far as I dared through the loophole, being just in time to hear Gros Jean read a letter from his daughter. Fortunately the innkeeper had to speak plainly, as his companions were foreigners, and for the same reason I had no difficulty in catching the drift of what the Turks said.

"The letter was quite short. It told him that H. had decided to leave France, and had made arrangements to proceed at once to Palermo, whither the writer would accompany him.

"One sentence I remember exactly: 'H.,' she wrote, 'has friends in Sicily, and he feels assured of a kind reception at their hands.'"

"Friends!" interrupted Brett. "That means brigands!"

"The information seemed to annoy the Turks very much. They were very angry at what they described as the enforced delay, and discussed with Gros Jean the quickest means of reaching Palermo forthwith. Then he told them that he had endeavoured to find out the trains running through Italy to Messina, but they could not leave Marseilles until to-night, and he thought it best that they should have a quiet talk on the situation before deciding too hurriedly upon any line of action.

"The rest of their conversation was inconsequent and desultory, alluding evidently to some project which they had fully discussed before. But it is quite clear from the drift of their remarks that an emissary from the Sultan had approached Hussein-ul-Mulk, and had offered such terms for the recovery of the diamonds that not only were the Young Turkish party in Paris eager to compromise with him, but they had succeeded in convincing Gros Jean that Dubois also would be likely to accept the proposition."

Brett smiled grimly. "The commissary in Paris always follows up the wrong person," he said. "Had he only used his wits yesterday morning he would have discovered that the agent of the Embassy was in touch with Hussein-ul-Mulk. Hence the presence of the quartette in Marseilles to-day."

Talbot was naturally mystified by this remark until Brett explained to him the circumstances already known to the reader.

"Was there anything else?" inquired the barrister, reverting to the chief topic before them.

"Only this. I gathered that Gros Jean did not know his daughter's whereabouts in Marseilles, but she had arranged that if circumstances necessitated her departure from the town she would leave a letter for him in the Poste Restante, giving him full details. Nevertheless, this presupposes the knowledge on her part that he would come to Marseilles, so I assume therefore that telegrams must have passed between them yesterday afternoon."

"Obviously!" said Brett. "Anything else?"

"Yes," and now Talbot's voice took a note of passion that momentarily surprised his hearers. "It seems to me that this underhanded arrangement, if it goes through, condones the murder of poor Mehemet Ali and his assistants, and places on me the everlasting disgrace of having permitted this thing to happen whilst an important and special mission was entrusted to my sole charge by the Foreign Office. Dubois has been able to commit his crime, get away with the diamonds, hoodwink all of us most effectually, and, in the result, obtain a huge reward from the Turkish Government for his services. I tell you, Mr. Brett, I won't put up with it. I will follow him to the other end of the world, and, at any rate, take personal vengeance on the man who has ruined my career. For, no matter what you say, the only effective way in which I can rehabilitate myself with my superiors is to hand back those diamonds to the custody of the Foreign Office. No matter how the panic-stricken sovereign in Yildiz Kiosk may sacrifice his servants to gain his own ends, I, at least, have a higher motive. It rests with me to prove that the British Government is not to be humbugged by Paris thieves or Turkish agitators. If I fail in that duty there remains to me the personal motive of revenge!

"No, Edith; it is useless to argue with me," for his sister had risen and placed her arms lovingly round his neck in the effort to calm him. "My mind is made up. I suppose Mr. Brett feels that his inquiry is ended. For me it has just commenced."

The young man's justifiable rage created a sensation which was promptly allayed by Brett's cool voice.

"May I ask," he said, "what reason you have to suppose that I should so readily throw up the sponge and leave Monsieur Henri Dubois the victor in this contest?"

"Do you mean," cried Talbot, starting to his feet, "that you will stand by me?"

"Stand by you!" echoed the barrister, himself yielding for an instant to the electrical condition of things. "Of course I will. We will recover those diamonds and bring them back with us to London if we have to take them out of the Sultan's palace itself!"

"And now, Lord Fairholme," he added, before Talbot could do other than grasp his hand and shake it impulsively, "we want your friend's yacht. We will set out for Palermo at the first possible moment. We must reach there many hours, perhaps a whole day, before Dubois, who is on a sailing vessel, and even with the start he has obtained cannot hope to equal the performance of a fast steamer. Let Gros Jean and his Turks travel overland. We will beat them, too. Come, now, no more talk, but action. You, Fairholme, go ahead and prepare Daubeney. I will see to your luggage being packed. Talbot and I will join you in half an hour."

"Eh! what is that?" broke in Sir Hubert. "Fairholme, Talbot, you–what are Edith and I going to do?"

"Mr. Brett, of course," said Edith, in her steady, even tones, "did not trouble to include us, uncle, because we shall be on the yacht first. A woman can always pack up much better than a man, you know, and I will look after you, dear."

Brett gave one glance at her flushed and smiling face, and forthwith abandoned argument as useless.

An hour later the *Blue-Bell* was skimming merrily past the outer lighthouse in Marseilles bay.

19
THE RACE

For a wonder, the Gulf of Lyons was not boisterous. They had a pleasant journey through the night, and Daubeney assured them that his handsome yacht was doing twelve knots an hour without being pressed.

Next morning they reached the Straits of Bonifacio, and here they had to slacken speed somewhat, for the navigation of that rocky channel was difficult and dangerous. Far behind them they could see a huge steamer approaching. As the morning wore, this vessel came nearer, and Daubeney, important now in his capacity of commander, announced that she was the P. and O. steamship *Ganges*, bound for Brindisi and the East, via the Straits of Messina.

"She left Marseilles at a late hour last night," he said, "and will call at Brindisi for the Indian mails."

An idea suddenly struck Brett. "Do you know how fast she is steaming?" he inquired.

"Oh, about thirteen and a half knots an hour. That is her best rate. The P. and O. boats are not flyers, you know."

"And does she stop at Messina?"

Daubeney now caught the drift of the barrister's questions.

"I don't think so, but Macpherson, my chief engineer, will probably tell us."

Macpherson was produced, a bearded and grizzled personage, hailing from Dundee. Being a Scotchman he would not commit himself.

"I hav'na hear-rd o' the P. and O. ships stoppin' at Messina," he announced, "but aiblins they wad if they got their price." And "Mac" would not commit himself any further.

Another hour passed, and the *Ganges* was now almost alongside. Although both ships were well through the Straits of Bonifacio, and the *Ganges* should have followed a course a point or two north of that pursued by the *Blue-Bell*, she appeared to be desirous to come close to them.

Suddenly the reason became apparent. A line of little flags fluttered up to her masthead.

"She is signalling us," cried Daubeney excitedly. "Here you," he shouted to a sailor, "bring Jones here at once."

Jones was the yacht's expert signaller. He approached with a telescope and a code under his arm. After a prolonged gaze and a careful scrutiny of the code, he announced—

"This is how the message reads: 'Turks on board. Stopping Messina.—WINTER.'"

For once the barrister was startled out of his usual quiet self-possession.

"Winter!" he almost screamed. "Is he there?"

A hundred mad questions coursed through his brain, but he realized that to attempt a long explanation by signals was not only out of the question, but could not fail to attract the attention of passengers on board the *Ganges*. This he did not desire to do. Quick as lightning, he decided that by some inexplicable means the Scotland Yard detective had reached Marseilles full of the knowledge that Dubois and the diamonds were *en route* to Sicily, and had also learnt that he, Brett, and the others were on board the *Blue-Bell*.

He had evidently taken the speediest means of reaching the island, and found himself on board the same ship as Gros Jean and the Turks. Hence he had approached the captain with the request that the *Blue-Bell* should be signalled.

"What shall we answer?" said Daubeney, breaking in upon the barrister's train of thought.

"Oh, say that the signal is fully understood."

Whilst the answering flags were being displayed Daubeney asked—

"What does it all mean?"

"It means," said Brett, "that if the *Blue-Bell* has another yard of speed in her engines we shall need it all. It perhaps will make no material difference in the long run, but as a mere matter of pride I should like to reach Palermo before Gros Jean. If I remember rightly, Palermo is six hours from Messina by rail. Can we do it?"

"Mac" was again consulted. Of course he would not commit himself.

"We will try damned ha-r-rd," he said.

And with this emphatic resolve the *Blue-Bell* sped onwards through the sunlit sea until, late in the evening, the *Ganges* was hull down on her quarter.

Macpherson came on deck to take a last look at the P. and O.

"It will be a gr-reat race," he announced, "and I may have to kill a stoker. But—"

Then he dived below again.

So rapidly did the *Blue-Bell* speed over the inland sea that as night fell over the face of the waters on the second day out from Marseilles the look-out forrard announced "a light on the starboard bow," and Daubeney, after scrutinizing it through his binoculars and consulting a chart, announced it to be the occulting light on Cape San Vito.

This discovery occasioned a slight alteration in the course. The *Blue-Bell* ran merrily on until the small hours of the morning, when everybody on board was suddenly awakened by the stoppage of the screw.

This is always a disturbing incident at sea when people are asleep. Travellers not inured to the incidents of ocean voyaging cannot help conjuring up vivid pictures of impending disaster.

It is useless to tell them that for the very reason the ship has slackened her speed it is obvious she is being navigated with care and watchfulness. Reason at such a time is dethroned by the natural timidity of the unseen, and it is not surprising therefore that the passengers on board the *Blue-Bell* should one and all find some pretext to gain the deck in their eagerness to find out why the vessel had slowed down. The answer was a reassuring one. She had burnt a flare for a pilot, and quickly an answering gleam came from afar out of the darkness ahead.

The pilot was soon on board. He was an Italian, but, like most members of his profession doing business in those waters, he spoke French fluently.

Brett asked him how long, with the north-easterly breeze then blowing, a small sailing vessel, such as a schooner-rigged fishing-smack, would take to reach Palermo from Marseilles.

The pilot seemed to be surprised at the question.

"It is a trip not often made, monsieur," he said. "Fishing vessels from Marseilles are frequently compelled to take shelter under the lea of Corsica or even Sardinia, but here—in Sicily—why should they come here?"

"Oh, I don't mean a schooner engaged in the fishing trade, but rather a small vessel chartered for pleasure, taking the place, as it were, of a private yacht."

"Ah," said the Italian, "that explains it. Well, monsieur, with this breeze I should imagine they would set their course round by the north of Corsica in order to avoid beating through the Straits of Bonifacio. That would make the run about 650 knots, and a smart little vessel, carrying all her sails and properly ballasted, might reach Palermo in a few hours over three days."

"Thank you," said Brett. "Is Palermo a difficult port to make?"

"Oh no, monsieur. There is deep water all round here, no shoals, and but few isolated rocks, which are all well known. The only thing to guard against is the changeful current. According to the state of the tide and the direction of the wind, sailing ships have to alter their course very considerably, for the currents round here are very strong and consequently most dangerous in calm weather."

Brett smiled.

"It would be an ignoble conclusion to the chase if the *Belles Soeurs* were wrecked with her valuable cargo. I most devoutly pray," he said to himself, "that the breezes and currents may combine to bring Dubois safely on shore. Then I think we can deal with him."

Soon after daybreak the *Blue-Bell*, after a momentary halt at the Customs Station, crept past the Castello a Mare, and amidst much gesticulation, accompanied by a torrent of volcanic Italian, she was tied up to a wharf in the Cala–the small inner harbour of the port.

Edith, who could not sleep since the advent of the pilot, made an early toilet and climbed to the bridge, whence she had a magnificent view of the sunrise over the beautiful city that stands on the Conca d'Oro, or Golden Shell–the smiling and luxuriant plain that seems to be provided by Nature for man's habitation. It lies beyond a lovely bay, and is enclosed on three sides by lofty and precipitous mountains.

Naturally Fairholme was drawn to her side as a chip of steel to a magnet.

"We are certain to have a furious row here," he remarked when they had exhausted their superlative adjectives concerning the splendid prospect opening up before their eyes.

"Why?" cried Edith wonderingly. "I understood that our present adventure may at any moment have exciting developments, but I do not see the association between the view and the possibility."

"It is this way," he answered. "I have not read a great deal, as you know, but I have always noticed in my limited way that wherever Nature is most lavish in her gifts, she seems to take a delight in setting people by the ears. Italy is a fine country, you know, yet there are more murders to the square inch there than in any other place on earth. Then again, it is likely that several armed policemen are at this moment chasing bandits among those hills over there," and he nodded towards the distant blue heights which looked so peaceful in the clear atmosphere, now brilliant with the rays of the rising sun.

Edith laughed. "Really, Bobby," she pouted, "you are becoming sentimental. I half expect to find you break out into verse."

"I can do that, too," he said, "though it is not my own. Hasn't Heber got a hymn which tells us of a place where 'Every prospect pleases, and only man is vile'. I forget the rest of it."

Miss Talbot faced him rapidly.

"Good gracious, Bobby, what is the matter with you? I never knew you in such a melting mood before?"

"How can I help it?" he half-whispered, laying his hand on her shoulder. "We have never been together so much before in our lives. Don't you realize, Edith, what it means to us if Mr. Brett discovers those diamonds within the next few hours or days?"

He bent closer towards her and his hand passed from her shoulder round her neck. "When we return to England, if you are willing, we can be married within a week."

A bright flush suffused her beautiful face. She bent her head and was silent. It is quite certain that Fairholme would have kissed her had not Daubeney shouted—

"Look here, you two, flirting on the bridge is strictly forbidden. You will demoralize the whole crew. Even the pilot cannot keep his eyes off you."

They laughed and giggled like a couple of children caught stealing gooseberries. Yet the incident and the words were fraught with a solemn significance which often came back to their minds in other days.

The party breakfasted on board and then set out to survey the hotels. Brett's first care was to ascertain the scheduled hours of the train service between Messina and

Palermo. To his joy he discovered that neither Winter nor the gang he was shadowing could possibly reach the city until a quarter to four in the afternoon. They decided in favour of the Hotel de France as being most modern in its appearance and centrally situated.

The next thing to do was to provide an efficient watch on all sailing vessels entering the harbour, and here the pilot proved to be a valuable ally. Brett explained to him that he was most anxious to meet some people who were coming from Marseilles on a fishing smack named the *Belles Soeurs*, No. 107. It was possible, he explained, that both the number and the name might be obliterated, so he wished the pilot, or any helpers he might employ for the duty, to take particular note of all strange boats answering to this description, and at once report their appearance. This the man guaranteed to do. He said that it was quite impossible for a French-rigged smack to enter Palermo without attracting his notice.

As the daily remuneration fixed for his services was far beyond any sum he could earn as a pilot, he set about his task with enthusiasm. He engaged two assistants to take turns in watching the harbour, and gave the barrister such assurances of devotion to duty that Brett felt quite satisfied that Dubois could not arrive in Palermo without his knowledge. Of course it was quite on the cards that some secluded creek along the coast might be preferred by the astute schemer as a point of debarkation, but this was a risk which must be taken.

By approaching the police authorities and requesting their co-operation, and also using Gros Jean and the Turks as a stalking-horse, Brett felt tolerably certain that the time would soon arrive when Dubois and he would stand face to face.

In making these manifold preparations the morning passed rapidly. The barrister insisted that his companions should go for a drive whilst he busied himself with the necessary details, and they should meet at the hotel for the midday meal. It was then that he singled out Sir Hubert for his personal share in the pursuit.

"You know Mr. Winter?" he said to the baronet.

"Yes, I remember him perfectly."

"In that case I wish you to go to the station and meet the 3.45 p.m. train on arrival. You will probably see the Turks and Gros Jean, but pay no attention to them. Keep a bright look-out for Mr. Winter. Walk up quite openly and speak to him, and the probability is that should Gros Jean have become suspicious of this Englishman who follows in the same track as himself, your presence on the platform will convince him that he was mistaken in imagining the slightest connection between Winter's journey and his own."

"That is good," said the major-general. "It would never have occurred to me. Any other commands?"

"None, save this," continued Brett, smiling at the old soldier's eagerness to obey implicitly any instructions given to him. "When you meet Winter, tell him, if possible, to so direct his movements as to find out Gros Jean's destination, if it can be done without giving the Frenchman the slightest cause for uneasiness. Otherwise the matter is of no consequence. I have already interviewed the chief of police here, and it will only be a question of an hour's delay before the local detectives effectually locate the quarters occupied by Gros Jean and the Turks."

20
CLOSE QUARTERS

Sir Hubert was all eagerness to undertake his mission. He reached the station at least half an hour too soon. Anyone seeing him there would readily admit that the barrister could not have chosen an agent less guileful in appearance. The very cut of his clothes, the immaculate character of his white spats, bespoke the elderly British gentleman.

At last the train arrived. The vast majority of its passengers were Sicilian peasants or business men returning to Palermo from the interior of the island. To Sir Hubert's delight, he at once caught sight of Gros Jean and the Turks, whom, of course, he quickly identified as the loungers on the tower of the Chateau d'If.

It occurred to him that there was a remote chance of recognition by Gros Jean, so he busied himself for an instant in a seeming scrutiny of the bookstall until they had passed. A little further down the platform he caught sight of Inspector Winter, that worthy individual being engaged in a fiercely unintelligible controversy with an Italian porter as to the possession of his portmanteau.

Sir Hubert hurried forward, and seized the amazed policeman by his hand, wringing it warmly. To tell the truth, Winter did not know for a moment who it was that accorded him such a cordial greeting, for, as it subsequently transpired, the policeman was not aware of Sir Hubert's journey to Marseilles, nor did he guess that Edith was with him.

The stolid detective, however, quickly recovered himself, and his first words were—

"Did Mr. Brett fully understand my signal?"

"I think so," said the other; "but he will tell you all about that afterwards. At present he wishes you to ascertain Gros Jean's intended residence."

Mr. Winter smiled with the peculiar air of superiority affected by Scotland Yard.

"Oh, that is too easy," he condescended to explain. "I have been talking to him."

"You don't say so!"

"Yes, I have. My French is bad, and his English is worse, but he understands that I am in the wholesale grocery trade. I have come to Palermo to buy currants!"

"Most extraordinary! How very clever of you!"

Mr. Winter drew himself up with an air of professional pride.

"That is nothing, sir," he said. "We often make queer acquaintanceships in the way of business. But Gros Jean is a smart chap. He eyed me curiously when he happened to hear that I was the fifth passenger who wished to leave the steamer at Messina, so I took the bull by the horns and made myself useful to him in the matter of getting his baggage out of the hold."

"Marvellous!" gasped Sir Hubert.

"The upshot of it was that he gave me some advice about currants. We stayed in the same hotel at Messina, travelled together in the train, and I am going to put up at the Campo Santo Hotel, where he will stay with the Turks."

Meanwhile the subject of their conversation had quitted the station, and Sir Hubert's respect for Mr. Winter's powers as a sleuth-hound yielded to anxiety lest the slippery Frenchman might vanish once and for all.

"Hadn't we better follow him?" he suggested.

Mr. Winter winked knowingly. "Don't be anxious, sir. He wants to be seen in my company. He believes I am here for trading purposes, and the association will be useful to him."

Nevertheless the baronet was glad to find that Mr. Winter's confidence was not misplaced, when, ten minutes later, he again encountered the Frenchman and the Turks at the door of the Campo Santo, a cheap and popular hotel near the square that forms the centre of Palermo.

The detective was eminently suited for the *role* he now filled.

"Ah, monsoo," he cried with boisterous good humour, "permittez-moi introducer un friend of mine, Monsoo Smeeth, de Londres, you know. Je ne savez pas les noms de votre companiongs, but they are tres bons camarades, je suis certain."

Gros Jean was most complaisant.

"It ees von grand plaisir, m'sieu," he said, whilst the Turks gravely bowed their acknowledgments.

The upshot of this extraordinary meeting was that when Mr. Winter had secured a room and the party had ordered dinner, the six men set out for a stroll through the town.

Sir Hubert strove hard to so manoeuvre their ramble that they should pass the Hotel de France, and perchance come under the astonished eyes of Brett and the others.

But this amiable design was frustrated by Gros Jean's eagerness to visit the post-office, which lay in a different direction.

One of the Turks, none other than Hussein-ul-Mulk, spoke English fairly well, and it puzzled the old baronet considerably to answer his questions.

Yet the situation passed off well. Gros Jean came out of the post-office, apparently without having obtained any missives—a letter, of course, could not possibly await him— and suggested that they should wander towards the harbour.

Sir Hubert strongly recommended the spectacular beauty of the street where the Hotel de France lay, but Gros Jean politely insisted that he wished to make some inquiries at the shipping office, and Mr. Winter backed him up, being ignorant of the baronet's real motive.

There was nothing to do but yield gracefully.

They walked along the Corso Vittorio Emmanuele. Sir Hubert, fresh with memories of his morning's drive with a guide, pointed out the chief buildings, becoming sadly mixed up in the names of some of them.

Still, this was a safer topic than his previous conversation with Hussein-ul-Mulk, so he persevered gamely.

They soon reached the quay. Sir Hubert became almost incoherent with agitation when they passed the *Blue-Bell* and came into full view of Edith, Jack, Fairholme and Daubeney, who happened to leave the hotel shortly before five o'clock in order to visit the yacht and secure a good cup of tea.

Brett refused to accompany them, on the ground that his Italian scout, the pilot, might bring news at any hour, and he must remain within immediate call.

It was a supreme moment when Gros Jean halted and called general attention to the smart-looking vessel and the tea-drinkers.

Sir Hubert keenly examined the top of the funnel, and tried simultaneously to yawn and light a cigar. In the result he nearly choked himself. Mr. Winter, somewhat more prepared for emergencies, endeavoured to interest Gros Jean in the wonderful clearness of the water.

But Hussein-ul-Mulk and his two sedate friends suddenly betrayed a keen interest in Fairholme.

When they last met the earl on the tower of the Chateau d'If they were so engrossed in the object of their visit to Marseilles that he had passed them unnoticed.

But now, looking steadily at him—for Fairholme was seated facing them, and was striving to maintain the semblance of an animated chat with Edith—there came to the Turks a memory, each instant becoming more definite, of an exciting scene in the Rue Barbette, and the opportune arrival of a stalwart young Englishman, backed up by a couple of gendarmes.

Hussein-ul-Mulk's swarthy countenance reddened with suspicious anger. He drew Gros Jean on one side and whispered something to him. The Frenchman started violently.

"They have recognized you, Bobby!" murmured the quick-witted Edith. "Oh, why didn't we remain with Mr. Brett!"

There is no knowing what might have happened had not Fate stepped in to decide in dramatic fashion the important issues at stake.

Whilst Gros Jean and the Turk were still conferring in stealthy tones, and the English people endeavoured to keep up an appearance of complete unconcern, a tramp steamer swung round the corner of the mole that protects the harbour.

In tow, with sails trimly furled and six people standing on her small deck—a lady and gentleman and four sailors—was the *Belles Soeurs*, fishing-smack No. 107, from Marseilles. Instantly a watcher, otherwise unperceived, ran off from the quay at top speed towards the Hotel de France.

Gros Jean, the Turks, Edith, Fairholme—each and every member of the two parties on the wharf and on the deck of the *Blue-Bell*—momentarily forgot the minor excitement of the situation in view of this unexpected apparition.

"*Voila! Ils viennent! Venez vite!*" cried Gros Jean.

He ran further along the quay, followed by the Turks.

"Quick, Bobby! Oh, Jack, do something! Mr. Brett could not foresee this, though he seemed to have an inspiration that kept him in the hotel. What can we do? Dubois and the girl will know you at once! Jack, shouldn't you keep out of sight?—go below—go and fetch Mr. Brett. Oh, dear, this is dreadful!"

Thus did Edith, for once yielding to feminine irresolution, appeal to her lover and brother, vainly seeking to discover the best line of action to follow in this disastrous circumstance, for she knew that the diamonds must now be in the personal possession of Dubois. It was a golden opportunity to recover the stolen gems. If once he eluded the grasp of his pursuers after landing they might–probably would–secure him, but not the diamonds.

Daubeney, now purple with perplexity, and Fairholme, swearing softly under his breath, sprang from the deck to the low wall of the quay. Almost unconsciously they joined Sir Hubert and Mr. Winter. Edith followed them. She glanced at her brother. He was gazing curiously, vindictively, at the two figures on the deck of the *Belles Soeurs*. There was a fierce gleam in his eyes, a set expression in his closed lips, a nervous twitching at the corners of his mouth, that betokened the overpowering emotions of the moment.

With a woman's intuition Edith realized that no power on earth, no consideration of expediency, would restrain him from laying violent hands on Dubois at the first possible opportunity. She knew there must be a struggle, in which Gros Jean and the Turks, perhaps the four sailors, would participate. They might use knives and firearms, whereas the Englishmen were unarmed.

So she ran back on board the yacht and cried to the Scotch engineer–

"Oh, Mr. Macpherson! Please come with some of your men! There may be a fight on the wharf, and Mr. Daubeney and the others will be outnumbered!"

Macpherson for once forgot his cautiousness. There was none of the characteristic slowness of the Scottish nation in his manner or language as he yelled down the fore-hatch: "Tumble up, there! Some damned Eye-talians are goin' to hammer the boss. Bring along a monkey-wrench or the first thing to hand. Shar-r-p's the wo-r-rd!"

Forthwith there poured from the hatchway a miscellaneous mob of seamen, firemen and stewards. Following Edith and Macpherson, they ran along the quay. Already there was something unusual in progress.

Loungers by the harbour, perceiving a disturbance, were running towards the scene of action.

A solitary Italian policeman, swaggering jauntily over the paved roadway, was suddenly startled out of his self-complacency.

"*Caramba!*" he shouted. Drawing his sabre, he broke into a run.

For matters had developed with melodramatic suddenness. Casting off the steamer's tow-ropes, the *Belles Soeurs* swung alongside the wharf much more easily and quickly than did the friendly vessel by whose aid she had so soon reached Palermo.

Both steamer and smack had already been searched by the Customs' officers, who boarded them in the quarantine station, and the reason that the schooner had not been earlier sighted from the shore was supplied by the mere chance that she was rendered invisible by close proximity to her bigger companion.

The instant that the fishing-boat was tied to the wharf, Mlle. Beaucaire sprang ashore. Gros Jean, breathless and excited, was there to greet her. But the greeting between father and daughter was not very cordial. The innkeeper seemed to be dumbfounded with surprise at her early arrival.

Dubois followed more leisurely. He took no notice of Gros Jean, and appeared to be looking around for a cab. Two of the sailors were handing up a couple of portmanteaus from the deck. Hussein-ul-Mulk and the two other Turks, unable to restrain their excitement, crowded round the pink-and-white Frenchman, jabbering volubly, but Mademoiselle and her father moved some slight distance away.

At this juncture Mr. Winter strode resolutely forward, seized Dubois firmly by the shoulder, and said—

"Henri Dubois! In the name of the King of England I arrest you for the murder of—"

The detective's words were stopped by a blow.

A wild struggle promptly ensued. The man turned on him like a tiger, and the Turks joined in. Gros Jean, too, ran back to take a hand in the fray. Fairholme, Sir Hubert, Daubeney and Talbot flung themselves on the would-be rescuers, and the four French sailors of the *Belles Soeurs* leaped ashore to assist their passenger in this unlooked-for attack.

Frantic yells and oaths came from the confused mob, and knives were drawn. Talbot had but one desire in life— to get his fingers on Dubois' throat. He had almost reached him, for Winter clung to his prey with bull-dog tenacity, when an astounding thing happened. The Frenchman's handsome moustaches fell off, and beneath the clever make-up on her face were visible the boldly handsome features of La Belle Chasseuse, now distorted by rage and fear.

"You fool!" yelled Talbot to Winter. "You have let him escape!"

Tearing himself from the midst of the fight, he was just in time to see the female figure, which he now knew must be Dubois masquerading in his mistress's clothes, jumping into a cab and driving off towards the Corso Vittorio Emmanuele.

"Come on, Fairholme!" he cried. "He cannot get away! Here comes an empty carriage!"

But now Macpherson and his allies had reached the scene. Using a "monkey-wrench or the first thing to hand," they placed the Turks, Gros Jean, and the crew of the *Belles Soeurs* on the casualty list.

Mr. Winter's indignation on finding that he had arrested a woman was painful. In his astonishment he released his grasp and turned to look at the disappearing vehicle containing the criminal he so ardently longed to lay hands upon.

La Belle Chasseuse, with the vicious instinct of her class, felt that Talbot's pursuit of her lover must be stopped at all costs.

She suddenly produced a revolver and levelled it at him. Fairholme and Edith alone noted her action. At the same instant they rushed towards her, but the girl reached her first.

With a frenzied prayer that she might be in time—for she had been told of this woman's prowess with a pistol— Edith caught hold of her wrist and pulled it violently. Her grip not only disconcerted Mademoiselle's deadly aim, but also caused her to press the trigger. There was a loud report, a scream, and Edith collapsed to the ground with a severe bullet wound in her left shoulder. Even her cloth jacket was set on fire by the close proximity of the weapon.

It is to be feared that Fairholme flung La Belle Chasseuse from off the quay into the harbour with unnecessary violence. Indeed, the Italian onlookers, not accustomed to sanguinary broils, subsequently agreed that this was the *piece de resistance* of the spectacle, for the lady was pitched many feet through the air before she struck the water, whence she was rescued with some difficulty.

[Illustration: "Fairholme flung La Belle Chasseuse with unnecessary violence." –*Page 278.*]

Careless how or where Mademoiselle ended her flight, the earl dropped on his knees beside Edith and quickly pressed out the flames of the burning cloth with his hands. He burnt himself badly in the act, but of this he was insensible. Then he bent closer and looked desperately, almost hopelessly, into her face.

"Speak to me, darling!" he moaned in such a low, broken-hearted voice that even Sir Hubert, himself almost mad with grief, realized how the other suffered.

Edith heard him. She opened her eyes, and smiled bravely.

"I don't think it is serious," she murmured. "I was hit high up—somewhere in the shoulder. Don't fret, there's a dear."

Then she fainted.

Not knowing why Fairholme did not join him, Talbot raced towards the carriage he had seen approaching. It was a smart vehicle, with a sleek, well-groomed horse, and he guessed that it must be a private conveyance. Gazing anxiously around, he could not see another carriage anywhere in the vicinity. There was nothing for it but the method of the brutal Saxon. Explanations would need precious time and might be wasted. So Talbot jumped into the victoria, hauled the coachman off the box, threw him into the roadway, seized the reins, and climbed into the vacant seat.

Brett, hurrying with the pilot from the Hotel de France, saw a veiled and curious-looking female vehemently urging the driver of a carriage to proceed up the main street of Palermo as fast as his horse could travel.

Even in the turmoil of thought caused by the pilot's intelligence he noted something peculiar in the lady's manner. Half a minute later he encountered Talbot, driving an empty vehicle and furiously compelling with reins and whip a lazy animal to exert himself.

Brett shouted to him. He might as well have addressed a whirlwind.

"I saw them all together on the yacht when I came away, signor," exclaimed the pilot. "That is, all except the old signor, who was walking with some Turks, a Frenchman, and another who looked like an Englishman."

"The old signor was walking with the Turks?" cried Brett.

"Without doubt. He conversed with them. I thought it strange that he took no notice of those on board the yacht, but just then the steamer—"

"Now," said Brett to himself, "Winter has arrested somebody. Talbot is on the right track!"

Yielding to impulse he stopped suddenly and called a cab.

"Here!" he said to the pilot, "ask the driver if he saw two carriages pass up the Corso just now at a very fast pace? Very well! Tell him to follow them if possible. Jump in with me. I may need your services as interpreter. We must overtake one or both of those carriages!"

21
THE FIGHT

Not often have the good people of Palermo seen three cabs pass through the Corso Vittorio Emmanuele in such fashion. The sight made loiterers curious, drove policemen frantic, and caused the drivers of other vehicles to pull to one side and piously bless themselves. Dubois had evidently offered his *cocchiere* a lavish bribe for a quick transit through the city, and the Italian was determined to earn it. Although he had a good start, and his horse was accustomed to negotiating the main thoroughfare at a rapid pace, nevertheless the half-starved animal was not able to maintain a high rate of speed for more than a few minutes.

By the time they reached the Corso Catafini, which carries the chief artery of Palermo out into the country–crossing the railway and passing the magnificent convent of San Francisco de Sale–the horse was labouring heavily notwithstanding the frantic efforts of the cabman.

It was at this point, when mounting the bridge, that Dubois knew for certain he was followed. Three hundred yards behind, he saw Talbot whipping an equally unwilling, but better-conditioned steed than that which carried his own fortunes. At the distance he could not recognize the Englishman, but instinct told him that this impassioned driver was an enemy.

Brett, of course, was not visible, being far in the rear.

"My friend," said Dubois, standing up in the small carriage and leaning against the driver's seat, "I offered you twenty francs if you crossed the city quickly. I will make it forty for another mile at the same pace. See, I place the money in your pocket."

"It will kill my horse, signorina."

"Possibly. I will buy you another."

The *cocchiere* thought that this was a lady of strange manner. There was an odd timbre in her voice, a note of domination not often associated with the fair sex. But she had given earnest of her words by a couple of gold pieces, so he murmured a prayer to his favourite saint that the horse might not die until the right moment.

Thus they swirled on, pursued and pursuers, until the villa residences on the outskirts of the town were less in evidence, and fields devoted to the pepper-wort, alternated with groves of olives and limes, formed the prevalent features of the landscape.

Now it became evident that the leading horse could barely stagger another fifty yards, notwithstanding the inhuman efforts of the *cocchiere* to make the most of the poor brute's failing energies. At last the animal stumbled and fell, nearly pulling the driver off his perch. It was sad, but he had more than earned his price, for Palermo lay far behind.

"My horse is done for, signorina," cried the cabman. "It is marvellous that he—*Corpo di Baccho!* It is a man!"

Dubois felt that his feminine trappings were no longer a disguise, only a hindrance. He had torn off jacket, skirt, hat and wig. The frightened cabman saw his fare—changed now into an athletic young man, attired in shirt and trousers, the latter rolled up to his knees—spring from the vehicle and vault over a ditch by the roadside.

Some portion of the discarded clothing lay on the seat of the carriage, but Dubois had thrown the skirt over his arm.

"Here! Come back!" yelled the Italian. "What about payment for my dead horse?"

But Dubois paid little heed to him. He was fumbling with the pocket of the skirt as he ran. Not until he had withdrawn a revolver from its folds—whereupon he at once threw away the garment—did the maddening remembrance come to him that he unloaded the weapon prior to the Customs examination, and had forgotten to reinsert the cartridges.

They were in the pocket of his serge coat, the coat which Mademoiselle wore. She, like a prudent young woman, had been careful to reload the revolver she carried, and which she transferred to her new attire when, at the last moment, Dubois suggested the exchange of clothing as a final safeguard in the most unexpected event of police interference with their landing.

Henri Dubois could not afford to expend his breath in useless curses. But his eyes scintillated with fiery gleams. He, the man who took no chances, who foresaw every pitfall and smiled at the devices of outraged law, to compromise his own safety so foolishly!

For an instant he was tempted to fling the weapon away, but he controlled the impulse.

"As it is," he thought, "this fellow who is pursuing me may not be armed, and I can terrorise him if he comes to close quarters."

Moreover, this superlative scoundrel could feel tightly fastened round his waist a belt containing diamonds worth over a million sterling. Such a ceinture was worth fighting for, whilst his pocket-book contained ample funds for all immediate necessities.

If the worst came to the worst he carried a trustworthy clasp knife, and he was an adept in the savate–the system of scientific defence by using hands and feet which finds favour with Parisian "sports."

On the whole, Henri Dubois made for a neighbouring wood in a state of boiling rage at his momentary lapse concerning the revolver, but conscious that he had many a time extricated himself from a worse fix. A hundred yards in his rear ran Jack Talbot. The Englishman, notwithstanding his recent imprisonment, was in better condition than Dubois. He was a good golf player and cricketer, and although in physique and weight he did not differ much from the Frenchman, his muscles were more firmly knit, and his all-round training in athletic exercises gave him considerable advantage.

Thus they neared the wood, neither man running at his top speed. Both wished to conserve their energies for the approaching struggle. Talbot could have come up with his quarry sooner, were it not for the paramount consideration that he should not be spent with the race at the supreme moment, whilst Dubois only intended to seek the shelter of the trees before he faced his opponent. The Frenchman did not want witnesses.

Neither was aware that Brett and the Italian pilot had by this time reached the place where the two leading carriages were halted in the roadway. Without wasting a moment the barrister leapt the intervening ditch and followed the runners across the field, whilst behind him, eagerly anxious to see the end of this mysterious chase, came the sailor.

On the edge of the wood Dubois halted and turned to face his pursuer. Instantly he recognized Talbot, and for the first time in his career a spasm of fear struck cold upon the Frenchman's heart. In the young Englishman he recognized the only man who had cause to hate him with an implacable animosity.

But the unscrupulous adventurer quickly recovered his nerve.

"So it is you who follow me so closely," he cried. "Go back, my friend. This time I will not tie you on a bed. You are becoming dangerous. Go back, I tell you!"

And with these words he levelled the revolver at Talbot's breast, for the latter was now within fifty yards of him. But Jack was animated with the mad elation of a successful chase, and governed by the fierce resolve that his betrayer should not escape him. For an instant he stopped. It was only to pick up a huge stone. Then he ran on again, and, careless whether Dubois fired or not, he flung the missile at him.

The Frenchman barely succeeded in dodging, as it passed unpleasantly close to his head. He instantly understood that here was a man who could not be deterred by idle threats. To attempt to keep him at arm's length by pointing an empty pistol at him would merely court disaster.

So now, with an imprecation of genuine rage, he flung the weapon at Talbot, who, in his turn, was so surprised by the action that he did not get out of the way in time. It struck him fair in the chest and staggered him for a moment, whereupon Dubois ran off again into the interior of the wood.

But Talbot's pause was only a matter of seconds. He did not trouble to pick up another stone. He felt with a species of mad joy that his enemy was unarmed—that he could throttle him with his hands, and wreak upon him that personal and physical vengeance which is dearer to outraged humanity than any wounds inflicted by other means.

Dubois reached a small glade among the trees before he comprehended that his ruthless adversary was still close at his heels. He stopped for the last time, resolved now to have done with this irritating business, once and for all. Talbot too halted, about ten yards from him. He felt that he had the Frenchman at his mercy, and there were a few things he wished to say to him before they closed in mortal combat.

"This time, Henri Dubois," he panted, "I am not drugged and strapped helplessly to a bed. You know why I am here. I have followed you to avenge the stigma you inflicted on my reputation and at the same time to recover the diamonds which you obtained by subterfuge and murder."

The Frenchman was quite collected in manner.

"I murdered no one," he answered. "I could not help the blundering of other people. If I am regretfully compelled to kill you to-day, it is your own fault. I am only acting in self-defence."

"Self-defence!" came the quick retort. "Such men as you are a pest. Like any wild beast you will strive to save your miserable life! But, thank Heaven, you must depend upon your claws. Lying and trickery will avail you no further!"

"How can we fight?" demanded the Frenchman calmly.

"Any way you like, you villain. As man to man if you are able. If not, as dog to dog, for I am going to try and kill you!"

"But you are probably armed, whereas I am defenceless? My revolver, as you saw, was not loaded."

"We are equal in that respect, if in no other," retorted Talbot.

An evil smile lit up the Frenchman's pallid face. He pulled out his knife with a flourish and hissed—

"Then die yourself, you fool!"

He advanced upon Jack with a murderous look in his face. Talbot awaited him, and he, too, smiled.

"You are a liar and a coward to the end!" he cried. "But if you had twenty knives, Henri Dubois, I will kill you!"

At that instant a cold, clear voice rang out among the trees, close behind the two men.

"Halt!" it cried.

Both men involuntarily paused and turned their eyes to learn whence came this strange interruption. Brett quietly came a few paces nearer.

He held a revolver, pointed significantly at Dubois' breast.

"Drop that knife," he said, with an icy determination in tone and manner that sent a cold shiver through his hearer's spine.

"Drop it, or, by God, I will shoot you this instant!"

Dubois felt that the game was up. He flung down the knife and tried even then to laugh.

"Of course," he sneered, "as I am cornered on all sides I give in."

Brett still advanced until he reached the spot where the knife lay. He picked it up, and at the same instant lowered the revolver. Then he observed, with the easy indifference of one who remarks upon the weather—

"Now you can fight, monsieur. My young friend here is determined to thrash you, and you richly deserve it. So I will not interfere. But just one word before you begin. Two can play at the game of bluff. This is your own pistol. It is, as you know, unloaded."

Dubois' cry of rage at the trick which had been played on him was smothered by his effort to close with Talbot, who immediately flung himself upon him with an impetuosity not to be denied.

Luckily for the Englishman he had clutched Dubois before the latter could attempt any of the expedients of the savate. Nevertheless the Frenchman sought to defend himself with the frenzy of desperation.

The fight, while it lasted, was fast and furious.

The two men rolled over and over each other on the ground—one striving to choke the life out of his opponent, the other seeking to rend with teeth and nails.

This combat of catamounts could not last long.

From the writhing convulsive bodies, locked together in a deadly struggle, suddenly there came a sharp snap. The Frenchman's right arm was broken near the wrist.

Then Talbot proceeded to wreak his vengeance on him. Unquestionably he would have strangled the man had not Brett interfered, for with his left hand he clutched Dubois' throat, whilst with the right he endeavoured to demolish his features. But the barrister, assisted by the Italian pilot—whose after-life was cheered by his ability to relate the details of this Homeric fight—pulled the young man from off his insensible foe.

Talbot regained his feet. Panting with exertion, he glared down at the prostrate form, but Brett, being practical-minded, knelt by the Frenchman's side, tore open his shirt, and unfastened the precious belt.

"At last!" he murmured.

Peering into one of the pockets, which by the way of its bulging he thought would contain the "Imperial diamond," he looked up at Talbot with the words–

"Now, Jack, we are even with him."

It was the first time he had addressed Talbot by his familiar and Christian name. The very sound brought back the other man to a conscious state of his surroundings, and in the same instant a great weakness came over him, for the terrible exertions of the past few minutes had utterly exhausted him.

"I cannot even thank you, for I am done up. But I owe it all to you, old man. If it had not been for you we should never have found him."

Brett's grave face wrinkled in a kindly smile.

"I think," he said, "we are even on that score. If you had not followed this rascal he might have escaped us at the finish, and my pride would never have recovered from the shock. However, go and sit down for a minute or two and you will soon pull yourself together again. I wish to goodness we had some brandy. A drop would do you good, and our prostrate friend here would be none the worse for a reviver."

The Italian pilot caught the word "brandy." Being a sailor he was equal to all emergencies. He produced a small flask with a magnificent air.

"Behold!" he declared. "It is the best. It is contraband!"

Brett forced his companion to swallow some of the liquor; then he gently raised Dubois' head and managed to pour a few drops into his mouth.

The Frenchman regained consciousness. Awakening with a start to the realities of existence, he endeavoured to rise, but sank back with a groan, for he had striven to support himself on his broken arm.

"Be good enough to remain quite still, M. Dubois," said Brett soothingly. "You have reached the end of your rope, and we do not even need to tie you."

With the aid of some handkerchiefs and a couple of saplings cut by the Italian he managed roughly to bind the fractured limb. Then he assisted Dubois to his feet.

"Come," he said, "we are regretfully compelled to bring you back to town, but we will endeavour to make the journey as comfortable as possible for you. In any event, the horses will certainly not travel so fast."

In the roadway they found the carriages where they had left them, whilst three wondering *cocchieri* were exchanging opinions as to the mad behaviour of the foreigners.

Brett and the Frenchman entered one vehicle, Talbot and the Italian pilot the other.

"But, gentlemen," moaned the disconsolate cabman who had headed the procession from Palermo, "who will pay me for my dead horse?"

"I know not," replied Brett. "In any event you had better occupy the vacant seat and drive those two gentlemen to the city, where you can secure the means of bringing back your carriage."

In this guise the party returned to Palermo, evoking much wonderment all the way through the Corso Vittorio Emmanuele, whence no less than six outraged policemen followed them to the Hotel de France to obtain their names and addresses.

22
PIECING THE PUZZLE

Palermo was in a perfect ferment. Not since the last revolution had people seen such a pitched battle in the streets, for Macpherson and his myrmidons had used no gentle means to pacify Gros Jean and the Turks, whilst the crew of the *Belles Soeurs* would not be in a fit state to go to sea for many days.

An excited mob of people surrounded the hotel when Brett and Talbot arrived with their wounded prisoner. Fortunately the Chief of Police came in person to ascertain the cause of all this turmoil. The first alarmist report that reached his ears made out that a species of international warfare had broken out in the harbour.

He told his subordinates to clear away the crowd, and explanations by Brett and Winter soon demonstrated the wisdom of an official *communique* to the Press that the row on the pier was merely the outcome of a quarrel between some intoxicated sailors.

The Chief of the Police politely offered to place detectives at the disposal of the Englishmen for the proper custody of their captive. Brett thanked him, but declined the proffered assistance, having decided to warn Winter not to interfere.

"The only prisoner of interest," he explained, "received such severe injuries during a struggle which he brought on himself that he will be quite unable to be moved for several days. His right arm is broken, and his face has been reduced to a pulp. There is a stout Frenchman named Beaucaire and three Turks who accompanied him, whom I recommend to your safe custody. We bring no charge against them, but it would be as well to keep them under lock and key until we have left Palermo."

"Do you mean the innkeeper Gros Jean and the Turks who accompanied him from Messina by train to-day?"

"Yes."

"You need not trouble about them. They have all been carried to the hospital."

"What!" exclaimed Brett. "How did they come to be injured?"

"I cannot tell you exactly, but they, together with some sailors from the fishing-smack, were knocked senseless by the crew of the steam yacht when the young lady was shot."

"What young lady?" demanded Brett and Talbot together. This conversation had taken place in the entrance of the hotel, whilst Dubois was being carried to a bedroom by the servants.

"Did you not know?" inquired the official gravely. "The young lady was of your company who stayed here with you—the niece of milord, the elderly gentleman."

"Edith! Shot, did you say!" cried her brother, leaning against the barrister for support.

"Yes, but not seriously, I hope. She has been brought here. The doctors are now with her in her room."

"Who shot her?" demanded Brett savagely.

"The person who was flung into the harbour by the other milord. It is stated that she is a woman, but really at this moment I have not heard all the facts. She was carried to the hospital with the others."

The two waited to hear no more. They ran upstairs, and Talbot would have fallen twice had not Brett supported him. Reaching the corridor which contained their apartments they found Sir Hubert, Lord Fairholme, Daubeney, and Mr. Winter standing silently, a sorrowful, motionless group, outside Edith's room.

"What terrible thing has happened?" Brett asked them. "Surely Miss Talbot cannot be seriously hurt?"

The only one who could answer was Mr. Winter.

"We hope not, sir," he said, "but the doctors will be here in a moment. They are extracting the bullet now."

Before the bewildered barrister could frame another question the door of Edith's room opened noiselessly, and two Italian gentlemen emerged. One of them spoke English well. He addressed himself to Sir Hubert Fitzjames.

"I am glad to tell you," he said cheerfully, "that the young lady's wound is not at all dangerous. It looks worse than it is. Most fortunately, the bullet first struck a large bone button on her coat. This, combined with the thick woollen material, and some small amount of padding placed beneath the collar by the maker, offered such resistance that the bullet lodged itself against the collar bone without breaking it. Consequently, although the wound has a nasty appearance, it is not at all serious. The young lady herself makes light of it. Indeed, she thought that an anaesthetic was unnecessary, but of course we administered one prior to extraction, and she is now resting quietly."

"You are not deceiving us, doctor? Tell us the truth, for Heaven's sake." It was Fairholme's voice, broken and hollow, that so fiercely uttered these words.

The kindly doctor turned and placed his hand upon the earl's shoulder.

"I would not dream of such a thing," he answered. "It would be cruel to raise false hopes if the young lady's condition were really dangerous. Believe me, there is nothing to fear. With the careful attention she will receive, she will be well able to travel within a week, though, of course, the wound will not be fully healed until later."

Sir Hubert managed to stammer—

"When can we see her?"

"As soon as she wakes from sleep. We have given her a small draught, you understand, to secure complete rest after the shock of the operation. My colleague and I will return here at eight o'clock, and then there will probably be no reason why you should not speak to her. Meanwhile be confident; there is absolutely no cause for alarm."

With this reassuring statement they had perforce to rest content. The medical men were about to take their departure when Brett intervened.

"There is yet another patient who requires your attention, gentlemen," he said. "You will find him in room No. 41. He is suffering from a broken arm and other injuries."

The doctors hurried off, and it was not long before they were able to make a satisfactory report concerning Dubois.

"The fracture of the ulna is a simple one," said the spokesman, "and will become all right in the ordinary course of nature. But what happened to the man's face?"

"He settled a slight dispute with my friend here," said Brett, indicating Talbot, who was leaning with his head wearily resting on his hands. The accident to Edith had utterly unnerved her brother.

"Then all I can say," remarked the doctor, when he took his leave, "is that the settlement was complete. Whatever the debt may have been, it is paid in full!"

The Englishmen were now safe in the seclusion of a private room, so Brett resolved to arouse Talbot from the stupor which had settled upon him.

"Listen to me, Jack," he said. "You must pull yourself together. Don't forget you have an important trust to discharge. Our first duty is to ascertain whether or not the diamonds are intact."

He laid on the table the belt taken from Dubois, and lifted out its precious contents with careful exactness. The men crowded around. Even amidst the exciting events of the hour, the sight of the fateful stones which had caused so much turmoil and bloodshed could not fail to be deeply interesting.

Predominant among them was the Imperial diamond, luminous, gigantic, awesome in its potentialities. Its size and known value rendered it one of the most remarkable objects in the world, whilst even in its present unfinished state the facets already cut by the workmen gave evidence to its brilliant purity.

Pulling himself together by an effort, Talbot advanced to the table and slowly counted the stones. There were fifty-one all told, and even the smallest of the collection was a diamond of great value.

"Yes," he said, "that is the correct number. I cannot be certain, but I believe they are the originals. The big one certainly is. It will be one of the happiest days of my life when I see the last of them."

"That day will arrive soon," remarked Brett quietly. "You and I, Mr. Winter, must sail on the *Blue-Bell* to-night for Marseilles. That is, if Mr. Daubeney is agreeable," he added, turning to that worthy gentleman, whose face was a trifle paler than it had been for years.

"I am at your service, gentlemen," he announced promptly.

"But what about Fairholme and the young lady," he went on, turning to Sir Hubert.

"I think I understand," replied the baronet. "Mr. Brett means that these wretched diamonds should pass officially out of the control of the British Government as early as possible."

The barrister nodded.

"That being so, no time should be lost. Edith, should all go well, will be compelled in any event to remain here for several days before she can be removed. You, Jack, and you, Mr. Brett, should you so desire, can easily return here from London, after having fulfilled the trust reposed in you."

"Then I only make one stipulation," put in Daubeney quickly. "The *Blue-Bell* will remain in Marseilles and bring you back."

His eagerness evoked a quiet smile all round, and it was generally agreed that this programme should be followed. In the brief discussion which ensued, Mr. Winter explained his earlier movements. The detectives attached to the British Embassy in Paris told him of Dubois' journey to Marseilles.

Learning that Brett was staying at the Hotel du Louvre et de la Paix, he went straight there on his arrival, only to learn that the barrister and some friends had quitted Marseilles that day on a private yacht bound for Palermo. The local police filled in some of the details, but chance did the rest.

Going to the P. and O. office to book his passage to Messina on the *Ganges*, he heard of Gros Jean and the Turks, and then knew that he was on the right scent.

There was a touching meeting between Edith and the others that evening. She was naturally pale and weak, but her buoyant spirit triumphed over physical defects, and she made light of her injuries. Even Fairholme was restored to a state of sanity by his brief visit, a fact that was evidenced by his quiet enjoyment of a cigar when he walked down to the quay to witness the departure of the *Blue-Bell*.

Before leaving Palermo Brett had another interview with the Chief of Police, the result being that unobtrusive but effective means were taken to safeguard the different members of the gang which had caused so much personal suffering and diplomatic uneasiness.

The reception of the party in London may be detailed in a sentence. The Turkish Ambassador was specially instructed from Constantinople to take charge of the diamonds, and Talbot had the keen satisfaction of personally handing them over to the Sultan's representative, in the presence of his chief at the Foreign Office. The unlucky gems were forthwith taken back to their owner, and no doubt repose at this moment in a special reliquary, together with other mementoes of the Prophet, for the project which led to their first visit to London was definitely abandoned.

Meanwhile daily telegrams from Palermo assured Talbot and Brett as to the continued progress of the fair sufferer, who had so nearly sacrificed her life in her devoted championship of her brother's cause.

At last a day came when the *Blue-Bell* again steamed into the harbour of Palermo, and the manner in which Fairholme shouted when he caught sight of Daubeney standing on the bridge was in itself sufficient indication that all had gone well during their absence.

The travellers were surprised and delighted to find Edith herself seated in a carriage with her uncle on the wharf. Were it not that she was pale, and her right arm was tightly strapped across her breast to prevent any movement of the injured shoulder, no one could have guessed that she had recently undergone such a terrible experience.

But Brett, delighted as he was to meet his friends again under such pleasant conditions, experienced the keenest sentiments of triumphant elation when he entered the apartment where Dubois was still confined under the watchful guard of two detectives.

Talbot accompanied him. The young Englishman had by this time quite forgiven his enemy. He felt that he was more than quits with him. Indeed, he was the first to speak when they came together.

"I am sorry to see it is your turn to be trussed up in bed, Dubois," he said. "How are you feeling now? Getting along all right, I hope."

The Frenchman did not answer him directly. A faint smile illumined his pale face. He turned to Brett with a nonchalant question—

"Mr. Brett, have you any influence with those two worthy Italian doctors?"

"Perhaps," said the barrister. "What is it you want?"

"I want a cigarette. They won't let me smoke. Surely to goodness, a cigarette won't hurt my arm."

The barrister turned a questioning glance towards the male nurse in charge of the patient, but the man did not understand what had been said. Brett, who spoke no Italian, indicated by pantomime what it was the Frenchman required, and the attendant signified his sentiments in silent eloquence–he turned and looked out of the window. So Dubois enjoyed his cigarette in peace. He gave a sigh of great contentment, and then said, lazily–

"Now, ask me anything you like. I am ready."

"There is only one point concerning which I am really at fault," began Brett. "How did your Turkish associates manage to murder Mehemet Ali and his secretaries so quietly?"

"Oh, that was easy enough," declared the Frenchman. "You understand I was in no way responsible for the blood-letting, and indeed strongly disapproved of it."

"Yes," replied the barrister. "I believe that."

"Well, the rest of the business was simplicity itself. Hussein–the Envoy's confidential servant–was in our pay. It was, of course, absolutely necessary to have an accomplice in the house, and his price was a small one– five hundred pounds, I think. The credentials we brought, which you, Mr. Talbot, examined, were not forgeries."

"How can that be?" cried Jack. "The Sultan would never be a party to a plot for his own undoing."

"Don't ask me for explanations I cannot give," responded Dubois coolly. "The exact facts of this story can only be ascertained at Yildiz Kiosk, and I do not suppose that anyone there will ever tell you. No doubt you saw for yourself that Mehemet Ali was convinced. Were it not for you, he would have given up control that night. But you and your policemen, and your confounded English notions of right and wrong, rendered necessary the adoption of the second part of the plan we had decided on, in case the first miscarried. After I left the house with you, Hussein brought in more coffee. That which he and my Turkish friends drank was all right. The beverage given to Mehemet Ali and his secretaries was drugged."

"Ah!" interrupted Brett, "that explains everything. But why was Hussein killed?"

"That is another matter, which only a Turk can understand. These fellows believe in the knife or a piece of whipcord as ending unpleasant difficulties most effectually. You see they were not ordinary rogues. They pretended to be conspirators actuated by pure political motives–motives which a common servant like Hussein could not really be expected to appreciate. So to close his mouth thoroughly they stabbed him whilst he was taking some loose cash from his master's pockets. Then it occurred to them that when Mehemet Ali and the others recovered from the effects of the drug, they also would be able to throw an unpleasantly strong light on the complicity of certain high personages in Constantinople. This was sufficient reason for the adoption of strong measures, so they also were peacefully despatched."

"But where did the knife come from?" pursued Brett. "It was not in their possession when they entered, nor when they left."

"No; of course not. Hussein brought it himself, to be used in case of necessity. He also brought the pliers which cut the wire blinds, and the material used for concealing the broken strands subsequently. Hussein was really an excellent confederate, and I was furious when I heard that he was dead. You know how the diamonds were abstracted from the house?"

"Yes," said Brett. "They were made up into a parcel and flung through the window into the Park. The knife and the pliers accompanied them, I suppose?"

"The third Turk–the gentleman who pulled you down on to the bed so unceremoniously, Mr. Talbot–was waiting there for the packet. But he had to hide in the Park all the night, until the gates were opened in the morning. It was a ticklish business right through. I did not know at what hour the police might discover the extent of the crime. The diamonds did not reach me until seven o'clock. And then I had some difficulty in persuading the Turks to give them up to me. You see, I had my own little plan, too, which these excellent gentlemen never suspected, as they already had paid me L5,000 for my help. But the real heads of the party were in Paris–Hussein-ul-Mulk and that gang, you know–and by representing the danger to their cause which would result from any attempt on the part of the Turks in London to reach France, they were at last persuaded. By nine o'clock that morning I got them safely off to the docks, where they boarded a vessel bound for Smyrna. Their passages were already booked in Armenian names. Gros Jean, who had no connexion with the affair personally, stayed at a little hotel in Soho in order to report all clear during the next few days. He happened by chance to travel with you and the other man. It was a clever scheme, I assure you, from beginning to end. By the way, may I trouble you for another cigarette?"

"These are not equal to Hussein-ul-Mulk's," said Brett, producing his case.

"No, he has an exquisite taste in tobacco. But I nearly fooled him with the dummy diamonds. I would have done so if it had not been for you. Do you know, Mr. Brett, I have always underrated Englishmen's brains. You are really stupid as a nation"–here Talbot almost blushed–"but you are an exception. You ought to be a Frenchman."

"I suppose I may regard that as a compliment?" remarked Brett casually.

"Take it as you like," said Dubois. "And now that I have told you all that you want to know, I suppose, may I ask you a question of some interest to myself? What is to become of me? Am I to be hanged, or imprisoned, or passed on to the Sultan for treatment?"

Brett was silent for a few moments. He had fully discussed Dubois' connexion with the British authorities.

"How much of the five thousand pounds given you by the Turks remains in your possession?" he demanded.

The Frenchman hesitated before replying–

"There is no use lying to you. I have not yet expended the first thousand, although I had to pay pretty dearly for a good many things."

Again there was silence.

"Why did you come here?" asked the barrister.

"Because I would be safe for some months with a few hospitable gentlemen whom I know up in the hills there." He nodded towards the window, through which they could see the blue crests of the distant mountains.

"And then?"

"Then Marguerite and I were going to the Argentine, to dwell in rural felicity, and teach our children to bless the name of Mahomet and Abdul Hamid."

"Marguerite is Mademoiselle Beaucaire?"

"Yes, poor girl! I hear she is ill and in prison, together with her excellent father. Really, Mr. Brett, I cannot help liking you, but I ought to feel anxious to cut your throat."

"In that case you would certainly be hanged. Are you married to Mademoiselle Beaucaire?"

The Frenchman darted a quick and angry look at his inquisitor.

"What has that to do with you?" he snarled.

Dubois' future had already been determined. The rascal was more fortunate than he deserved to be. Owing to the lucky chance that his crime had a political significance he would escape punishment. By no known form of European law could he be brought to trial on any charge and at the same time gagged in his defence. The slightest public reference to either the theft of the diamonds or the Sultan's original intentions with regard to them would create such a storm in the Mohammedan world that no man could prophesy the end.

When the Ottoman Empire is next torn asunder by civil war other thrones will rock to their foundations. Half unconsciously, though he had a glimmering perception of the truth, Henri Dubois was saved by the magnitude of the interests involved.

Brett knew exactly how to deal with him. But a fantastic project had arisen in his mind, and he determined to graft it upon the drastic expedient adopted by the authorities. He abruptly broke off the conversation and told the Frenchman that he would call again during the afternoon.

True to his promise, Talbot and he visited the injured man some hours later. This time they were accompanied by a stout individual and a closely-veiled lady–Gros Jean and his daughter.

The meeting between Henri and Marguerite was pathetic. It was at the same time exceedingly French, and somewhat trying to the nerves of the Englishmen.

At last the couple calmed their transports, and Brett promptly recalled them to a sense of their surroundings by reminding them that there was serious business to be discussed.

"I am commissioned to inform you," he said, addressing Dubois, "that if you proceed direct to the Argentine, never attempt to revisit France, and keep your mouth closed as to your attempt to purloin the Sultan's jewels, you will be set at liberty here, and no effort will be made by the French or English police to arrest you. The infringement of any of these conditions will lead to your extradition and a sentence of penal servitude for life."

"*Ma foi!*" cried the Frenchman, looking intently into the barrister's inscrutable face. "Why such tenderness?"

Brett would not give him time for prolonged reflection.

"I have not yet finished," he said drily. "I imagine that Mlle. Beaucaire cannot produce a marriage certificate. She will be supplied with one, to permit her to travel with you as your lawful wife."

The pair were startled. They somewhat relaxed the close embrace in which they sat. The man's handsome face flushed with anger. The woman became a shade paler and looked from the barrister to her lover.

"Good," growled Gros Jean. "Quite right!"

"We can manage our own affairs," began Dubois savagely; but Brett again took up the parable.

"You owe this lady a deep debt of gratitude for her unswerving devotion to you. She has helped you to lead an evil life; let her now assist you in a better career. You have your chance. Will you take it?"

La Belle Chasseuse sat mute and downcast. This personal development came as a complete surprise to her. Pride would not permit her to plead her own cause. Dubois glanced at her covertly. He was still annoyed and defiant; but even he, hardened scoundrel and cynic though he was, could not find words to contest Brett's decision.

The barrister deemed the moment ripe for his final smashing argument. He came somewhat nearer to the bed, and said with exasperating coolness–

"There is a secret room in the Cabaret Noir, the contents of which have not yet been too closely examined by the police. It is in their charge. At my request, backed up by the British Foreign Office, they have thus far deferred a detailed scrutiny. Perhaps if the external influence is removed they may press their investigations to a point when it will be impossible to permit your contemplated voyage to the Argentine. You know best. I have nothing further to say."

Dubois looked at him in moody silence. The Argentine–with L4,000? Yes. But a wife!

Suddenly all eyes were attracted to Gros Jean, who emitted a gasping groan. His fat cheeks were livid, and huge drops of perspiration stood on his brow. Feeling that the others were regarding him intently, he made a desperate effort to recover his composure.

"It is nothing!" he gurgled. "The English gentleman's proposal with regard to my daughter interested me, that is all."

Dubois and the innkeeper gazed intently into each other's eyes for a few trying seconds. Then the Frenchman drew Marguerite closer to him, with his uninjured arm, and said–

"Let us get married, *ma p'tite*. It is essential."

And married they were forthwith, a priest and an official from the Mayor's office being in waiting at the hotel. Whilst they were signing the register Gros Jean motioned Brett to one side.

"Allow me to thank you, M'sieu', for the kindness you have shown," he murmured. "Touching that hidden room in the Cabaret, now. Do the police really know of it? You were not joking?"

"Not in the least."

"Then, M'sieu', I accompany them to the Argentine," and he jerked his thumb towards Dubois and his wife. "Paris is no place for me."

Soon after the ceremony Mme. Dubois asked to be allowed to visit Edith. When the two women met Marguerite flung herself impulsively on her knees and sobbed out a request for forgiveness. Miss Talbot should have been very angry with her erring sister. She was not. She took the keenest interest in the Frenchwoman's romantic history. They talked until Fairholme became impatient. He had not seen Edith for two whole hours.

*   *   *   *   *

Six months later, when the Earl and Countess of Fairholme returned from a prolonged wedding tour on the *Blue-Bell* through the Norwegian fiords, Brett was invited to dinner. Talbot was there, of course, and Daubeney, and Sir Hubert.

"Constantinople must be a queer place," observed Jack after the first rush of animated converse had exhausted itself.

"Surely there are no more diamond mysteries on foot!" cried his charming sister, who looked delightfully well, and brown as a berry with the keen sea breezes of the hardy North.

"Not exactly; but I made some inquiries through a friend of mine in the Legation. Hussein-ul-Mulk and his two Paris friends are quite important functionaries in the palace. You remember that the other pair of scoundrels escaped to Smyrna?"

"Yes," cried everybody.

"Well, Mehemet Ali's relatives heard the truth about them by some means. Within a reasonable time they were chopped into small pieces, with other details that need not be repeated."

"Dogs, or pigs?" inquired Brett.

"Dogs!"

"I wish you wouldn't say such horrid things," protested Edith. "Is there any news of Monsieur and Madame Dubois, and the fat man Gros Jean?"

"You will receive some in the drawing-room, Lady Fairholme," said Brett; and not another word of explanation would he give until dinner was ended.

In the drawing-room her ladyship was delighted to find a splendid cockatoo, magnificent in size and white as snow, save for the brilliant red crest which he elevated when they all crowded round his handsome cage.

"The happy couple in the Argentine sent him to me to be presented to you on your return," explained the barrister. "He is named 'Le Prophete,' and he talks beautifully—indeed, his language is most emphatic, but it is all French."

"What a darling!" cried Edith. "I do wish he would say something. *Cher Prophete, parlez avec moi!*"

And immediately the cockatoo stretched his wings and screamed–

"*Vive Mahomet! Vive le Sultan! A bas les Grecs! a bas! a bas!*"

FINIS

Resurrected Press Mysteries From Louis Tracy

The Albert Gate Mystery
Four men murdered and a fortune in diamonds belonging to the Turkish Sultan stolen, while the Foreign Office official in charge has gone missing. Was it a common jewelry theft or was it a case of international intrigue? This is the question that barrister detective Reginald Brett must solve.

The Bartlett Mystery
When Ronald Tower is murdered on his way to a bridge game on the yacht Sans Souci it at first appears a common crime. But as Rex Carshaw finds, a tragic case of mistaken identity leads to political scandal among the rich and powerful of New York.

The Strange Case of Mortimer Fenley
When the wealthy Mortimer Fenley is struck down by a shot from an express rifle on the steps of his mansion, detectives Winter and Furneaux of Scotland Yard must find the culprit. Was it the artist who claimed he was painting a picture at the time of the shot? The disaffected younger son? Or is there another suspect?

The Stowmarket Mystery
For five generations the Fergus-Hume family has been cursed. Each of the baronets has met a violent end. When the fifth baronet is found slain by a ceremonial Japanese dagger, suspicion falls on his cousin David. It falls to barrister detective Reginald Brett to prove his innocence and find the real murder in a case that spans two continents and as many centuries.

Resurrected Press Mysteries by J. S. Fletcher

The Orange-Yellow Diamond
When an elderly pawnbroker is murdered in the London parish of Paddington, a young, down on his luck writer is accused of the crime. But then it's found the pawnbroker had had in his possession an extraordinary South African diamond worth over eighty-thousand pounds — a diamond that's now missing. It falls to Melky Rubenstein to unravel the mystery and prove the young man's innocence.

The Middle Temple Murder
When an elderly man's body is found on the steps of chambers in the Midde Temple, one of the Inns of Court, it falls to newspaperman Frank Spargo and Detective-Sergeant Rathbury to solve the crime. The murdered man, for indeed it was murder, was found with no money or identification on his person except for a piece of paper with the name and address of a young barrister. Who is the victim? Why was he killed? Who is the murderer?

Scarhaven Keep
Bassett Oliver, the famed actor, has gone missing. When Oliver fails to show for a rehearsal, aspiring playwright Richard Copplestone finds himself sent to the small village of Scarhaven on the northern coast of England to track down the actors movements. What he finds is mystery. Find the answers as Copplestone unravels the mystery of Scarhaven Keep.

Visit www.resurrectedpress.com

Resurrected Press Mysteries by Fergus Hume

The Green Mummy

Professor Braddock hoped to compare the burial practices of the Egyptians with those of the ancient Peruvians with his latest acquisition, the mummy of the last Inca, Caxas. But on arrival, the packing case proved to hold not the mummy, but the body of his assistant Sidney Bolton. It falls to Archie Hope to discover the murderer if he is to marry the professors step-daughter, Lucy Kendal. Who killed Bolton and where is the mummy? Was it the sea captain Hervey? The mysterious Don Pedro? Cockatoo the Polynesian servant? The professor, himself? And what has become of the emeralds? These are the questions that Hope must answer amongst the secrets of the past in The Green Mummy.

The Mystery of a Hansom Cab

"Truth is said to be stranger than fiction, and certainly the extraordinary murder which took place in Melbourne Friday morning goes a long way towards verifying that saying." Thus opens The Mystery of a Hansom Cab, the best selling mystery of the nineteenth century. When a man is found dead in a hansom cab one of Melbourne's leading citizens is accused of the murder. He pleads his innocence, yet refuses to give an alibi. It falls to a determined lawyer and an intrepid detective to find the truth, revealing long kept secrets along the way. Fergus Hume's first and perhaps most famous mystery... The Mystery Of A Hansom Cab.

Visit www.resurrectedpress.com

Resurrected Press Mysteries from the Dr. John Thorndyke Series

Dr. John Thorndyke - Lecturer on Medical Jurisprudence and Forensic Medicine. Before Bones, before CSI, before Quincy, M.E– there was Dr. John Thorndyke solving the most baffling cases of Edwardian London using the latest tools of medical science. Read about his cases in:

The Eye of Osiris
John Bellingham, noted Egyptologist has vanished not once but twice in the same day. Now Dr, Thorndyke must unravel the tangled claims on his estate, solve the riddle of the missing man and find the "Eye of Osiris".

The Mystery of 31 New Inn
When Dr. Jervis is whisked away in a coach with no windows to an unknown location to treat a man in a coma from undivulged causes it is Dr. Thorndyke who must come up with the solution.

The Red Thumb Mark
The first of Dr. Thorndyke's cases finds him trying to prove the innocence of a young man accused of being a diamond thief despite the fact that his finger print was found at the scene of the crime.

John Thorndyke's Cases
More cases of medical mysteries as told by his trusted assistant Jervis, M.D. Eight stories of crime and deduction in Edwardian London.

Visit www.resurrectedpress.com

Resurrected Press Mysteries by John R. Watson & Arthur J. Rees

The Hampstead Mystery

High Court Justice Sir Horace Fewbanks found shot dead in his Hampstead home, a butler with a criminal past, a scorned lover and a hint of scandal. These are the elements of the Hampstead Mystery that Detective Inspector Chippenfield of Scotland Yard must unravel with the assistance of the ambitious Detective Rolfe. But will he be able to sort out the tangled threads of this case and arrest the culprit before he is upstaged by the celebrated gentleman detective Crewe. Follow the details of this amazing case at it plays out across Hampstead, London and Scotland until it reaches a stunning conclusion in the courts of the Old Bailey.

The Mystery of the Downs

When Harry Marsland was caught in a sudden down pour he sought shelter at Cliff Farm. Met at the door by a young woman clearly expecting someone else he is only too glad to get inside to wait out the storm. When they hear a noise upstairs in the deserted house they investigate only to discover the body of the farm's owner, Frank Lumsden, dead of a gunshot wound. Who then, killed Lumsden, and why? Who was the woman expecting and did she have any roll in the murder? These are the questions that private detective Crewe must answer in The Mystery of the Downs.

Visit www.resurrectedpress.com

Other Resurrected Press Mysteries

Mysteries on a Train

Before the Orient Express there was:

The Rome Express by Arthur Griffiths
A man is found dead in his first class sleeping compartment on the express from Rome to Paris. Who was his murderer? The Countess? The English General? His brother the clergy man? The maid who has disappeared? Is the French justice system up to solving the crime? Read about it in The Rome Express.

The Passenger from Calais by Arthur Griffiths
Colonel Basil Annesley finds he is the only passenger on the train from Calais to Lucerne. That is until a mysterious woman shows up at the last minute to book a compartment. Who is after her? What is her secret? Is she a criminal or a victim? Read about it in The Passenger from Calais

Visit us at www.resurrectedpress.com

About Resurrected Press

A division of Intrepid Ink, LLC, Resurrected Press is dedicated to bringing high quality, vintage books back into publication. See our entire catalogue and find out more at www.ResurrectedPress.com.

About Intrepid Ink, LLC

Intrepid Ink, LLC provides full publishing services to authors of fiction and non-fiction books, eBooks and websites. From editing to formatting, from publishing to marketing, Intrepid Ink gets your creative works into the hands of the people who want to read them. Find out more at www.IntrepidInk.com.